GUILTY ACTS

A Cass Leary Legal Thriller

ROBIN JAMES

Robin James Books

Copyright © 2021 by Robin James

All Rights Reserved

No part of this book may be reproduced or transmitted in any form or by any means, electronic or mechanical including photocopying, recording, or by any information storage and retrieval system, without the written permission of the author or publisher, except where permitted by law or for the use of brief quotations in a book review.

This is a work of fiction. Names, characters, businesses, places, events, and incidents are either the products of the author's imagination or used in a fictitious manner. Any resemblance to actual persons, living or dead, or actual events is purely coincidental.

Chapter 1

ONE LOOK at Bryson Ballard and I knew why Jeanie called me in. Young. Skinny. Baggy jeans, a wrinkled tee shirt, and shaggy black hair three weeks overgrown. Someone might have taken care of this kid once but they weren't doing it anymore.

He looked up when I entered Jeanie's office, his blue eyes swollen from crying. He sniffled, sat up straighter, tried to cover for whatever had caused his breakdown. Jeanie was barely holding it together herself. At seventy-four, she was one of the pioneer female lawyers in Woodbridge County. She started her practice at a time when male judges thought it was okay to tell her how cute she looked in her little suits when she showed up for court.

A long time ago, a different boy, just like Bryson, sat in her office crying even bigger tears. My little brother. Matty. Her decision to fight for him and for all of us changed the course of my life. As I sat down in the chair next to Bryson Ballard, I knew Jeanie meant to change the course of his. And mine with it.

"Cass," she said. "Bryson's had a bit of a tough year. Kiddo? You think you're up to telling Cass what you told me?"

Bryson ran his palm over his pant leg, then held it out to shake mine. I took it.

"My mom," he said. "She ... and my dad. Um, my stepdad. He didn't like me to call him that. He was my dad."

Bryson's voice broke on the word dad. He'd used the past tense. Even if he hadn't, this boy's grief wrapped around him with weight, bending his spine, ravaging his voice.

"I'm sorry," I said. Lord. He did look a heck of a lot like my little brother, Matty. Like my older brother, Joe, too. And he was alone. Just like we'd been after our mother died and my own father had disappeared. That was on his good days. On his bad ones, he was drunk and dangerous.

"They want me to say what I heard," he said. "She told me I have to. She told me not to lie."

It was then I noticed the heavily creased piece of paper in front of him. He'd tried to smooth it out and laid it on Jeanie's desk. A subpoena. Jeanie's expression told me that paper held the crux of this boy's problem today. I reached over and picked it up and read the caption.

People of the State of Michigan versus Juliet Ballard Clay. His notice to appear was three months from now to testify at trial. I tried to keep my expression neutral as I read the signature on the bottom. This came from the prosecutor's office.

"They want me to testify against my mom," he said. "I told her lawyer I can't. I won't."

He broke down again. Jeanie turned and opened the mini fridge she kept behind her desk. She pulled out a small bottled water and handed it to Bryson. He took it and thanked her. His hand shook as he unscrewed the cap.

Juliet Clay. Of course I recognized the name. I looked up and found Jeanie's eyes again. She'd been on the news. Some kind of local TikTok star.

"No," I mouthed. "Oh no."

I plastered on a fake smile as Bryson turned his head. This felt like an ambush.

"I'm not your mother's lawyer," I said. "My understanding is she's been assigned a public defender."

"He sucks," Bryson said. "Never returns her calls. He was supposed to get me out of this. How can they make me testify against my own mom?"

"Bryson," Jeanie said. "Why don't we handle one crisis at a time? If you're serious about the other matter we discussed, I think I can help you. In the meantime, though, do you have a place to stay tonight?"

Bryson nodded. He reached for a tissue on Jeanie's desk.

"Good," she said. "Why don't you give Cass and me some time to talk?"

He rose dutifully, like a soldier. I had to curl my fists at my sides to stem the urge to put an arm around him.

"Thanks, Mrs. Mills," he said. Jeanie smiled rather than correct him on the Mrs. part. Gold help any man who tried to get Jeanie to change her name.

"I'll call you tomorrow afternoon. Will you be home right after school?"

"Uh, yeah," he said. "I'm staying with some friends. I'll text you the address. Three thirty should be good. I'll get those documents together you asked for. If I can find them. They might still be at the house."

"We can make arrangements to get them," Jeanie said. "Don't worry about that. I'll figure out a solution if you hit a snag. And if you'd like me to go with you to your parents' house, I can do that too."

Bryson's shoulders sagged with relief. "Yeah. Yeah. Maybe that would be a better idea."

"Fine then. Are you sure I can't drive you? You're sure you're okay taking the bus?"

He nodded.

"Okay," Jeanie said. "Then we'll talk tomorrow."

The boy pursed his lips and shook my hand once more before he left. I waited until I heard the front door quietly close before turning to Jeanie.

"Are you …" I started. She held a hand up to cut me off.

"Just listen," she said. "That boy's a wreck."

"I can see that."

Jeanie looked over my shoulder and waved someone else in. Tori, our associate. Young. Pretty. Blonde. She had the youthful energy of my past twenty-year-old self, but had so far avoided my questionable life choices.

"Juliet Clay," I said. "She's been charged with first degree murder. Cops are saying she poisoned her husband?"

"Yep," Jeanie answered. "Nathan Clay. Did you know him?"

"I knew of him," I said. "Personal injury lawyer. We didn't cross paths very much but he had a good reputation. I referred a couple of people to his firm."

"So did I," she said.

"What does the kid know?" I asked.

"Not a lot. He told them his parents argued quite a bit and had their issues," she answered. "His more immediate problem is his living arrangement. Juliet, his mother, was Nathan's second wife ... Judge Castor denied her bail. She's in the county jail for the duration. Bryson's been staying with friends and neighbors but their good will is starting to run out. He turns seventeen in two months. I want to help him get emancipated before he ends up in foster care."

"How awful," I said. "Where's the rest of his family?"

"Nonexistent. His biological father hasn't been around since he was a baby, if ever. Nathan married his mom ten years ago. He was the only dad the kid's ever known. If Juliet gets convicted, he's gonna be on his own."

"Is there money at least?" I asked. "I thought Nathan Clay had a healthy law practice."

"It's hard to say," Tori said, taking the seat Bryson had vacated. "It's not clear now how liquid he was. Everyone's assuming money was a motive in his murder. Clay has ... er ... had a law partner. It'll take some doing to untangle whatever there is and liquidate it."

"What about this?" I asked, indicating Bryson's crumpled-up subpoena, tattered on the edge of Jeanie's desk.

"That," she said. "The rumor is the kid's the state's star witness. I told you. They got him to admit his parents had a lousy marriage. Feels like he was forced to. He's tearing himself up over it."

"I see," I said. Jeanie was trying to be coy. I knew her too well.

"Jeanie ..." I said.

"It wouldn't hurt you to just poke around and see what kind of evidence they have against the woman."

"Does Bryson think his mother is guilty?" I asked.

"I didn't ask him that," Jeanie said. "That's beyond the purview of my representation."

She had a wry smile. I shook my head. "No," I said. "Juliet Clay already has a lawyer."

"A court-appointed one," Jeanie said. "And one who apparently doesn't answer her calls."

"I don't take court-appointed cases anymore, remember? Plus, I told you. No more murder cases. Hell, that was your idea. A one-year moratorium. By my calendar, I've got at least seven months to go."

"Cass," she said. "I'm just asking you to poke around a little. See what's being done."

I waved the subpoena at her. "The woman goes to trial in three months!"

"Oh, you could get a continuance."

"You're a sucker for lost causes," I said.

"Lucky for you!" she answered. It's how she always answered.

"There's no money," I said. "Somebody has to keep you paid and the lights on, Jeanie. You too, Tori."

"There's an online fundraising page set up. It's pretty sizable. The kid wants to hire someone else. He wants to hire you," Jeanie said.

It was quick and subtle, but the glance she exchanged with Tori told me these two had probably rehearsed this whole meeting.

"Just take a look," Jeanie said. She had a folded piece of paper in her hand. "That's all I ask." She slid the paper closer to me. I had to catch it before it fell to the floor. I cocked my head sideways to read it. The moment I did, my pulse thrummed as I read the current balance of the fundraising page she mentioned.

"This should be for the kid's education, shouldn't it?" I asked.

"He's got a trust fund set up for that if I can get him access to it," Jeanie said. "What he wants is his mother to get a fair shake."

Jeanie tried to stifle her knowing smile a beat too slow. She knew what I'd say from the get-go. So did Tori. This was enough money to pay Tori's salary for a year and then some. Enough to tempt me out of my vow to stay away from murder trials for a while.

"All right," I said. "I'll take a look at the case."

Both Jeanie and Tori started to beam. "A look!" I warned them. "No promises though. No amount of sad puppy eyes will help if I'm dealing with a guilty client."

"I'll bring you the worst of it," Tori said. She started to walk out, then paused.

"How bad is the worst?" I asked.

Tori turned back to me but didn't answer.

"Tori?"

"Well, it more or less looks like Juliet Clay recorded herself giving the poison to her husband."

"Was it more or less?"

"And also recorded him drinking it," she said.

"What?"

"And ... um ... posted it all online."

"Tori!"

Chapter 2

"This is all of it," Tori said the next morning as she handed me a flash drive. "Most of Juliet Clay's social media accounts have been taken down but the internet and the Wayback Machine are forever."

She paused and looked at me. "Oh, the Wayback Machine is an online archive where …"

I laughed. "I know what the Wayback Machine is. How old do you think I am?"

"Ancient. Do you want me to get your readers? I mean, you'll be turning forty."

She was teasing. She shivered in fake revulsion. I scratched my forehead with my middle finger. Tori had a gleam in her eye and color in her cheeks that was new. This girl always carried the weight of the world on her shoulders and I welcomed the change in her.

"You look good," I said. "Happy."

She bit her lip and I worried maybe I'd overstepped. It was hard not to. We'd become like family in this office. I had a big, complicated, real one anyway. Tori was alone. She'd been easy to love and to take in.

"Thanks," she said. But darkness shadowed her eyes. I had said too much. She was keeping a secret. I'd bet the firm's receipts on it.

"So, Juliet Clay," I said. "What have you been dying to show me? I called a friend of mine at the jail last night. The woman's proclaiming her innocence to anyone within earshot. Whoever she's got representing her doesn't seem to have control of her. She shouldn't be talking to anyone about the case at all."

"I think Bryson's right about the quality of her defense lawyer. In the meantime, though, I've compiled her TikToks relating to Nathan over the last year and a half. You *do* know what TikTok is?"

She was teasing again. I was glad to see humor light up her face. Whatever personal secret I'd touched on earlier was forgotten.

I stuck out my tongue and snatched the drive from her and plugged it into my laptop. Tori took the chair beside me and settled in. Two files popped up. She'd named one "PreciousJules Timeline" and the other "PreciousJules Smoking Gun."

"You can either watch chronologically, or, well, bite-her-in-the-ass mode. @PreciousJules827 is her internet handle."

"That's fairly terrible," I said.

"Let's just say Juliet Clay is someone the internet loves to hate. Before her account got pulled, she had fifty thousand followers."

I clicked on the timeline file and Juliet's first thirty-second video pulled up. She was young. Very pretty with straight blonde hair, delicately applied make-up, and big brown eyes. She stood in front of a full-length mirror with perfect lighting wearing black leggings, a fitted tee shirt, and hot-pink cardigan.

"This is no joke," she said. "Two months with these shakes. I thought I'd hate it."

A before picture popped up showing Juliet perhaps ten pounds heavier but still perfectly thin. I paused the playback.

"Please tell me you don't expect me to watch hours of promo videos for a diet shake."

"It's relevant," Tori said. "The prosecution's working theory is that Juliet slipped poison into those shakes and fed them to Nathan Clay."

Tori reached over and clicked on a few videos in the Smoking Gun folder. The first showed Nathan Clay sitting in his home office. He had readers perched on the end of his nose and smiled as Juliet walked in. He wore a faded Detroit Lions tee shirt, pajama pants, and dark-blue slippers. He had a thick head of brown hair with gray at the temples. Not a bad-looking guy by any means. But he carried every minute of the twenty-plus years he had on his wife. In the video, Juliet handed Nathan what looked like a chocolate shake with a red-and-white-striped paper straw.

"Come on, baby." She giggled. "Give it a try. You promised." She sat on her husband's lap. He smiled, rolled his eyes, then drank the shake.

"It's not bad, right?"

"It's tolerable," he grumbled.

The next series of videos took place over the course of a few months at the beginning of the year. In each one, Juliet caught her husband drinking the same chocolate shake. But week by week, he was slimming down.

"Why is this interesting to people?" I asked.

"I told you," Tori said, closing the laptop. "People kind of loved to hate her. She went viral about a year and a half ago, posting videos of herself trying on clothes from the local discount stores. Style tips for everyday women. That kind of thing. Her account's been monetized."

"How much money was she making with this crap?" I asked.

"Don't know," Tori said. "But I'm sure you'd get that in discovery." She grinned.

"Not you too," I said. "It's bad enough Jeanie's on me about this case. Why are you?"

She got a faraway look in her eye. "I don't know. It's Bryson, really. I know what he's going through."

The room got quiet and I felt like a jerk. It should have been immediately clear to me why this case would hit close to home for Tori. Her father had gone to prison for a murder he hadn't committed when Tori was just a kid too.

"Do you think she's innocent?" I asked.

Guilty Acts

"I don't know," she said. "Probably not. It's just ... it seems so stupid to post videos of herself handing poisoned drinks to her husband for months."

"Unless she figured that's exactly what everyone would think. It's stupid, yes. But maybe more calculated than everyone's giving her credit for."

"Maybe," Tori said. "Only I've been in Bryson's shoes. I knew my dad's public defender wasn't doing him any good at the time. Nobody would listen to me. Things might have turned out different for him if he'd had someone like you from the get-go. And look, maybe she's guilty. She probably is. But if she at least has qualified, good representation Bryson won't have to torture himself like I did."

I sat back in my chair. Tori paused one of Juliet's videos where she was looking straight at the camera. It's impossible to see into someone's soul through their eyes. That's a myth, in my opinion. Certainly you can't do it on a laptop screen. But as Juliet Clay stared back at me, I saw quiet desperation. She came off as needy in those videos.

"The diet shake company was paying her," Tori explained. "They're getting a heap of negative press from all of this. It's in their interests to make sure Juliet gets convicted. And again, I'm not saying she's not guilty. I'm just saying there are other people who need her to be guilty even if she's not."

"Who's her lawyer?" I asked.

"A guy named Rodney Reid. He normally practices in Ann Arbor. Not even sure why he's on a Woodbridge County court-appointed list. Don't be mad. I already talked to him."

"And said what?"

"Well, he was pretty interested when I told him I worked for you. Cass, I think he wants off this case. I got the impression he views it as a headache for him. Something he regrets getting involved in. He wouldn't specifically confirm it, but I really think I'm right. I think there's someone out there who wants Juliet convicted no matter what. Maybe it's someone connected to the diet shake company. I don't know. But he asked me point-blank if Juliet asked you to take over. He went so far as offering to send his file to me."

"He what?" I asked. I pulled up a browser and typed Reid's name into the bar directory. I could tell by his State Bar number he'd only been in practice for six years. He was listed as a solo practitioner. That alone didn't mean anything, but I'd never heard of him. Tori asked the right question. What was he doing taking Woodbridge County court appointments?

"He said this was his first murder case," she said. "He's not ready for it. He didn't say as much, but I'll bet anything he assumed he'd just be brokering a plea deal for Juliet. I don't think he planned on actually going to trial."

"Unreal," I said. "Has he done any discovery at all?"

"He said if you wanted to talk to Juliet, he wouldn't have a problem with that."

She started biting her lip again. Another secret.

"What else did he say, Tori?"

"He said Juliet's been trying to fire him. The court won't let him withdraw unless she's got substitute counsel lined up. Cass, she can afford you."

"You've been in cahoots with Jeanie for days, haven't you?"

She smiled. "Don't be mad. And it's your call. Juliet's probably lying about everything. She probably is just that dumb. You don't have to take the case. Jeanie will help Bryson. She'll make sure he's got the support he needs if his mother gets convicted. But maybe if you just talked to her. Your instincts are good. Even if she's guilty, she deserves a good defense lawyer."

I heard footsteps in the hallway. Jeanie had made her way up the stairs. I got the distinct impression that these two had rehearsed this whole meeting and maybe even Tori's speech.

"You might as well come in," I said.

Jeanie at least had the decency to flash me a sheepish grin as she walked into my office.

"Fine," I said. "I can't fight off the two of you. And let me guess, you've already got Miranda on your side. She's probably already spent the retainer checks."

From the first floor, I heard my secretary, Miranda, shout up. "Just take the meeting, kid!"

I couldn't help but laugh. "Fine! I'll talk to the woman. But just talk. No promises. I'll take a look at my schedule."

More footsteps as Tori and Jeanie's co-conspirator climbed the stairs. Miranda handed me a pink note. "Tomorrow," she said. "Nine a.m. You're meeting Juliet Clay at the county jail."

Outplayed and outnumbered. I took the piece of paper and slipped it into my bag.

Chapter 3

SHE WAS PRETTY. Not beautiful. But without all the make-up and filters she used in her videos, Juliet Clay looked more like twenty-five, not thirty-five. She wore her blonde hair tied back; about an inch of light-brown roots showed. When she saw me looking, she put a hand on her forehead to hide it.

"I didn't think you'd come," she said. "When Bryson called, I told him he was wasting his time."

"Does he come visit you?" I asked.

"Just once," she answered. We sat in the common room. I was just a regular visitor, not her lawyer. We almost had the room to ourselves. Two female deputies stood by the only exit and in the far corner, another inmate spoke in hushed tones to her boyfriend. She was crying. I tried not to eavesdrop, but he was breaking up with her.

"I don't want Bryce to see me like this," she said. "He's been through enough. This is harder on him than it is on me. He's lost weight. His skin's a mess."

"I'm not your lawyer," I said. "But I don't think it's a great idea for you to be having conversations with Bryson. You know he's been subpoenaed to testify in your trial. He'll be asked to disclose what you talk about."

"Oh, we never talk about my case," Juliet said. "And we don't talk about his dad. I just ask him how he's doing in school. Whether he's eating right. If he's got enough money. I'm still his mom."

She hiccupped on the last word. Tears filled her eyes.

"Well, he's very worried about you. And he seems to think I can help you."

She reached for me. "Can you? I mean, will you?" Her fingers cut into my wrists. I don't think she could have held me harder if she were dangling from a cliff. I realized at that moment she was.

"Mrs. Clay," I said. "This is a little complicated for me. I'm not technically your attorney. I tried to get a hold of Mr. Reid. He should know we're meeting."

"Let me guess," she said. "He wouldn't take your call. He's been ghosting me too for three weeks. I keep getting some blow-off answer from his secretary. He's in trial on another case. Everything's under control with mine. Meanwhile, as you mentioned, my son's been subpoenaed to testify against me. That can't happen. They can't put him through that."

"Well, I was given permission to tell you that my partner, Jeanie Mills, has agreed to represent Bryson. He's going to file for legal emancipation."

"I'm glad," she said. "It was my idea. That way if anything ... if things don't work out for me, he can chart his own path. And you should know, that's all I wanted. It's the only reason I suggested Bryson go to your office. I'm not trying to ambush you or guilt you into helping me."

"I appreciate that," I said. "Fortunately, I'm in the position in my career where I can pick and choose which cases or clients interest me."

"Do I interest you?" she asked. Something flickered in her eyes. She was scared. That was plain. At the same time, I couldn't help feeling that Juliet Clay was far more cunning than she currently wanted to let on.

"Yes," I said. "I'll admit, Bryson's easy to want to help. He's a sweet boy caught in the crosshairs of something horrible. He has everyone in my office smitten. Jeanie will take care of him. You don't have to worry about that."

It was then she broke down. Tears spilled freely from her eyes and she buried her face in her hands. "I can't ... I don't know how to thank you. How can he survive all of this? How can he ever have a normal life again?"

I remember asking myself those questions about my younger brother and sister twenty-five years ago. Our mother died. For all intents and purposes, we lost our father then too. It had just been me and my older brother, Joe, holding things together. Bryson Ballard didn't have anyone.

I wouldn't tell her what everyone else probably had. That kids are resilient. They are. Yes. But Bryson was going through the defining trauma of his life.

"I think you can't try to solve his entire life in one day," I said. "Or yours. I think you just have to work on getting through the day you're on, then do the same thing tomorrow."

She straightened her back. "Thank you. I think that's the first honest thing anyone's said to me during this. My friends mean well. Those who will still talk to me, anyway. But they keep telling me God will see me through. Like I've got a fairy godmother who will just swoop down and wave some magic wand and fix things."

I smiled. "I don't think that's how God works."

She got quiet. She studied me. Sized me up. Was I someone she could trust? Did I want to be?

"I told you the truth. I didn't send Bryson to your office on my behalf. But now that you're here. I'm going to ask you. Will you help me? Will you look into my case?"

I paused, sizing her up in turn. Had she slowly poisoned her husband to death while the internet watched? Did it matter in terms of my representing her? Tori made a compelling argument. Even if Juliet was guilty, she deserved a competent defense. It was still possible the elusive Rodney Reid was giving her that.

"I won't promise you anything," I said. "I have a lot of questions and you aren't even the principal person I need to ask them of."

"I understand," she said.

"But this, right now, has become a legal consultation. Do you know what that means?"

She ran her finger along a seam in the table. "It means that what I tell you is confidential."

"That's right."

"Are you going to ask me?" she said, meeting my eyes. "Are you going to ask me if I killed Nate?"

I took a beat. "No. I'm not. Not right now."

She nodded quickly, beating back fresh tears.

"Why don't you give me some background. Let's start there. Tell me about you and Nate."

She smiled. A real one. "He took care of me," she said. "He always took care of me. There's a role everyone wants to put me in. Trophy wife. Homewrecker. I'm none of those things. We had a marriage. A real partnership. Nate was drowning when I met him. He was rotting from the inside out. Ulcers. High blood pressure. Panic attacks. Everything was work, work, work. His first wife, Alison? They were completely dysfunctional together. She nagged him constantly. Wanted to change who he was. People don't understand it because of our age difference. But I fell in love with Nate's soul. I believe we'd always been destined to be together. Life mates. I know it's hokey. Nate used to tease me about it, but I'm certain we always find each other. Like in past lives. And maybe someday, in some other incarnation, we'll find each other again. Like I said, I know how that sounds. It's just, our love was transcendent. That's all I'm trying to say."

"That's a good story," I said. Though I knew it was decidedly different than what her son told the cops. "But there's no such thing as a perfect marriage. You had problems. And you have to know that every one of them will be played out and dissected in court."

She looked down. "I know. I do. I promise. I'm bad with money. We fought about that a lot. And we made unconventional choices. But I'm telling you, it was mutual. I refused to let Nate ever feel like our marriage was a prison. That's what he had with Alison."

I crossed my arms in front of me. "So you had affairs. Or he did."

She shook her head and focused on the ceiling.

"Look," she said. "A lot of people want to say a lot of things about me. I deserve it. I put myself out there. That's why so many people related to me online. Some of it was embellished for clicks. I won't deny that. But what you see is what you get with me."

"You didn't answer my question," I said. "Were you cheating on Nate?"

Her eyes snapped back to mine. "Not cheating. Cheating implies you're breaking the rules. I wasn't breaking the rules."

"The rules," I said. "You're saying you and Nate had an open marriage?"

"Yes."

I reached into my battered leather messenger bag and pulled out a pad of paper and pen. I slid them across to Juliet. "Names," I said. "Time frames. Who were you sleeping with? Who was Nate sleeping with? Has Rodney Reid gone over all of this with you?"

"I don't know who he's talked to," she said. She wrote down three names and slid the pad back to me.

"Have the police talked to these men?" I asked. It would be in their report. There would be witness statements. But I wanted to hear Juliet's version first.

"I assume so," she said.

"Hasn't Reid shared the police report with you?"

"No," she answered. "We've had two conversations. I told you. I don't know what he's doing."

"All right," I said.

"Will you ask me now? What I think happened to Nate?"

"No," I said. "Not here. Not now." I motioned to the two deputies standing by the door and the other couple in the corner. If they overheard anything Juliet said, they could testify about it.

"I'll pay a visit to Rodney Reid myself," I said. I pulled a form out of my bag and slid that to Juliet. "He'll need a release from you in order to talk to me about your case. This isn't an agreement that I'll represent you. Not yet."

She signed it quickly and slid it back. "What do you need? What will convince you to take my case? I'll say it again. I didn't send Bryson to you for me. But that doesn't mean I don't know how good you are. I need good. I need great. I think you are."

"I don't know," I said. "That's the honest answer. I haven't decided anything yet."

"What can I do? You know there's money. I can pay. There wasn't before. But Bryson set up that fundraising page. I'll be damned if I'll let Reid get his hands on it for doing nothing."

"I told you I have the luxury of choosing my clients."

"Then what? I'll do anything. Ms. Leary, I truly believe that unless you agree to help me, they're going to put me in jail for the rest of my life."

"We can start with a polygraph," I said. "If we go forward, I need you to take a lie detector test."

"Those aren't admissible," she said. An odd answer if she were an innocent woman.

"It will just be for me," I said. "And it's a deal breaker."

She looked back at the ceiling. Her hands trembled. Finally, she met my eyes once more.

"Okay," she said. "I'll do it. How soon can you set it up?"

Chapter 4

"Nice bass!" I shouted as I made my way down the porch steps. My niece, Jessa, held up her gleaming silver catch. Its tail flopped and caught her under the elbow. She squealed and tried to hand her pole off to my brother.

"You take it off, Uncle Joe," Jessa said.

He laughed. "No way. You're old enough to do that by yourself."

"He's too wiggly!" Jessa argued.

Joe stood with his arms crossed. Jessa's pout didn't work on him. He'd raised a daughter of his own and it seemed like yesterday I saw him having this same argument with my other niece, Emma.

I stepped onto the pontoon where my sister Vangie, Jessa's mother, watched the goings-on with a smile on her face.

"Don't look at me," she told Jessa. "My pouting never worked on him either."

Jessa screwed her face with determination, then tried to pull the hook out of the fish's gaping mouth.

"Not that way!" Joe and my other brother, Matty, shouted in unison. Matty stood on the fishing boat moored to the other side of the dock casting his own pole. The pair of them had been trying to teach her how to bait her own hook and take a fish off the line for a while now. Only she had them both wrapped around her finger so it wasn't always clear who was teaching whom.

"He swallowed it," Jessa said. Matty reached down and pulled a small pair of pliers from a toolbox underneath one of the boat seats. He tossed them to Joe who went about teaching Jessa how to deal with it.

"She's got a birthday coming up," I said to Vangie, pouring her a glass of lemonade from the pitcher I brought out. "Can we have the party here?"

Vangie thanked me for the glass I handed her, then tucked her bare feet beneath her once more. "She'd love that. It looks like it's going to stay warm for another couple of weeks."

It was. Eighty degrees in the last week of September, the leaves were already starting to change color. We might just be able to scrape two or three more weekends before I had to pull the boats and the dock.

"So," Vangie asked. "Should I send an invitation to Eric then?"

She tossed a look at both of my brothers and shrugged. I nearly spit out my lemonade, laughing.

"Smooth," I said. Clearly, the three of them had been working out how to ask me about my relationship status.

With Jessa's fish properly rescued and dispatched, he threw it back in the water and stepped onto the pontoon. Matty reeled in his line and stuck his pole in the PVC holster he'd attached to the dock. He took the captain's chair and my three inquisitors faced me.

"Sure," I said. "You can invite Eric. But I don't know if he'll be back in town."

I calmly sipped my lemonade, trying not to show any emotion. Probably a waste of my time. Joe at least could easily read me.

"Well, I don't like it," Joe said. "I don't like seeing you pining over someone who saw fit to abandon you."

I set my lemonade down. "I am not pining, and Eric didn't abandon me. Not like it's any of your business."

My siblings all looked at each other and burst into simultaneous laughter. I couldn't help but join them. Personal boundaries weren't something we Learys stuck to for very long.

"Five months though," Matty said. "And you haven't heard from him?"

"I've heard from him," I said, but wouldn't go much further. Detective Eric Wray and I had a complicated history. He'd left Delphi last spring after a deep personal tragedy. I missed him. But I understood his need to sort through it all on his own.

"His wife died," I said. "He's allowed to grieve for her. And he's allowed to do it without his current girlfriend asking him about it all the time."

"She was barely his wife. That marriage had been over for years," Vangie said. "Her death doesn't make her a saint now."

"Let's not," I said. "Let's just let Wendy Wray rest in peace. I've got plenty of other things to keep me occupied. I am *not* pining."

"You're pining a little, Aunt Cass," Jessa chimed in from the dock. She'd just caught another smallmouth bass. This time, she got it off the line herself with no trouble at all.

I put a hand over my heart. "You too? Man. Talk about an ambush."

Matty's deep laughter rocked the boat. He looked good. Great, actually. He had color in his cheeks and finally a decent haircut. I poked him in the ribs and felt his hardened stomach.

"Oooh," I said, delighted to train the spotlight on someone else. "Lift your shirt. What's that?"

I pulled at the hem of my brother's shirt and peeked under it. He had a true six-pack. Joe laughed.

"Someone's been working out," I said. Matty blushed and gently pulled my hand away. I tousled his hair.

"Baby brother's got some guns too," I teased.

"Sun's out guns out," Vangie added.

It was great seeing Matty looking so healthy. He'd struggled with his addictions but for the last year and a half, turned a real corner.

"It's a girl," Jessa said, putting her pole into the holster beside Matty's. "Do you have a girlfriend, Uncle Matty?"

"Back off," Matty said, but he was still blushing. "You're all a bunch of weirdos."

My barking dogs drew our attention. Two mallards had gotten close to the shoreline. Marby and Madison charged after them, but never got close enough to do anything tragic.

"Well," I said. "Are you going to keep us in suspense? Who is she? What's she do for a living? Is she Irish? Does her father know how to work power tools?"

Joe laughed the hardest. Vangie and Matty were too young to remember but those were standard interrogation questions from our Irish grandmother.

"Stop," Matty protested. "There's nothing to tell."

"Don't lie," Vangie said. "My friend Melanie said she saw you driving around in Chelsea and there was a blonde woman in the car with you. You went by too fast for her to make her out."

"Nice move," Joe said. "But Chelsea's not far enough if you're planning some intrigue."

"Apparently not," Matty said. There was an edge to his voice that all of us respected. Whatever was going on with him, he wasn't ready to let us in. I said a silent prayer to St. Joseph that whoever had him hitting the gym and sneaking off to Chelsea was worthy of him. And also that her father knew how to work power tools.

"So Melanie also told me you went to visit Juliet Clay at the jail the other day," Vangie said.

"Give me a break with this Melanie," I said.

"Clay will make 'em pay," Joe said. "That's her husband, right? From the billboards on 127?"

"Yeah," I said. "And it was just a consultation. Nothing to get excited about yet."

"I thought you were going to take at least a year off murder cases," Matty asked.

"It was just a consultation," I repeated. "And you know I can't tell you any more than that."

"Oh, she's all over the internet," Vangie said. "Poisoned him with health shakes and did it all online. She bragged about how he lost forty-seven pounds in four months on those things. It was sick. There's one where he even chimes how good the things taste and calls them a miracle."

"Yikes," Joe said. "Sounds like another lost cause. I'm sure you'll be filing an appearance by the end of the week."

"Don't joke," I said. "There's a kid in the middle of all of this. That's how any of it came onto my radar."

"Ah," Matty said. "Jeanie strong-armed you. Is she taking care of the kid?"

"She is," I said.

"Katie knows the first wife," Joe said. "Alison was her name. She used to babysit Katie and her sister."

"Has she talked to her lately?" I asked. "What's Alison been saying about all of this?"

"Katie talked to her a few months ago. Ran into her while they were both waiting for an oil change. Alison doesn't live in

Delphi anymore but she was in town visiting her mother and took her car in for her. It was right after Clay died. I don't even think they were saying it was murder at that point. Alison was pretty talkative. She's remarried. Katie got the impression Alison was still on good terms with Nate."

"What's the story there?" Vangie asked. "Everyone assumes Juliet was a home-wrecker."

"Katie!" Joe yelled. My sister-in-law had been inside the house making chili for all of us. She came through the screen door and walked down. She wore an apron and wiped her hands on it before she stepped onto the boat to join us.

"Cass is asking about your conversation with Alison Clay."

Katie raised a brow. "She's Alison Densmore now. It wasn't very in depth. I didn't want to pry. I could tell she was pretty shaken up about Nate's death."

"I might like to talk to her myself," I said. "I wasn't in town when he married Juliet. What was the scuttlebutt?"

"I'd always assumed Nate was catting around with Juliet. I mean, she was your typical pretty, blonde nightmare of another woman. She was in her twenties. Nate was what, twenty, thirty years older? I know Alison was in love with him. I can't speak to what really broke their marriage. But Juliet's always just been ... I don't know. Let's just say she's not too popular with the other PTA moms. Maybe that's unfair. But Alison is well-liked. Juliet isn't."

"Just because of her marriage to Nate, or is there something specific people said? And I mean before Nate's death. Now it's easy for everyone to say whatever they like about her."

"I didn't know her well," Katie said. "Her son is four or five years younger than Emma. But I do know she was asked to step down from the football boosters board."

"Why?"

"Juliet was always trying to sell something. Like she'd use those meetings to try to rope other parents into whatever get-rich-quick pyramid scheme she was peddling. Those diet shakes were just the latest. She always seemed desperate to be liked. I think if she could have just settled down and not tried so hard, people might have taken to her better. Nate, on the other hand; everyone loved him. He came to all the meetings. Volunteered wherever he was needed. He donated a sizable amount to the school. I don't know. The two of them were just polar opposites."

"I see," I said.

"Do you think she did it?" Vangie asked, directing the question to Katie, not me. I found myself on the edge of my seat, waiting for her answer. It didn't matter. Only evidence did. But I was already trying to decide how a future jury might view Juliet if I decided to take the case.

"I don't know," Katie said. "I can tell you one thing for sure. And I don't like to spread rumors. Particularly of this kind. But Cass, you should know. The reason Juliet Clay got kicked off the boosters wasn't because of her pyramid schemes. The real reason is because she was sleeping with the football coach behind his wife's back."

Great, I thought. Joe was right. Another lost cause. My specialty. Only my gut was telling me something far different. Just then, my phone vibrated with a text message. It was Tori. Rodney Reid was willing to see me first thing in the morning.

Guilty Acts

I clicked my phone shut and smiled, not daring to let any more on to my family.

Chapter 5

Rodney Reid made me hate him in all of five seconds. He had the kind of office that made me cringe. Disarray with files stacked everywhere on top of each other. He kept me waiting in his lobby for almost thirty minutes and when he finally did usher me in, he immediately took a phone call.

"Sorry," he said upon hanging up. "I'm in trial next week in Lenawee County. I'm due at a deposition in an hour so we're going to have to make this quick."

"Quick?" I said. "Mr. Reid, you have a first-degree murder trial scheduled in ten weeks."

"Yeah. I've got a secretary to manage my schedule. You here to apply for the job?"

His lips curved in a smirk. Was I supposed to laugh at that? He was older than me. Maybe fifty. Only I knew he'd only been practicing for just over five years. Miranda sleuthed out he'd worked for his father's shipping company before that. When the old man sold it off and retired, Rodney Jr. here apparently tried to find a new purpose in his life.

"Look," I said. "I'll be frank. I've met with Juliet Clay. I don't know if you're aware, but my law partner is handling Bryson Ballard's emancipation petition."

"Who's he?" Reid asked. My blood heated.

"He's your client's son. Are you aware he's been subpoenaed to testify against her? Have you even met with him?"

Reid's blank expression told me hadn't. Unbelievable.

He reached behind him and started rifling through the nearest mountain of paperwork. He pulled out a stack of unopened mail. Most of it bore the Woodbridge County Prosecutor's Office as the return address.

Before he could review any of it, his secretary buzzed his landline intercom to let him know he had a call waiting.

"Just a minute," he said. It took me a beat to realize he meant me, not the secretary.

As Reid reached to pick up his receiver, I reached my breaking point. I leaned over his desk and caught the receiver before him. I picked it up and slammed it down, hanging up on whoever he had waiting.

"Enough," I said. "You're going to give me fifteen minutes of your undivided attention. I don't know who the hell you think I am, but you're going to show me some professional courtesy."

His face reddened, but Reid sat back in his chair and locked eyes with me.

"What do you want?" he said.

"Your client came to me asking for help. I wasn't going to judge you by anything she said." I bit off the next sentence I wanted to utter. I was judging this guy plenty by how he'd conducted himself in the last hour.

"Fine," he said. "Your office is gonna help out Juliet Clay's kid. That's good. Just send me a copy of anything you file. I'm going to need to interview him at some point, of course. So you're planning to be present for that? Leave your card with my girl out front and we'll make sure to coordinate schedules."

So many reasons to punch this jerk in the throat. I curled my fists in my lap.

"I said my partner was taking Bryson on as a client. Juliet Clay asked me to look into *her* case for her. I came here as a courtesy. I haven't decided if I want to be involved or not."

Reid laughed. He had nicotine-stained teeth. Even seated, I could tell he was tall. He had a long, lanky frame and as he pushed his chair back, I caught a glance at his foot as he crossed it over his knee. He wasn't wearing his shoes and his gold-toe sock had a hole in the heel.

"She wants to dump me. Music to my ears. I'll file a motion to withdraw before the end of the day."

He went for his phone again and buzzed to the front desk. "Dawn, can you get in here and bring a Substitution of Attorney form?"

"I haven't said if ..."

"What's she paying you?" he asked. "Did she sign a release? Never mind. I'll take your word for it. Dawn, bring an empty banker box too."

"What are you doing?" I asked.

"I'm giving you everything I have," he said.

I could not believe what happened next. Dawn, his overworked, likely underpaid secretary came in with the banker box he asked for. Rodney Reid dumped a stack of paperwork and files inside of it, filling it to the brim. Then he shoved the whole box across the desk toward me.

"All yours," he said.

"She hasn't signed a full release," I said, incredulous.

"You said you consulted with her. I trust you're good for it. I'll have my last bill to the court clerk."

"Have you even looked at any of this?" I asked, rising. At a quick glance, most of these documents looked like copies of the police file. I saw no pleadings filed by Reid, but it was a big stack of papers.

"Anything you need to know, you can ask Dawn," he said. Reid had already turned his attention to his computer screen. Dawn, on the other hand, gave me a very pointed look that told me she was well aware of this bozo's idiocy.

"Why did you even agree to take this case in the first place?"

"I regret it," he said. "I was working my way up to suggesting that lunatic find substitute counsel. So this will work out for everybody."

"Once again, I haven't agreed to take it on. At the moment, it's pretty clear to me that you've left a mess of it. I'm not taking these files."

On the other hand, it occurred to me if I didn't, who knows what Reid would do with them. One thing was clear. In Reid's hands, Juliet was as good as convicted already.

"Well, let me know," he said. "You wanna look through those? Be my guest. You can use my desk. Now I really do have to get going."

Reid slipped into a pair of loafers and grabbed a wrinkled suit jacket from a coat rack in the corner. He extended his hand to shake mine, then hustled out the door, leaving me in his office, my jaw still on the floor.

"He can't ... is he really ..."

"Afraid so," Dawn said. She was young. College-aged, well dressed in a crisp, cream-colored suit and heels. She looked more professional than her boss by a mile.

"You're a law student, right?" I guessed.

"Third year," she said.

"Okay, well, Dawn? I think you need to take that guy as an example of everything you're not supposed to do in the practice of law."

She laughed. "I'll keep that in mind. I've been after him to let me organize his files for months. He says he knows where everything is and I'm not supposed to touch it. He hired me as an intern. I was the only one of my law school friends who got a paid gig after first year. He keeps promising to let me do more than answer phones and schedule his appointments though."

"Well, you deserve better," I said.

Dawn's expression went grim. "Listen, so does Juliet Clay. If you're on the fence about taking her case. Um ... maybe you should."

She stepped around me and cleared a few piles off Reid's desk. The idiot had left his computer on, giving me a full view of the settlement letter he was working on for another client. Dawn noticed it too and quickly hit the power button on the monitor. "You can take all the time you like," she said. "I eat lunch at my desk. I can order you something too if you'd like."

"No, thank you," I said. I had half a mind to just storm right out. To the extent taking Juliet's case would act as any kind of favor to Rodney Reid, I was disinclined. But I thought of what Tori said and what she went through as a kid. A buffoon very much like Reid had bungled her own father's murder trial. I promised her I'd take a look. And so I would.

Dawn excused herself and left me alone with Reid's mangled file.

I found Reid's copy of Bryson's subpoena. Unopened, of course. There were several others just like it. As far as I could tell, Reid had done no discovery or investigation on his own. The whole box was filled with everything the prosecutor's office sent under mandatory disclosures.

I set aside a copy of the full police report. It was the thickest file in the box. I flipped to the tab with Nate Clay's autopsy report.

There were no surprises in the listed cause of death. Acute thallium poisoning. Amelia Trainor, our county coroner, theorized he'd ingested the stuff over a period of weeks. More lab results showed analysis of the protein shake mix found in a plastic blender bottle in the kitchen. It tested positive for thallium and Juliet's fingerprints were all over it. That, the videos of her feeding the things to Clay, and several witness statements presented a pretty damning case against Juliet. It was actually worse than I thought.

But there was one more report that caught my eye. Supplemental findings from Amelia's examination.

"I'll be damned," I muttered.

"Is everything okay?" Dawn appeared, startling me. I checked the clock on the wall. Nearly an hour had gone by. I was due in court myself in half an hour.

"You've read through all of this yourself, I take it?" I asked.

"Most of it, yes," she said.

"Including these?" I asked, waving the summary of Nathan Clay's medical reports.

"Yeah," she said.

"This hasn't been part of any news stories on the case. The press doesn't have it."

"Nope," she said.

I flipped through the report again, wondering if I'd misread it. I hadn't. Amelia Trainor's physical findings during the autopsy conclusively confirmed it. Juliet never mentioned it to me. Not once. As far as I knew, not even Bryson Ballard knew the contents of these files.

"Do you think any of that matters?" Dawn asked me, her genuine curiosity written plainly in her eyes.

"I don't know," I said. "It depends on a lot of things. But according to this, even if Nathan Clay hadn't ingested poison, he would have been dead a few weeks later anyway."

Chapter 6

When it came to administering polygraphs, Norma Savoy was the best in the business. She'd been at it long enough, coming up through the ranks during Jeanie's era. That's how I first met her. With eyes cold as steel and the backbone to match, Norma wasn't afraid of anyone. She'd gone head-to-head with some of the worst killers in Michigan and saw through everything.

"Thanks for doing this one on such short notice," I said to her. Topping nearly six feet, Norma towered over me. She had a head of braided black hair with wiry gray through it. She'd been overweight most of her life, but twenty years ago, on her fiftieth birthday, Norma decided to become a bodybuilder. She dropped a hundred pounds and replaced it with solid muscle that rippled through her arms as she offered her hand to shake mine.

"Let me guess," she said. "You're expecting a rush on the results too." There was no edge to her voice. Instead, her eyes twinkled as she said it.

"You know I'm good for it," I said.

She laughed. "Damn right you are. I'm charging you double my normal rate plus my rush fee."

"Ouch," I said, but I was teasing too.

"I got your email," Norma said. "Anything special you want to add today?"

"Just what we went over," I said. "But I'd like you to probe her about her husband's medical condition. I'd like to figure out if she knew he was dying."

"Poor bastard," Norma said. "My dad died of pancreatic cancer. This was fifty years ago so there was pretty much nothing they could do for him. There isn't much now. But at least you can get some oxy or something to take the agony away. It's a rough way to go."

"Not as rough as the kind of poison they found in his system," I said.

"Man," Norma said. "Well, you know there's a limit to what I can tell you. But even without the machine, I'm a good read."

"Your gut feeling means a lot to me," I said. "Maybe even more than that thing."

I pointed to the roll cart Norma dragged behind her. It contained all of her equipment. She refused to work with an assistant, preferring to hook her subjects up to the complicated sensors by herself.

Just then, two deputies met us and ushered us into the bowels of the county jail to their biggest conference room where Juliet Clay waited.

I hadn't had a chance to talk to her since I had a look at Rodney Reid's file. My decision to delve any deeper rested on the outcome of today's examination.

"You sitting in?" the deputy asked me.

"She is not," Norma answered for me. "I want two of you outside that door and there better not be any recording devices in there."

"Of course not," the deputy answered. She seemed flustered in Norma's presence. A common occurrence. She opened the door and Juliet was already inside. She rose, adjusting her orange jumpsuit.

"Hi, Juliet," I said. "I'd like to introduce you to Norma Savoy." I waited for the deputies to leave us alone. Word would get out that Norma showed up to see her today, but no one but the three of us would ever know how this all played out.

"Thanks for doing this," Juliet said. "I've been anxious to get started. I've been waiting so long to ..."

"Stop," Norma interjected. "Not another word until I get you hooked up and start asking questions."

"Come with me," I said to Juliet. "I've made arrangements to use the office next door for a couple of minutes while Norma gets ready for you. I won't be staying through the test so this is our only chance to really talk."

One deputy went back in the room with Norma, the other led us into the adjoining office. Juliet sat in the nearest chair, her wrists still cuffed but they'd removed her ankle chains.

"We'll just be a minute," I told the deputy.

"I'm nervous," Juliet said. "Will that make any difference?"

"No," I said. "People are always nervous about these things. Ms. Savoy will factor that in when she interprets your results. She'll ask you a series of questions to get a baseline."

"Okay," she said. "I mean, I've only seen this kind of thing on television. I'm not scared of the questions. I know the truth."

"I met with Mr. Reid," I said.

"So then you know what I've been talking about," she said. "That man is a menace. I'm screwed if I can't find someone better. If you won't …"

"One thing at a time," I said. "Let's just get through today. Just follow Ms. Savoy's instructions. I'll call you in a day or two once I've had a chance to review your results. Then we'll take it from there."

"Have you seen Bryson? Is he okay?"

"I haven't," I said. "But he's in good hands with Jeanie. You don't need to worry about that."

"Thank you for doing this," she said. "It's a lot more than Rodney's ever done. He doesn't believe me. I know it. I can see it in his eyes. He just wants to cash in whatever the county pays him. I'm so glad he never got his hands on that fundraising money. I think he thought I'd accept a plea deal."

"Has the prosecution even offered one?" I asked.

"Heck if I know. He doesn't tell me anything."

"Well, he'd have to tell you that," I said. "He has an ethical responsibility."

"Ethics? Rodney Reid wouldn't know ethics if it smacked him in the ass. Oh sorry. I know I shouldn't swear."

"I need to head back to the office," I said. "You're in good hands with Norma. Just follow her instructions and answer truthfully."

"That's all I've ever done!" Juliet said. "But everyone wants to believe the worst of me. They're jealous. All of them. The second I was able to carve out something for myself, they found a way to tear me down."

"Who's they?" I asked, not liking this side of her. I'd probably never put her on the stand even if I went to trial for her. Still, it mattered that she could keep her cool under pressure.

"Everyone. People. I don't know. Nathan's friends never liked me. They blame me for his divorce from Alison. I didn't even meet Nate until after they were already separated."

"Okay," I said. "There will be time for all of that later. Norma should be ready for you. I'm going to leave you to it. I said I'll be in touch in a couple of days and I meant it. I'll have an answer for you one way or another. If I can't take your case, I'll help you find someone who can."

"No!" she nearly shrieked. "No. You have to help me. You just have to."

The deputy rapped softly on the door. I called her in.

"She's ready. Are you ready?"

"Yes," I said.

"Aren't you going to go with me?" Juliet asked, her indignance faded. Now, she just looked and sounded very scared.

"Not this time," I said. "You can trust Norma. Your statements to her are confidential too. The results of your poly won't be made public either. You've got nothing to be afraid of today. That's a promise."

I hoped that was true. As many questions as I had about Juliet's story, I knew Rodney Reid would bury her, just as she feared.

The deputy walked back into the conference room with Juliet. I waited long enough for the door to close behind her, then took the opportunity to meet with another inmate client of mine before heading back to the office.

Chapter 7

I found Jeanie and Miranda waiting for me in my office when I got back at the end of the day. Miranda stood in the doorway while Jeanie paced.

"What now?" I asked. "Please tell me there's no more bad news."

"That's what I'm waiting to hear from you," she said. "How'd the poly go?"

"I don't know yet." I checked the wall clock. It was just past five. Norma probably finished with Juliet Clay by noon. She hadn't specifically said whether she'd have results for me by the end of business today.

"She put a rush on it," I said. "Relax. And I haven't agreed to anything anyway."

I hadn't filled either of them in on what I'd learned about Nate Clay's cancer diagnosis.

"Well," Jeanie said. "I've got a hearing on Bryson's emancipation petition at the end of next week."

"That was fast," I said. "How's he doing in the meantime?"

"He's okay. Anxious. He had to move in with a different friend the other day. I'm working on getting him some temporary housing if his petition's granted."

"Any worries that it won't?" I asked. "His seventeenth birthday is only two months away."

"The bigger issue is going to be financial," she said. "Nate's stuff is still tied up in probate. What he left for Juliet is up in the air pending the outcome of her trial. On that ..."

I put a hand up. "No way. You know better than to ask me. As long as you're representing Bryson, there's a conflict of interest. You're walled off. Completely."

"I just wish I had some good news to give the kid," she said.

"Me too," I said.

"Well," Miranda chimed in. "Word on the street is Rodney Reid showed up to court today inebriated. He actually fell asleep in Judge Ivy's courtroom."

"He's lucky if he can hold on to his license, let alone win a murder case."

"I know," I said. "You know I can't offer you details, but let's just say I got a good look at the inner workings of Reid's law practice. It wasn't pretty. I will tell you that I told Juliet I'd find her suitable representation if it wasn't me."

I glowered at Jeanie as she gave me her own hard look. I would not be bullied into this. Not even by her.

"What else happened today?" I said, changing the subject for all our sakes.

The pair of them exchanged another glance that got my hackles up.

"Spill," I said. "You've both been acting weird since I walked in."

It was then I noticed Miranda had been holding an envelope. She took a breath and gently set it on the desk in front of me.

It wasn't a business mailing. Instead, it had the size and shape of a greeting card. I picked it up and flipped it to the return address.

My heart did a little flip as I recognized the handwriting. Coupled with the Raleigh return address, I knew Holmes and Watson over here had sleuthed it out, too.

It was from Eric. By the weight of it, I guessed there might be a letter inside along with whatever card he'd sent.

"When's the last time you heard from him?" Jeanie asked, not even attempting subtlety. Suddenly I wished she were just grilling me about Juliet Clay's case.

"It's been a couple of weeks," I said. "Thanks for bringing me this."

"No calls? No texts?" Miranda blurted. "What on earth is he thinking?"

"I don't know." I laughed. "Call him yourself if you're so curious." I tried to play it off, but I was almost as desperate to hear from him as these two were. When Eric left, I knew there was a chance he might not come back. Delphi held a lot of pain for him. I wanted to think he still had a good reason to stay though I refused to put pressure on him. We left things open. I would give him his space. But the card in my hand weighed heavily on me.

Did I love him? Did he love me? We'd both been so ripped raw after his ex-wife's murder it got hard to think straight about each other. My brother Joe said we'd been using Wendy Wray's fate as an excuse not to deal with our relationship. I argued, but maybe Joe had a point. For the first few weeks after Eric left for Raleigh, we'd stayed in daily contact. But then, as the summer faded into fall, his texts and mine to each other became less frequent.

It hurt. It killed. But until Eric decided whether he wanted to be in Delphi for good, I had to guard my heart.

"He loves you, you know," Jeanie said. "He's waiting for you to tell him."

"Jeanie, don't start," I said.

"We just want you to be happy," Miranda said.

"I appreciate that," I said. "I really do."

"You two need a push," Jeanie said. "I'm sorry if you don't like it, but you're both too stubborn for your own good. I'm about to call him up myself and tell him to fish or cut bait."

I smiled. "That's what Joe and Matty say. And seriously. You can stand down. We'll figure it out or we won't."

"Is it Killian?" Miranda asked. "Are you still thinking about your own ex?"

Killian Thorne had been more than my ex. He'd been my most important client when I worked for the Thorne Law Group in Chicago for his brother. A career that had almost cost me my life and my law license.

"No," I said. "I'm not thinking about Killian anymore. So just pipe down, you two. And what's so wrong about me just being single for a while?"

They exchanged an impatient look. They had something to say, but some nonverbal cues between them kept them both quiet. Jeanie looked back at the unopened letter on my desk. I reached for it, then flipped it over in my hand.

I wouldn't get the chance to open it. Not then. Instead, my phone buzzed with an incoming text. I'd set it on the desk and both Jeanie and Miranda could read it.

Norma Savoy. She wrote, "I've got your polygraph results. Is now a good time to talk?"

"Out," I told the two of them. I waited for the door to shut before picking up my phone.

Chapter 8

I HELD my breath as if that would help. Norma shuffled some papers on the other end of the phone.

"Well," she started. "The nutshell of it is your girl is telling the truth."

I exhaled.

"Okay."

"You'll have my full report in your inbox by tomorrow morning."

"Don't email it," I said. "I'd rather have Tori come pick it up. She can be there whenever's convenient for you." I wasn't sure Tori would appreciate an hour and a half drive to Novi, but the Clay murder case was about to become her life as well as mine.

"Whatever floats your boat."

"Give me the highlights, Norma," I said.

"No deception detected on any of the money questions, Cass. I asked her if she killed him, poisoned him, wanted him dead ... oh, on that one, she said sometimes. That's about the most honest answer I've ever gotten from a spouse."

"Wow."

"All the conspiracy questions. She admitted she'd been sleeping around on him."

"I already knew that," I said. "They had an arrangement."

"Different strokes, I guess."

"What'd you get when you asked her if she knew the husband was terminal?" I asked.

"That was a little soft," she said. "She got pretty emotional during that one. I can't tell you if it was genuine. I've written some detailed notes in my report."

"Thanks, Norma, I really appreciate it. I know you had to bump a lot of things to do this for me."

"I don't mind it every once in a while. You know that."

"I do," I said. "You just let me know when you're ready and Tori will be there."

"You got it," Norma said. She clicked off. She was like that. Norma Savoy wasted no words or time saying goodbye when the conversation was over. I kind of liked that about her. I set my phone down and took a moment.

She passed. Juliet Clay had passed her polygraph. I knew it wasn't admissible, but for me, it might just be the ballgame.

Miranda had a sixth sense. Or she'd heard me end my conversation. She knocked on the door, then let herself in.

"Well?"

"She passed her poly with flying colors."

Miranda smiled.

"Don't say anything to Jeanie. I mean it. If I'm going to move forward with this, she's walled off."

Miranda saluted. "You want me to give Reid's office a call? I can get his complete file by the end of the day."

Miranda had a small file folder tucked under her arm. Knowing her, I could pretty much guess what it was. She confirmed it with a sheepish grin.

"So when's my hearing on the substitution of attorney?" I asked.

"Judge Castor's willing to do it on the pleadings," she said. "If you hurry, you can get in to see him first thing in the morning before he takes the bench."

"I don't know how you do what you do." I laughed. "You're never allowed to retire."

"Thanks. I think. Do you want to know when your appointment at the prosecutor's office with Rafe Johnson is?"

"Let me guess. About thirty minutes after I'm supposed to see Judge Castor."

"Forty-five," she said, handing me the small file with my substitution motion. She'd tabbed it for my signature. I signed and handed her back the file.

"Now get on home," she said. "But get back here early. If you can catch Castor after his coffee but right as he starts in on the donuts Nancy brings in on Thursdays, he'll be in the best mood he gets into all week."

"You're a gem, Miranda. I could kiss you."

I followed her down the stairs. She made copies of my motion and slipped them into the outside pocket of my leather bag before scooting me out the door.

CASTOR'S OFFICE WAS EASY. Ten minutes after the clerk's office opened in the morning, I had my substitution order and filed my formal appearance on Juliet Clay's behalf. That weasel Rodney Reid had already submitted a final billing to the county. As I waited for my file stamped copies of my order, Nancy Olson, the county clerk, gave me a fresh earful on him.

"I regret ever giving this appointment to him," she said. "I've had a bad vibe from that guy from day one."

"Wouldn't be the worst thing in the world if his name got dropped from the system," I said.

Nancy gave me a knowing wink. "Rumor is, he's got some issues in Ingham County too."

"What kind of issues?"

She clammed up as two attorneys got in line behind me.

"Thanks," I said, as she handed me my file back.

"Good luck on this one," she said. "You're gonna need it. Reid already asked for two extensions. Castor's gonna be disinclined to grant any more."

It meant I'd likely be in trial with Juliet in eight weeks. It might as well be eight minutes.

"Why do you let me do these things to myself, Nancy?"

"Oh, you'll get up to speed in no time. We all have faith in you. Besides, if you show up with a pulse, you'll be better for that woman than her previous lawyer."

I thanked her and stepped aside. Castor's office and Nancy were efficient, but I was already late for my meeting at the prosecutor's office.

I hustled down the courthouse steps. Johnson's office was only two blocks away. An early fall breeze lightened the air. As I rounded the corner, I saw my brother Matty's brand-new blue pickup truck pulling up to the stop sign. He had a huge smile on his face. He threw his head back in a laugh and that's when I saw he had someone sitting in the passenger seat.

Quickening my step, I tried to get to the crosswalk before it was his turn to pull forward. Waving, I tried to catch his eye, but he turned his head to the person beside him. Hands went around his neck, threading through his hair. He leaned in.

They were kissing. Oh boy.

"What are you up to, little brother?" I muttered. If I hadn't been wearing heels, I would have broken into a run. Matty hadn't said a word about seeing anyone. But he'd been in a damn good mood the other day and I wondered if this mystery woman might be why. The car behind him honked. Matty straightened. He waved to the driver of the honking car as the passenger-side door opened. Matty said something to the woman as she exited, then pulled through the intersection.

I froze as I saw who it was.

Tori.

She was still smiling and laughing as Matty pulled away. She stared after him for a moment, unaware of anything else going on around her. I ducked behind a street sign so she wouldn't see me. Then waited as she turned on her heel and started walking toward our office.

Thunderstruck, it took me a moment to collect myself. Matty. And Tori. Tori and Matty. That was no innocent, friendly drive into town for convenience. They were intimate. And by the looks of it, it had been going on for a while.

"Cass!"

A deep voice drew my attention away from Tori as she sprinted down the sidewalk. She was too far away to hear my name being called.

I turned as Rafe Johnson walked briskly toward me. "Glad I caught you," he said. "I'm due in court in a few. I'm going to have to miss our appointment unless you're good with a walk and talk."

"I am," I said, plastering a polite smile on my face. Whatever was going on with my brother and Tori, I'd have to make brain space for it later. I turned and started walking back toward the courthouse with Rafe.

"You'll hear as soon as you get in there," I said. "But I just filed an appearance on behalf of Juliet Clay."

"Ah," he said. "I'm glad to hear it. I was concerned she wasn't being well served by her court-appointed counsel."

"On that," I said. "I was hoping you wouldn't fight me if I asked for an adjournment on the trial date. It's coming up."

Rafe stopped walking. "That one's out of my hands," he said. We both knew that was bull. "My office is under a bit of pressure on this one. Nathan Clay was very well liked. This case is getting some attention."

"Right," I said. "I suppose you think you need a win."

It was a light dig, but a dig, nonetheless. Rafe was still new in this town. He hadn't had any big wins yet. A high-profile murder conviction would be the perfect feather in his cap. It was a long shot to even ask. But we both knew the real reason Rafe would be disinclined to do me any favors.

"I really do wish I could help. I should tell you, I'm also not authorizing any plea deals. This case is a ground ball for us if ever there was one."

"Rafe, I was just brought on board. I don't even have Rodney Reid's full file on this case."

"Christ," he muttered. "I'm sorry about that, but I can't help you. I really wish I could. Your client should have taken my offer when I made it last month."

Neither Reid nor Juliet had mentioned a single thing to me about any proffered deals.

"Rafe," I said. "Are you sure Rodney Reid took your offer to Juliet? I gotta be honest, your concerns about him are the same as mine."

His face went blank. "That son of a ..."

"Was there anything sent in writing?" I asked.

"Look, I'm glad you're on the case. But be careful, Cass. Reid was a menace. I just wouldn't want you getting dragged after this woman files her appeal, alleging ineffective assistance of counsel. Because she will be convicted. I'm as sure of this case as any I've ever tried."

"Thanks for the pep talk, Rafe. Can I at least count on you to cooperate with me if I need to fill in any gaps from whatever Reid sends over?"

"Of course," he said. "And good luck. You're really going to need it."

He was posturing, of course. At the same time, I had a nagging feeling there was a landmine somewhere in the depths of Rodney Reid's mess of a file.

Chapter 9

"I don't know," Tori said. She stood in front of the war room white board. For the last day and a half, she'd been carefully arranging photographs of the main witnesses in Juliet Clay's case and taping them to the wall.

I sat at the table watching her as she mulled over each face and read off the main thrust of what they'd told the police. I had yet to ask her about seeing her with my brother. In all honesty, I wasn't sure what to make of it myself. If he'd just hooked up with her, I'd kill him. If it was serious ... that would present a whole other mess of potential problems.

"What's the main evidence against her?" I asked. It was a test. Tori had been handling mostly estate planning since she'd passed the bar. She wanted to sink her teeth into litigation and I had plans to broaden her role. Juliet's case seemed like the perfect opportunity.

"Well," Tori said. "There's the poison. They've got Amelia Trainor, the M.E., who'll tell the jury it was Nathan's cause of death. Then you've got the method of delivery. Those shakes.

The cops found thallium residue in the blender bottle by Nathan's bed. His fingerprints and Juliet's were on the bottle. How are you going to counter that?"

"The best I can do with Amelia is make her admit she can only testify about how Nathan died. She can't conclude who gave him the poison."

"That's weak though," Tori said. "She's also going to be able to talk about how horribly sick Nathan would have been in the last days. Thallium poisoning is a rough way to go. The weight loss. Hair loss. He complained of debilitating stomach pain."

"But he was also dying of pancreatic cancer."

"Right," she said. "But what difference does it make? He didn't die of it."

"I think we need to explore that further," I said. "Can we find a competing medical expert who might conclude cancer is what ultimately took his life? It doesn't mean Juliet's off the hook, but if he flat out didn't die from thallium poisoning, well, they can't prove murder."

"Only attempted murder," she said. "That's good, Cass. Do you mind if I work that angle?"

"I was hoping you would," I said.

"When are you meeting with Juliet again?"

"Soon," I said. I walked to Tori's side and pointed to two witnesses she had just taped up.

"Donovan McNamara," she said. It was a grainy blow-up of a photo ID badge. McNamara was Juliet's most recent lover. He worked in a lab where they manufacture optic lasers.

"So he's the hook," I said. "Berriman labs. You're saying thallium is used in laser manufacturing? That's what they're hanging their hats on?"

"That's what's bad, Cass. They can prove motive, means, and opportunity through this guy."

"Maybe," I said. "Only he hasn't been charged."

"I think that's the strongest thing you've got going then," she said. "Thallium isn't something you can just go pick up at the farm store. It was banned in the United States decades ago. People used to use it for rat poison."

"The cops just can't prove he was involved," I said. "It doesn't mean the prosecutor won't be able to use him."

"But there's no there, there. Sure, he had access to thallium and Juliet had access to him, but there's no record of that chemical going missing. That's why he wasn't charged."

"I'll handle McNamara's cross," I said. "I'm sure the prosecution is going to try to call him as a hostile witness. He's going to testify he saw nothing, knows nothing, and was never asked by Juliet or anyone else to acquire thallium at all, let alone in enough quantity to kill somebody over the course of several weeks or months."

"But they'll call somebody from the lab. You have to assume they'll be able to prove that McNamara had access to the stuff."

"Tori," I said. "I want you to handle the laboratory witnesses. Do you think you can? You know what you need. You can hammer home the points you just said. Did anyone see McNamara take anything he shouldn't have? There was none missing from the records."

Her face lit up. "You want me to cross-examine some of the witnesses? At the actual trial?"

"Yes," I said. "I'll be there the whole time. But I think you're ready."

"It's a first-degree murder case," she said. "Cass, are you sure?"

"We wouldn't be having this conversation if I wasn't. And I know I don't have to tell you how high the stakes are on this. I'm going to do what I can to try to buy more time. Rafe Johnson has already told me he'll oppose it. This trial has been postponed twice already. We have to be prepared for the worst-case scenario. And that is, jury selection in seven weeks. That's no time at all."

"I understand."

My stomach filled with dread. I didn't want to be having this conversation and knew how much I hated it when my siblings poked their noses into my private life.

"Tori," I said. "You've seen me when I'm in the middle of a murder trial. You know the toll it takes on my personal life. Frankly, I don't have a personal life for the duration. Can you commit the time this will demand?"

"Of course!" she said without hesitation.

"I'm pretty much going to be living in the office for the next two months."

"Cass," she said. "I know. I'm ready. I know what this takes."

I felt like a jerk for not just coming out and asking her, but this was brand-new territory we were treading. "Is there anyone in your life who might need to know that too?"

She caught my eye. Unspoken dialogue rose up between us. She knew. I think she even knew I knew. This was her opportunity to tell me about Matty. I watched a variety of emotions flicker over her. Then, she finally seemed to settle on cold resolve. She swallowed hard and pursed her lips.

"There's nothing in my life that would get in the way of me giving one hundred percent to trial preparation on this. I won't let you down. I promise."

I felt like a first-class jerk. I should have just come right out and asked her what I meant. Whatever was going on between Tori and my brother wasn't something she felt comfortable disclosing to me. Would I have even asked her these questions if it wasn't Matty I'd seen her with? But these were two people who meant a great deal to me. If Matty hurt her ... he had a lousy track record with the women in his life. I knew where the bodies were buried. Only Tori's answer and demeanor spoke volumes. She didn't consider this my business until she told me otherwise.

"What about Bryson Ballard?" she asked. "Do you really think they'll put him on the stand against his mom? Maybe that subpoena was just a scare tactic. A ploy to get her to reconsider a plea deal."

"Rafe was pretty adamant he wasn't offering one anymore. The McNamara connection came late in the game, after Juliet was charged. He said they offered her second degree at first but withdrew it after they figured out where McNamara worked."

"But he was cleared," Tori pointed out again. "I just don't get it. They know you'll make it crystal clear to the jury there's no proof he stole any thallium on Juliet's behalf."

"The viral videos and the diet shake connection are the clincher," I said. "Unless I can figure out a way to keep the jury from seeing those videos of Juliet actually giving Nathan the shakes, they're a killer."

"Have you read any of the online comments?" Tori asked. "There are whole hate groups that have popped up. People are out for blood. Juliet just seems to represent a lot of really negative stuff for people. She's pretty. Trim and fit. She projected this perfect Instagram life that triggered a lot of people. Now they're just waiting to watch her get torn apart."

"I want to talk to her team leader at the diet shake company," I said. "If I can at least plant a seed that someone else might have had access to those shakes."

"Like was someone trying to poison her instead?"

"Maybe. It's worth a few questions anyway. But she had her blood drawn after she was arrested. There was no trace of thallium in her system. There's no evidence that she ever ingested any of it. Only Nathan."

"Did they test Bryson?" Tori asked. She started sifting through some of the reports on the table.

"He was negative too," I said.

"What do they want him to say at trial?" she asked.

I pulled Bryson's statement to the police. He gave it before Juliet became a person of interest.

"He was asked about Nathan and Juliet's relationship," I said. "Were they getting along? Did they have a fight? Bryson said they did. There was an incident a couple of weeks before Nathan died. One of the neighbors actually called the police to report on a domestic disturbance. Bryson said they both yelled a lot. And it says in there Nathan made a statement to the effect that Juliet would be the death of him."

"Everyone says that kind of stuff. Lots of married couples yell a lot," Tori said. "It's just so awful for that kid. He doesn't want to be put in the position of helping the prosecution put his mom in jail for the rest of her life."

"It is awful," I agreed. "But it could backfire. There will be mothers on that jury. Sons too. Rafe needs to be very careful not to overplay his hand by how hard he goes at Bryson."

"Are you even planning to subject him to cross?"

"I don't know yet. When Jeanie thinks it's okay, I'd like to talk to the kid again."

"Okay," she said. "So what's next? Cass, thank you. It means everything that you're trusting me taking a more active role in this trial. You're great at this, you know. Maybe one of the best I've ever seen."

I laughed. "You're young. You haven't seen enough yet."

"Stop. Take a compliment. I mean it."

"Thanks. I've said this before but I think you're better than I was at your stage in my career. We'll make a good team."

"Okay." She blushed. "So really. What's next?"

"Follow up with Donovan McNamara's coworkers and boss. Flyspeck their records. Make sure we don't leave a single i undotted. I don't want any surprises from the prosecution on that point. I've got an appointment to talk with Nathan Clay's law partner. Juliet said the two of them weren't on the best of terms before Nathan died. I want to see if there's something there the cops might have missed."

"Do you really believe she's innocent? I know she passed her poly, but …"

I paused, really considering how to answer Tori's question. "I believe she's telling the truth."

Tori cocked her head to the side. "Cass, you realize that's not what I asked you. I asked you if you think Juliet is really innocent."

"I know," I said, smiling.

Tori's jaw dropped. I left her that way among the mountain of reports as I headed for the stairs.

Chapter 10

I ENCOUNTERED A VERY different Juliet Clay at our next jailhouse meeting. Gone was the damsel-in-distress vibe. She was clear-eyed, rigid-backed, and ready to work.

"We have to be ready to go to trial in seven weeks," I said. "Johnson's office isn't cooperating on my request for a continuance."

"Good," she said. "I don't want one. I want to get this over with and get my life back."

"Seven weeks is no time, Juliet," I said. "I've only scratched the surface of your file. Rodney Reid left it in disarray. There are witnesses he's never interviewed. Leads he never followed up on."

"I didn't poison Nate," she said. "And now you know I'm telling the truth. I'll tell the jury the same thing. They'll believe me. I'm good with people, Cass. I know how to build a following. I can build one with those twelve jurors. I know I can."

I tapped my pen on the legal pad in front of me. "You can't take the stand."

"I can't not. People will think I've got something to hide. I don't. I've lived my life as an open book. I put everything out there for the world to see and to dissect. I'm not afraid of negative opinions. I know I've got a fair number of detractors too. They tell you not to, but I've always read all my negative commenters and trolls under every video or blog post I've ever done. I'm not afraid."

"That's good," I said. "But keyboard warriors are one thing. Facing a seasoned prosecutor during cross-examination is something quite different. And the results of your polygraph won't be admissible. Any mention of it could be grounds for a mistrial."

"But I can tell them I'm innocent in my own words. They'll believe me."

Half the time, I wasn't sure I believed her. I kept that revelation to myself.

"Let's table that topic for now. We have bigger issues to talk about. It's my counsel to you that we pursue a continuance. I know it means more hurry up and waiting. It's difficult for you to be here. But my job is to tell you what I think is best for your case."

"I don't want it, Cass," she said. "The not knowing is killing me. Even if things don't go my way, I'd rather know that sooner rather than later. This limbo I'm in is torture."

"Juliet, it might feel that way, but a conviction after a hasty trial and facing life without parole is not better than putting off your trial date for a few weeks. It's just not."

She got quiet. Tears welled in her eyes and the damsel was back.

"Listen," I said. "I need to talk to you about two of the more problematic witnesses. Johnson's office will call. Donovan McNamara is going to hurt you on the stand. He's a critical component to their case. They'll argue he's how you got a hold of thallium."

"Except I didn't," she said, nearly shrieking. "Until this nightmare, I didn't even know what thallium was. How could I have possibly asked someone to get it for me? See, that's what you need to let me tell the jury in my own words."

"It's self-serving," I said. "As much as you want to proclaim your innocence, that's what regular people would expect you to do. My greatest concern is Mr. McNamara's whereabouts. He's not taking my calls. My assistant went to his house and he's not living there anymore. He's renting it out. I have every expectation the prosecution might miraculously find him before trial. I need to do it first. Reid had the benefit of discovery. He should have interviewed him months ago while he was still considered a person of interest in your case."

"Mac's useless," she said. "Seriously, Cass. We dated for a while last year. I wasn't in love with him or anything."

"That's not what he told the cops," I said. "He told them he broke things off because you were getting too clingy. He said he didn't like your energy. Granted, his statements are also self-serving. At the time, they were trying to pin him as an accessory to murder."

"He's a spineless weasel. I'll tell you. The only silver lining in all of this? It takes a murder charge to reveal who your true friends are. Do you really think whatever Mac says will hurt me that badly?"

"Maybe. Maybe not. It hurts that he had access to thallium. A lot. Only nobody saw him take it. There doesn't appear to be any amount of the stuff missing from Berriman labs in the relevant timeframe. He's denied his involvement and he's never actually been charged. It means the cops couldn't make a case against him. It's all speculation and innuendo. I'll fight like hell to keep his testimony out. But I'll lose. We have to assume Mac is going to take the stand and do everything he can to throw you under the bus."

"It's ridiculous!"

"But you met him at work. There's a record of you going to visit him after hours. They've got you on tape walking into a section of the lab not very far from where the thallium was kept."

"I don't even know what it looks like," she said, waving me off.

"It's a thin thread," I said. "But it's there. If the jury really wants to believe you poisoned Nate, it might be enough of an explanation for them no matter what Mac says."

"What do you need from me then?"

"I need you to think. I have to talk to Mac myself. If there's any friend or relative or place you know of where he might be hiding out, tell me."

"I don't know," she said.

"Well, think about it. Hard."

She nodded, but fear lit her eyes.

Guilty Acts

"Now," I said. "We need to talk about someone else. Tell me everything you can about your husband's law partner. What do I need to know about Ted Gorney?"

Fear left her eyes and anger took its place. "What's he saying about me now?" she asked.

"I'm meeting with him the day after tomorrow at his office. How were things between Nate and Ted? What did Nate tell you about their practice?"

Juliet clasped her fingers together. "I can tell you if there was anyone who really wanted to hurt Nate, it was Ted."

"How were they getting along?" I said. "Can you tell me anything about their dynamic I can use? Were there any disgruntled clients? Anything else between them that would have put them at odds?"

"Nate didn't talk about work very much. He was a lawyer when I met him. He was in practice with Ted Gorney before I met him. But Ted's always been jealous of Nate."

"How do you know that?"

"Just the way he presented himself. He'd drive over with whatever new hot rod convertible he bought to rub Nate's face in it. Boats. This ridiculous condo in Florida. He's one of those people who has to always tell you how much he pays for everything. How many square feet his house is. On and on."

"But what makes you think he wanted Nate dead?"

"I told you. Nate and I had an unconventional marriage. It worked for us. I'm not saying Nate wanted to hear every detail of any other men I was with, but he respected it. I was always upfront. I was just as open to any comfort he might seek outside the marriage."

She was veering wildly from what I'd asked her.

"Did Nate ever actually seek comfort outside the marriage though?"

Juliet bristled at the question. Nowhere in the police report or any of Reid's notes such as they were mentioned a current or former girlfriend of Nate Clay's.

"I don't know."

"But you said you were entirely open to the idea if he had. So do you think he just never told you or he never actually had any extracurricular dalliances?"

"I don't know!"

"Juliet, if we're going to get through this together, you're going to have to be completely straight with me. Did Nate have a mistress? Either at the time of his death or any time during your marriage?"

"No," she said. "Okay? No. He looked. He looked plenty. We'd joke about it. Anytime we went out to dinner and a pretty girl or handsome guy walked by, I'd ask him how attractive he thought they were. And he would tell me. I was fine with it. It was actually useful. You know. For me to really know who and what he found attractive. What got his juices flowing."

"But as far as you know, your open marriage was one-sided. And you're absolutely sure he knew about Donovan McNamara and every other lover you took?"

"Yes," she said. "I mean I was never that clumsy with the way I said it. Not so blunt. I would call them my friends but Nate knew."

"You're sure?"

"Yes."

I paused. "I believe you. I'm just not sure you'll get a jury that is quite so open-minded."

"You're not," she snapped. "I know you're judging me."

"I'm not. Whatever two people do within a marriage or a relationship that is consensual and legal is no one else's business. I don't judge people for who or how they love."

"But others might," she said.

"But others might." I agreed. "Now, you've managed to change the subject of Ted Gorney. Tell me why. Why don't you want to talk about him?"

"He's not a fan of mine," she said. "I wasn't just honest about my relationships with Nate. I was honest with him about his. I told him not to trust Ted. I told him about the night Ted Gorney made a pass at me."

There it was.

"Now tell me."

"It was after a Christmas party we had at the house. Ted was drunk. So was I. So was Nate, for that matter. I was getting our coats and Ted found me under the mistletoe. He took it a little too far. He grabbed my behind and pulled me into him. He grabbed me really hard. I was bruised the next day. I told him to knock it off. That I wasn't interested in him that way and that I didn't appreciate him taking liberties like that without my consent. Ted pretty much called me a slut. Said he knew all about my, what was the word you used? Dalliances. He threatened to tell Nate. I told him Nate already knows. At that point, Nate walked in. He'd seen and heard enough to know what was going on. He grabbed Ted and threw him into the wall. He defended me. He told Ted if he ever came near me again, they were through. It was ugly and awkward."

"This was last Christmas?" I asked. "Three months before Nate died?"

"Yes."

"So Nate and Ted remained law partners? This altercation didn't end their relationship?"

"Not their professional one anyway," she said. "But I overheard Nate arguing with Ted on the phone a couple of weeks before Nate died. Nate said I don't owe you anything and I'm not going to ruin my own career to save yours. He hung up on him. When I walked in and asked Nate what was going on, he was pretty much purple in the face. Angry. But he stormed off and wouldn't tell me what was going on."

"I see," I said, jotting a few points down from her story.

"Can you use it?" she asked.

"Maybe," I said. "But even if I thought it was worth the risk to put you on the stand, which I don't, anything you heard Nate say would be considered hearsay. It wouldn't come in. Did anyone else witness the incident at the Christmas party?"

"I don't know," she said. "There were people around, but we were in the backroom. I already told this to the police. They questioned Ted but of course he denied it all. He'll deny it to you, too. It happened though. I swear it. Isn't there any way you can talk to the other people in Nate's office?"

"I'm going to try," I said. "But this was something Rodney Reid should have done months ago. I'll start with a conversation with Ted Gorney himself. This is extremely helpful in preparation for that. I'll let you know how it goes."

The deputies knocked on the door to tell us our time was up. Adrenaline coursed through me as I gathered my notes. I couldn't wait to get Ted Gorney in my crosshairs.

Chapter 11

TED GORNEY DODGED me for four days. It finally took a bribe to the bartender at Mickey's to find out when he was there alone on a Thursday, taking a liquid lunch. He thought I was the waitress when I approached the table and actually asked me for a seven and seven.

"Sorry," I said, helping myself to the empty booth opposite him. I slid my card across the table but I could tell by his expression he already knew very well who I was. Everyone in this town did.

"You're wasting your time," he said. "And I hope you got your full retainer in advance. You're about to get your ass handed to you in court."

"Ah," I said. "So I guess I can skip the part where I ask you if you think Juliet Clay killed her husband."

He laughed. When the waitress did walk by, he gestured to his empty rocks glass. He at least had the decency to ask me if I wanted anything.

"No, thanks," I said.

"Well, we can talk as long as it takes me to finish my next drink."

"I appreciate that," I said. "You've been subpoenaed to testify in Juliet's murder trial. I figured it was long past time for someone on her team to talk to you."

"I gave my statement to the police. I have nothing to add to it."

I had a copy of Gorney's statement in front of me. There wasn't much to it. He'd been out of town a few days before Nate died. He wasn't complimentary about Juliet.

"Look," I said. "You just said you were willing to talk to me. So why don't you let me ask a few questions? What's the harm?"

"Ask away."

"So how long did you know Nate Clay?"

The waitress brought his drink. Smiling, Ted tapped his watch to remind me of what he'd agreed to. He wasn't a bad-looking guy. I knew he was in his mid-sixties. He still had a full head of dark-brown hair with only a few strands of gray in it. His gray suit was well tailored. Ted gave me a pleasant smile and his nostrils flared in a way that made it seem genuine even though I knew it was bullshit. Charming. I'd heard around town that back when they started, Ted would bring in the clients while Nate would do the work that brought the rain.

"Twenty-five years or so," he said. "I started out at a major firm in Farmington Hills. I clerked for a Michigan Supreme Court justice right out of law school before that. When I came back to Delphi to start my own firm, Nate was finishing up his law degree. He tried solo practice for a little after that. It was tough in those days if you were on your own."

"Still is," I said. It occurred to me Ted's career trajectory didn't sound too different from mine.

"Anyway," he said. "Nate and I had occasion to work on a few cases together. A couple times on opposite sides, then a couple of times as counsel for co-plaintiffs or co-defendants in some civil stuff. We had a good rapport. My business was expanding and I needed to take on a partner. I offered him the gig. We were just shy of our twentieth year together."

"That's a long time," I said. "Most law partnerships don't last that long."

"We outlasted both of our first marriages, and my second," he admitted.

"Did you consider him a friend too?" I asked.

Ted jutted his jaw to the side. I had no doubt there was something he wanted to say, but didn't. He was giving me a sanitized version of their relationship, if Juliet told me the truth.

"Did Nate know you made a pass at his wife?" I asked him. It was a risk. Juliet had only told me this little tidbit. Rodney Reid had at least kept her from talking to the police. So I had no idea if they knew that part of Juliet's story.

Ted slammed his glass down. Clear liquid sloshed up the side, spilling over the wooden tabletop.

"Your client is a liar," he said. "If she's telling you she didn't kill Nate, that's the biggest lie of all. I'd advise you not to believe anything that nut job has to say. You can be sure that's exactly what I plan on telling a jury if I do get called."

"Ted," I said. "You're aware I have access to some of your business records as part of the prosecution's discovery. If there were any billing disputes, I'm going to figure it out. It's better if you come clean about it with me now."

"You think you're going to use me to muddy the waters at trial?"

"I'm just trying to get a clear picture of the last few weeks of Nathan Clay's life. That's all. You're getting awfully defensive. Nate was your partner. Your friend of a quarter of a century. I would think you'd want to be as forthright as possible to make sure whoever murdered him is held accountable."

"Nate and I weren't perfect," he said. "You're bound to have disputes if you're in business with someone that long. From time to time, we'd disagree about the direction of the firm. What clients to take. That kind of thing. But at the end of the day, we stayed partners. I wasn't off doing things behind his back like Juliet was. If she's telling you anything happened between us, it's a lie."

"How did you feel about her?" I asked. "I mean, as a partner for Nate. Do you know how they met?"

Suddenly, Ted's posture changed. He got more comfortable in his seat. I recognized a spark in his eye that I'd seen a thousand times in witnesses during cross-examination. He had a story to tell and had just been waiting for someone to give him the floor to tell it.

"She stalked him," he said.

"Stalked?"

"Yeah. Her friend was a client of mine. I represented her in a wrongful death action. Med mal. Gallbladder surgery that went south. Juliet would come with her to the appointments at first. Well, one day, I got up to get something from the front desk and I saw Juliet in Nate's office. She was sitting on his desk, flashing legs, tits, and teeth. He was eating it up."

"Was he married at the time?" I asked. Juliet had maintained their relationship started well after he'd separated from his first wife.

"I don't know if he was technically divorced yet. Somehow Juliet got Nate's private cell phone number. He never told me how. But she started sending him racy photos of herself. Calling him all hours of the day and night. He loved it, mind you. She was like twenty-five at the time Nate was pushing fifty, going through a divorce. He'd put on a little weight. It was a real thrill for him."

"He showed you the texts she sent?" I asked.

"Oh sure. He couldn't believe it."

"How long did they date before they got married?" I asked.

"I wouldn't call what they were doing dating," he said. "But I don't know. I wasn't privy to the conversations they had. Nate just used to brag a lot about all the stuff she was into."

I tried to keep my face neutral. The picture Ted would paint on the stand became clear. This was classic slut shaming. Juliet the man-eater. The attention seeker. The murderer.

"They eloped," Ted said. "It was really sudden. Like one week, Nate was just describing this girl he had a wild weekend with. The next, he put a ring on her finger and off they went to Hawaii to tie the knot."

"But he was happy," I said.

"Yeah. For a while. But Juliet always wanted more and more. He tried to put her on a budget but she'd blow through that. Clothes. Cars. About a thousand pyramid schemes. She sold leggings online. Then she sold nail polish. Hair care products. If there was an MLM for desperate housewives, Juliet would sign right up. Once I went over to their house and damn near had a stroke when I saw all the boxes of crap she had out in the garage. And Nate had a big four-car garage. It was filled with all this inventory Juliet was forced to buy and then sell. My wife at the time got fed up with her always trying to rope her in to be on her team to sell more of this junk."

Ted made air quotes around the word 'team.'

"Then there was her blog," he continued. "And her YouTube channel, and on and on. Trying to get followers. Trying to be internet famous."

"Until she was," I said.

"Yeah," he said. "She went viral, making Nate gulp down those awful shakes. But I gotta say, it looked like they were working. I told you Nate had gained some weight before they got married. Juliet was always trying to get him to slim down. Different fad diets she'd put him on. She made him join a gym. He just let her do what she wanted. Happy wife, happy life, he'd tell me. But I knew he wasn't happy."

"How did you know that?" I asked.

"Because he changed. Nate used to be funny and outgoing. But that woman just nit-picked him all the time. We used to play in a golf league, go on vacations together. Juliet put a stop to all of that. She kept him on a tight leash."

"What about the last few months before he died?" I asked. "What were Nate's spirits like?"

"I gotta be honest," he said. "I saw a change in him. He started losing weight, finally. He looked great. He seemed more like his old self. Freer, if that makes any sense."

"Ted," I said. "Did Nate tell you he was sick?"

I knew the police had already covered this ground with him. I wanted to see his demeanor when I asked myself.

"No," he said, his head dropping. "I had no clue. Nobody did, as far as I know. God, I wish I had."

"How were the two of you?" I asked. "Before he died, I mean."

Ted shrugged. "I'll admit, we weren't as close as I would have liked. But that's how friendships go. There's an ebb and flow. I was happy Nate looked so good. That's why I was so floored when it came out he had pancreatic cancer. You never would have known it. Those last two weeks he took some time off so maybe it was starting to get to him. But whatever he was doing, he hid it. And now, to think that bitch was poisoning him to death on top of it all."

"Ted," I said. "How was the business going? Were you paying your bills?"

"Yes. I turned over everything the police asked for. You already know that."

"How'd you two split the work?"

"I told you. I turned over everything the police asked for."

"Look," I said. "I'm trying to do my job. You're not a suspect in this case. But what you might be able to do is help me figure out if the right person is going on trial for murdering your friend."

He regarded me, took another swig of his drink, then folded his hands on the table.

"It changed over the years," he said. "We always split our profits fifty-fifty. But I was trying to slow down. Nate handled anything that went to litigation over the last five years. He loves ... loved being in a courtroom. I'm over it."

"So you didn't share clients? Was there a clear delineation between who you worked with and who he did?"

"Most of the time, yes," he said. "I took on more of a managing partner role."

"No recent grievances filed against Nate that you know of?" I asked.

"Not that he told me about."

"Come on," I said. "We all have disgruntled clients. Can you think of anyone who had an axe to grind against Nate?"

"If I did, that would be privileged," he said. "And I would have told the cops if there was anything to tell."

"Ted, there were several large draws taken out of accounts payable in the year before Nate died."

"Stop," he said. "We work on contingency. Cases settle, we get paid. You should know how that works."

"Any grievances filed against you lately?" I asked.

He stiffened. He took one last swig of his drink and slammed it on the table.

"Time's up," he said, rising. I rose with him.

"You know I'm going to check," I said. "And I'm going to start talking to as many of Nate's former clients as I can."

"That's your business," he said.

"You're about to be called as a witness in a first-degree murder trial involving your law partner. If there's some skeleton in the closet, wouldn't you rather get ahead of it?"

"Right," he said. "You just want the truth and justice. Sure. Go to hell, Leary. I'm done talking."

"Ted ..."

He grabbed me by the arm. "I'm done," he said. I jerked my arm away, but not before Scotty at the bar loomed in my field of vision. He gave Ted Gorney a look that would melt steel.

"You want to know what was going on between Nate and Juliet? Start talking to their neighbors. His friends outside the office. Because trust me, they'll give you an earful. It won't be pretty."

He threw a twenty-dollar bill on the table and stormed off under the punishing glare of Scotty the bartender and the men sitting in the booth opposite us. I waved them off when they asked if I needed a hand.

Chapter 12

By the end of the week, two rulings came down that would shape the next few weeks of my life and the rest of Bryson Ballard's. I'd taken a rare afternoon to work from home with the intention of trying to relax and enjoy these last bits of straggling summer that hadn't yet been told it was technically fall. That's one of the beauties of living on a lake year round. If you had a rare October Saturday where the weather topped seventy and the wind cooperated, you could spend it pontooning long after the weekenders and Airbnb crowd went back to the cities.

That was my plan, anyway. As Jeanie pulled into my winding driveway with Bryson in tow, her grim expression told me plans would have to change.

She held folded papers in her hand. Peeling off one set, she handed it to me. I didn't have to read it to know what was up. I'd been waiting for this one.

"Hot off the presses," she said. "Castor's denied your motion for a continuance. The trial date is set in stone. November eleventh. He wants this case wrapped up before Thanksgiving."

"Thirty-four days," I said. "I've got a lot of work to do."

"Will it be enough?" Bryson asked. I think he'd grown even taller. He had a good haircut now. Short on the side, with a little of length on top. A grown-up haircut. It was easy to see the handsome man he would soon become. His muscles hadn't yet caught up with his lengthening bones. When they did, he'd cut an imposing figure.

"And this," Jeanie said, waving the second set of papers. Judge Pierce granted Bryson's petition for emancipation.

"Congratulations," I said to Bryson, extending my hand to shake his. This was big. Important. It meant Bryson could choose his own destiny. Most immediately, he could decide where he wanted to live without threat of going into foster care. I knew for the moment he was staying with Jeanie. I also knew how well she'd take care of him, waiting on him hand and foot, making sure he wanted for nothing. Fresh sheets. A warm house with no threat of the gas or the lights being shut off. Clean clothes every morning as she stayed up late doing laundry. If it was cold when he went to the bus stop, she'd put his coat in the dryer for a few minutes before he left the house. Jeanie had no biological or adopted children of her own, but she had stepped in to mother all of us at one point or another. I hoped Bryson knew how lucky he was. The way he kept close to Jeanie, I suspected he did. The hard part would come when it was time to send him off on his own.

"Come inside," I said. "Have either of you had lunch yet? I ordered takeout from that Chinese place you like, Jeanie. I overbought."

"As usual." She laughed.

Though I didn't know the orders would come down, I'd been expecting Jeanie and Bryson. We had to go over his testimony again. Judge Castor's deadline made that even more important now.

Bryson wolfed down a carton of shrimp fried rice and two egg rolls. He settled himself on the couch, taking in the view as the waves crashed against the sea wall. There'd be no pontooning today with this wind. But it was nice to be able to keep the windows open at least.

"I've talked to your stepfather's law partner," I said. "Mr. Gorney. How well do you know him?"

Bryson shrugged and took a sip of his Orange Crush straight from the bottle. My brother Joe liked to buy the retro ones from the convenience store at the other end of the lake.

"I knew him some," he said. "Dad didn't really bring business home. That was a rule my mom always had. He seemed fine. But one of those people you know just isn't used to being around kids. He always talked to me like I was four. Always making sarcastic jokes instead of asking me anything real or listening to what I was saying."

"How did your mother feel about him?" I asked.

"She never talked about him," he said. "I don't remember having conversations about him with her. I know she didn't ever want to go on vacation with him. He had some kind of timeshare in Florida or something. Once, a couple of years ago when my dad told her Mr. Gorney offered it to us, she didn't want any part of it. She said she had no interest in going anywhere with him."

"Did she say why?"

"That's really all I remember. Once my mom said what she wanted, that was it. Nate would make sure she got it."

He cast his eyes downward, seeming uncomfortable with the revelation. I had to be careful here. I'd read through Bryson's statement to the police. It wasn't helpful. He described a volatile relationship where his parents argued constantly. He told the police Nate often complained Juliet was out to get him. Though I'd argue that was inadmissible, I knew why the prosecution really wanted him. Bryson had been with Nate toward the end and could describe in detail how much he suffered. Only I could in no way coach Bryson on how to make my job any easier at trial. Even having him here at the house might be frowned upon.

"Do you think you can win?" he asked, his eyes not leaving the bottle in his hand.

"I think I can put on a good defense. And that's all I can say. Mr. Gorney suggested I speak to your neighbors. Which ones were your parents close with?"

"My mom wasn't really close to anyone. She wasn't the kind of person to have a big group of girlfriends. She was always pretty negative. You know, judging other women for what they wore. If they were fat or not. I got in arguments with her about that. Like, why can't you just be positive for once? She was ... is ... just really insecure. That's the thing people don't realize. She's really good at faking it."

His words went through me like a knife. If he said anything like that on the stand, Juliet was in trouble.

"Do you want me to say I don't think she killed him?" he said, though I hadn't asked. "If they put me on the stand, is that what I should say?"

"I'm afraid you won't get the chance to say that," I said. "It won't be admissible. You'll be asked primarily about what you directly observed between your parents in the months leading up to Nate's death. And you'll be asked what incriminating things your mother might have said to you."

"But that's hearsay, isn't it? I thought you couldn't talk about what other people tell you. Like there have to be special circumstances before you can say that stuff."

"It's complicated," I said. "Since your mother is the defendant, if she said something to you against her own interests, it's not considered hearsay."

"That doesn't make sense," he said.

"Bryson, you'll be asked about conversations you had with your mother about your father. I just want you to be prepared for that."

"She wasn't a saint or anything," he said. "She'll be the first to tell you that. People say all kinds of things. They don't mean it. My mom has a temper. She gets really mad really fast, but it burns out pretty quick. We just learned to ride the wave with her."

"She lost her temper with your father in front of other people," I said. "Often?"

"She's like one of those little lap dogs. The ones who growl at you but then flip over for you to pet them after a few minutes. It's just how she is."

"I see," I said. I wanted to probe deeper, but by Bryson's shifting posture, I knew he was getting uncomfortable. The key to getting him through his testimony was keeping him calm.

"Just tell me what to say," he blurted. "How do I say all that so people will understand her?"

I looked at Jeanie. "Bryson, that's the one thing I can't do. I cannot tell you what to say or how to say it. You have to be honest and forthright when you testify. Don't worry about how you say things. But you also don't have to offer more than what you're asked. If a question calls for a simple yes or no, then only answer with a simple yes or no."

He nodded, then put the pop bottle down. "That makes sense. I'm not feeling very good. Can I use your bathroom?"

"Of course," I said, pointing toward the hallway. "First door on the right."

Bryson excused himself. Jeanie and I walked back out to the porch, well out of Bryson's earshot.

"He's a basket case," she said. "It'll get better once he's had a chance to process today's ruling on his emancipation. So many things have been up in the air for him. I'm working on permanent living arrangements for him and helping him with his finances. He'll be okay."

We went down the dock and sat on the deck chairs I kept on the new platform Joe had built me this summer. The wind kicked up harder, blowing our hair every which way.

"So, do you think you can win?" It was the same question Bryson had asked.

"I honestly don't know," I said. "The law partner is interesting. I got the strong sense there was major bad blood between him and Nate towards the end. I want to talk to some of their mutual clients. See if I can kick up any disputes they might have had."

"You're going to offer him up as someone else with a motive to off Nate?"

I smiled but didn't directly answer. "I'm just interested in how well the police pursued other possible leads."

"Bryson has a meeting with the prosecutor's office next week," she said. "I may not be able to sit in. I'm working that angle."

"With Rafe?" I asked.

Jeanie shook her head. "Nope. It looks like Rafe has someone new in the office who might be handling the actual trial."

I raised a brow. "Really? I hadn't heard that. He's actually throwing this case to a rookie? I would have thought for sure he'd want it as a notch in his own belt. Maybe he thinks he's going to lose."

"Or maybe he thinks it's a ground ball so he's not afraid to let the newbie cut their teeth."

"Thanks," I said. "That's the worst pep talk ever. And it's pretty much word for word what he said to me. Let's talk about something else."

Without missing a beat, she turned to me. "Okay," she said. "You want to tell me why you haven't opened that card from Eric sitting on your kitchen counter? That's the one you got at the office a week or so ago."

"You're the worst," I teased.

"That's no answer. When's the last time you talked to him? And what are you afraid of? Do you think that's a Dear Joan letter?"

My first instinct was to protest. Jeanie knew me too well. That was exactly what I thought. And I wasn't quite prepared to look at it if it was.

"Come on, Cass," Jeanie said. "He loves you. If he was going to dump you, he'd have the balls to do it in person. Plus, you love him too, right?"

I took a breath. "Yes."

"Cass," she said. "Have you bothered to tell him that yet?"

I didn't answer right away. Which was an answer in and of itself. "There's been a lot going on," I said. "His wife died, for crying out loud. And with everything that happened after, Eric needed some space to grieve without me witnessing it. I understand that. He's been trying to spare my feelings."

"Well, that's just crap," Jeanie said. "You're not some fragile little flower. He knows that. You should call him. And you should at least read his card. Let me go get it."

"No!" I said. "I'll do it when I'm ready. Right now, I want to keep my focus on Juliet's case. The simple fact is, no, I'm not at all sure if I can win this. Everything about that woman just looks bad. She's the perfect villain in all of this."

Jeanie smiled. "Well, that's never stopped you before, honey. I have faith in you."

There was movement inside the house. With the heavy wind and lapping waves, I knew Bryson probably couldn't hear what we were saying, but I didn't want to take the chance.

"Just take care of that one," I said. "If he can keep from cracking on the stand, he'll get through it fine. I'm afraid the more I try to prepare him, the more nervous he's going to get. That's no good."

"I agree," she said. "You don't have to worry on that score."

We got up and headed for the house. Bryson was ready to go. I reassured him that we'd get through all of this and hoped I was right.

After they left, I finished my dinner alone. Almond chicken with a side of white rice. It was delicious. I opened my fortune cookie.

"Things you fear will only lead you to new opportunities."

It might as well have been Jeanie talking in my ear. Eric's unopened card seemed to taunt me from the other end of the table.

I wanted to ignore it. Just like I'd done a dozen other times. But the thing filled my thoughts later that night as I tried to fall asleep. No amount of thrashing under the covers made it better. The phrase nagged at me.

The things you fear will lead you to new opportunities.

The card was still there, taunting me early the next morning as I went down to make coffee. Eric's card sat there, stuffed fat with unopened promise. Or bad news I didn't want to deal with. I thought about just throwing the whole thing through the shredder.

Jeanie was right. I was afraid to open it. Afraid to feel that little jolt of excitement and trepidation if I saw Eric's familiar block handwriting. Just plain afraid.

"Screw it," I said to no one, grabbing the card. I picked it up and walked back outside. The dogs came with me, imploring me to take them for a proper walk.

"Just a second," I said. "I don't need either of you chasing after a cat tonight."

Marbury cocked his head sideways as if to say, "Who, me?"

Madison yapped at me and stomped an indignant paw. I turned to grab the double leash I kept on a hook by the front door.

As I turned, the pair of them started barking something fierce and tore up the gravel drive as headlights flashed. Someone was coming.

Clutching the leash and the letter in one hand, I went to see what the dogs did. My heart twisted as the car rounded the curve and came to a stop. The driver stepped out.

The sight of his lopsided smirk sent an electrical current from the tip of my spine to my toes. Detective Eric Wray shielded his eyes from the setting sun and came toward me with a long, confident stride.

Chapter 13

I HAD A HUNDRED FEELINGS. A thousand questions. But when Eric walked up and put a hand on my shoulder, it left me speechless. He was here. Whole. Warm. His twinkling gray eyes held questions of his own.

"It's been a long time," I said.

He looked good. There was color in his cheeks that hadn't been there six months ago when he'd left to grieve on his own. The Outer Banks air and his mother's home cooking had healed him. Perhaps in a way I couldn't, but that was a different reckoning. For now, I was just glad he was here.

"I should have called," he said.

"It's okay," I said. "Come inside. We should talk."

I still clutched his unopened card. I set it face down on the kitchen counter as he followed me. He saw it. Puzzled, he picked it up.

"You haven't opened this?" he asked. I deflected.

"Are you hungry?" I asked, using my grandmother's time-honored Irish greeting that served as hello, goodbye, how are you, and a variety of guilt trips when the need arose.

"I ate on the plane," he said. "I didn't know if you'd be here."

"Where else would I be?" I asked, turning to him. His smile fell a little

"I came straight here," he said. "I haven't even been at the house yet."

"When did you decide to come back? Why didn't you text me?"

He lifted the card, opened it, then handed it to me. It was a simple, thinking-of-you card. On the inside, he'd written, "I miss you, Cass. If I came over, would you open the door?"

My fortune was still sitting on the counter right next to where the card had been. The things you fear may lead to new opportunities.

"Are you staying?" I asked. Screw the card. Screw everything else. It had been six months.

"You got anything to drink?" he asked. Before he'd left, that wouldn't even be a question. My home was everyone's home. He knew where to find the beer. But now we felt like strangers. In a sense, I guess we were.

"Always," I said. He took an awkward step, then regained that smile and stepped around me to reach for the fridge. He cracked open a beer. He was a Coors man. My brother liked Bud. I kept stock of both.

"You want anything?" Eric asked.

"I'm good."

We made our way to the front porch. Eric took in the view. Light rain had started, but the porch kept us dry. We sat together, silently for a moment, then finally, Eric took a breath and laid it all out.

"How mad are you at me?"

My codependent wiring put an automatic answer in my head. I'm not mad at all. I'm fine. But as Eric stared straight at me, I knew he was one of the few who could see through all of that.

"First, I was just worried. Then I was sad. But yes, I was also mad for a while."

"You're the one who stopped texting," he said. He saw something in my expression and quickly shut up.

"I needed you to figure out where you wanted to be without me putting pressure on you."

He said nothing. So I did.

"Have you figured out where you want to be?"

"Here," he said, without hesitation. "I've always belonged here, Cass."

"Have you worked out whatever you left to work out?"

"Why didn't you open my card?"

"I don't know," I said. Because I was afraid.

He stared out at the lake. "Me too."

"So how was North Carolina?" I asked. "Does your sister still hate me?"

He laughed. "Maybe. But I don't want to talk about them. Right now, I just want to hear all about you."

"Okay," I said, but I knew he likely already knew what I'd gotten up to. His smirk confirmed my suspicions.

"I'm working on a murder case."

Eric shook his head. "Yeah."

"Juliet Clay. First degree."

"Yeah."

"Did you know Nathan Clay, her husband, the victim?"

Eric's whole posture changed. If we'd been unsure of each other, that melted away. He was Detective Wray all over again and it had been too long since he'd used that muscle. His eyes sparked with curiosity.

"I knew him," he said. "But we didn't cross paths much. Ambulance chaser, right?"

"I'm not fond of the term, but in essence, yes."

Before I knew it, I'd given Eric the highlights of the case. All the things that were part of the public record. He asked me all the pointed questions and I enjoyed watching his analytical mind turn the evidence.

"You want in?" I found myself asking.

"In?"

"How much longer is your leave of absence from Delphi P.D.?"

He pursed his lips. "That's an open question at the moment and one of the things I came back to resolve."

"This is a Woodbridge County case," I said. "If you served as a consultant to my firm, there'd be no conflict of interest. I could use you. Jeanie's sidelined. She's representing Juliet's son. I've got Tori, and she's fantastic, but I'm going to admit something I haven't said out loud yet."

He locked eyes with me.

"Yeah?"

"Yeah," I said. "Eric, I don't think Juliet's guilty. Which makes me a rarity around town. But the simple fact is, I don't know how to win this case yet. So are you in?"

He cocked his head to the side, still smiling. "Yeah," he said. "Count me in."

"You say that now. I haven't told you what I'm up against."

"Well," he said. "Keep talking. I need another beer. You?"

"Sure. And help yourself to whatever's left in the fridge. It was Chinese takeout last night."

He grabbed the pint of pork fried rice and rejoined me. We moved to the couch. I gave him the highlights of the case against Juliet Clay. I grabbed my laptop and pulled up the photo evidence the police had as well as my digital copy of the police file. Eric slowly sifted through it all. His eyes darted across the screen as his mind worked.

"Thallium residue in the empty glass beside his bed," I said. "More in a plastic container of shake mix in the kitchen. The videos of Juliet actually handing Nate said shakes and him drinking them."

"And Trainor's not budging on the ultimate cause of death?" he asked.

"Not so far. I'm trying to find an expert who can speak to whether it was the cancer that got him anyway."

"That's not a win," he said. "She'd still be up on attempted murder."

"It's my last-ditch strategy," I said.

"So what's your first-ditch strategy? Cuz I gotta tell you, I'm not seeing anything wrong with the warrants or the way they were executed. All this stuff, the cup by his bed. The shake mix in the kitchen. That was in plain sight. Plus, according to this, Juliet agreed to let them search the house."

"Honestly, that's my biggest plus. Juliet never acted like a guilty person, Eric. She cooperated with the cops from the word go."

He played one of the videos Juliet had posted to social media. It was one I knew Rafe Johnson's office would definitely try to get in front of the jury.

"Drink it all, baby," she said in a bright sing-song voice. Nate was off screen. With a jerky tilting of her phone, she focused on him. Nate Clay wore a Jim Beam tee shirt as he sat on the sun porch at the back of their house. He took the chocolate shake mixture from Juliet. She had it in a plastic tumbler with the words "Seize the Day" written in bold red.

Nate sucked down the shake and gave the camera a thumbs up.

"How many pounds are you down?" Juliet asked off camera. Nate was handsome. He was every man on the planet, rolling his eyes at his wife while humoring her all the same.

"Eight pounds," he answered.

"In two weeks!" she squealed.

Juliet stabilized the camera as she hopped on her husband's lap. They smiled at the camera together as an animated cartoon shake with feet danced across the screen.

"God," Eric said. "They're gonna think she's nuts."

"But are they gonna think she's crazy enough to poison her husband in front of her fifty thousand followers and a million views?"

Eric closed the laptop. "Well, she's either that stupid or that smart."

"If we're asking, so will the jury," I offered.

"You sure you can make reasonable doubt on that alone?"

"No," I confessed. "I know I can't."

"And she passed a poly? Who gave it?"

"Norma."

Eric whistled.

"Exactly," I said. "If this were your case, that alone would make you think twice before writing an arrest warrant."

"Was she offered a poly by the sheriffs?" he asked.

"She was, but her public defender at the time refused it. I can't say I blame him for that. Johnson knows she passed mine. He still likes his chances."

"So if she didn't do it, what's your theory of who did?"

I grinned. "See, I think that's maybe where you come in. If you could snoop around. Kinda freelance, like. Nate Clay's partner was really cagey when I met with him. I want to sniff around with the clients they shared. See if he's got money problems. He turned over his books and there were a couple of large draws that went to Gorney alone. There's some there, there. I feel it."

"Drugs, hookers, or gambling," Eric said.

"What?"

"Is there a malpractice case against him? A civil filing?"

"None," I said.

"Who's lead on the case for the county?"

"Sofia Blackfoot," I said.

"Hmm. She's good," he said. "If she didn't pursue Gorney, there's a reason."

"Probably," I agreed.

"So if you think he's stealing money from clients, is it for drugs, gambling, or hookers? So you're looking for a dealer, a bookie, or a liaison. That's where I'd start."

I sat back further on the couch. "I don't know that he was stealing. I just know there were a few high five-figure draws out of their business account payable to Gorney. I just want to know why and wasn't satisfied with his answer."

Eric sipped his beer and stared off into space.

"So you'll do it? You'll sniff around a little? I think if you do it, Gorney won't see you coming. With me, he gave me your basic slut-shaming story about Juliet. His old buddy Nate was never the same after that gold digger came into his life. You could probably recite it back to me word for word."

"Sure," Eric agreed. "But Cass, it doesn't mean it's not true."

"I don't think the prosecution can prove how Juliet would have gotten her hands on thallium. They've got a tenuous connection with an AWOL former boyfriend who worked for Berriman Laboratories. But there's no corroboration and the guy was never charged as an accessory."

"But he's gonna testify for the prosecution? This boyfriend?"

"Assume he will if he ever turns up again."

Eric paused. I knew that look. He was just as puzzled by some of the facts of this case as I was.

"Well?" I finally said.

"Well, I think I still like Rafe Johnson's case better than I like yours. But I'd also like Johnson's case even better if the sheriff's office had gone a little harder at Gorney or potential other suspects. So …"

"You'll do it for me!"

He laughed. "I don't know what my hourly rates are, Cass, but I won't be cheap."

"Deal!"

For the first time in weeks, I felt a lifting of the load off my shoulders. Of course, Eric couldn't promise a specific outcome. He might find something even more damaging to Juliet's case than the reverse. But it was worth a shot. And it felt good to be on the same side as him for once.

We'd talked for hours. I had a million missed calls from Miranda on my phone. There would be questions lobbed at me from all sides about why I went AWOL from the office today.

Eric met my eyes. Once upon a time, I might have asked him to stay over. Or I wouldn't have asked him at all. It would have been understood. But today was different. We still had a long way to go.

"It's getting late," he said, smiling. I rose with him and walked him to the door. He took my hands in his and kissed my forehead. "It's good to have you back," I whispered, my throat feeling thick.

It was a start.

Chapter 14

It only took three days for my decision to recruit Eric to bear fruit.

"I've got somebody you'll want to talk to," he said as I was walking out of court on a different matter. "You sitting down?"

I paused on the courthouse steps, allowing four deputies to pass ahead of me.

"I'm listening,"

"I've got eyes on Donovan McNamara. He's sitting two tables over having lunch at Digby's Bar and Grill in Ann Arbor. How soon can you get here?"

A rush of adrenaline went through me. "How? You know what, no. Maybe I don't want to know. Can you keep him there?"

"Sure," Eric said and I knew he was smiling.

"Give me an hour," I said. "And Eric. Thank you."

"I know," he answered, then clicked off the phone.

I started running. I called the office. "Miranda," I said, breathless. "Can you shuffle my afternoon appointments? I'm not coming back to the office until, well, maybe not at all today. Is there anything we can't move?"

I heard her tapping on her keyboard. "Nothing earth-shattering or nothing Tori can't handle for you."

"Great!" I cut off the call before Miranda could ask me any other questions. I had this strange superstition that if I told anyone else about Eric's get, it might slip away. The fewer people in the loop, the better. They'd grilled me constantly about him coming back to town as it was.

I got a lucky break out of town and avoided any traffic snarls on the highway. I found a spot on Liberty Street in downtown Ann Arbor right away, another miracle. And threw two quarters into the meter.

Digby's was a darkly lit Irish pub. Eric had McNamara pinned into a corner booth at the very back. The guy was red-faced and sputtering obscenities as I approached. Eric scooted over so I could sit.

"I told him," McNamara said, "I'll give you ten minutes. I know I don't have to talk to you."

"Then we can skip the pleasantries," I said. "You know who I am. And you know what I'm after."

"I've done nothing wrong," he said. "The cops in Delphi cleared me of everything. If you want to know anything else, you should talk to my lawyer."

"I'm not the cops or the prosecutor," I said. "I'm not legally required to talk to your lawyer, Mr. McNamara. And if you've got nothing to hide, why have you been dodging phone calls and subpoenas for three months? You've been living like a guy on the lam. Why, if you've got nothing to hide?"

"I don't want anything to do with Juliet Clay ever again. My lawyer says I don't have to."

Eric leaned forward. "You're a material witness to a murder case," he said. "Grow up."

"Do you have any idea what this shit has done to my life?" McNamara spat. He was movie-star handsome. I could see why Juliet went for him. He had a thick head of blond hair and bright-green eyes that were currently narrowed to slits as he stared me down. Strong jaw. Broad shoulders. In a lot of ways, he was the physical opposite of Nathan. He was also thirty years younger than him. Younger even than Juliet herself.

"You're not facing charges," I said. "As far as I know, you're not under investigation anymore."

"I lost my job over this," he said. "My name's been associated with this thing. I was making great money at Berriman as a quality inspector. Now I can't find anything comparable. And my family won't talk to me because now they know I was involved with a married woman. They're deeply religious. I tried to explain it's not what they think."

"So what was it?" I asked.

"What's she told you?" he asked.

"Juliet is my client," I answered. "I can't divulge our conversations. And I'm not here to make things more difficult for you. But you are going to have to face a jury. The prosecution will call you as a witness. If they don't, I might."

I reached into my bag and pulled out a fresh copy of Donovan McNamara's subpoena. I handed it to Eric. Without missing a beat, he slid it across the table to McNamara.

"You've been served," he said.

McNamara took the paper but crumpled it in his fist. I had no idea if I'd even use it. Mac was a better witness for the prosecution. But I wanted to keep my options open.

"Look," I said. "Just as you said, you've been cleared of any wrongdoing in Nathan Clay's murder. Nobody can prove that you acquired thallium for Juliet. But you know full well the prosecution is going to try to get a jury to believe you did anyway. They're going to put that possibility in the jury's mind. I get why you're angry. You're being used as a pawn. What I'm offering is a chance for you to get your story out your way. And first."

"I never gave her that stuff," he said through gritted teeth. "I passed a polygraph for the cops. I volunteered to take it. There's no record of the stuff going missing at Berriman. I couldn't go in or out of that lab without keying in with my security badge and cameras recording all of it."

"But you did take Juliet to work with you once," I said. "There's a record of her being on the premises with you."

He sat back hard against the leather booth. "I left my wallet in my office. We were going out to dinner and we swung by to pick it up. I never took her anywhere near where the chemicals were stored. Anybody who tries to say differently is lying."

"Is someone trying to say differently?" I asked.

"I don't know," McNamara waved a dismissive hand. "You people like to twist words until they suit your purposes. You put me on the witness stand, you might not like what happens."

"Is that a threat?" I asked. Eric bristled beside me. From the corner of my eye, I saw he was carrying.

"I don't know," McNamara said. "What you haven't asked me is whether I think she did it or not."

"You're right," I said. "I haven't."

"Well, you should."

"Your opinion on Juliet's guilt or innocence isn't admissible at trial," I said. "What is admissible is whether she told you she wanted Nathan dead? There's nothing like that in your statement to the police. Do you plan on changing your story?"

"She never said she wanted him dead," he said. "We didn't have that kind of relationship. We really didn't talk about Juliet's husband at all. But what she didn't do was tell me she was married at first."

"How did you two end up together?" Eric asked.

"We met online," he said. "Through a dating app. I've got ... or had ... a busy life. I worked seventy, eighty hours a week at the time. I didn't have time to meet women. Juliet found my profile about a year, year and a half ago and we started talking. She was a good listener. After maybe three months of chatting online and a few phone calls, we went out on a date. It wasn't until we'd been involved for maybe six months that she told me she had a husband."

"How did she characterize her marriage?" I asked.

All of a sudden, McNamara's guard dropped. He clearly had fond memories of his early time with Juliet. "She swore up and down that he knew she'd been talking to me. She said they had an understanding. They could both date. It threw me at first. I almost broke it off. But I really liked her and I wasn't looking for a long-term commitment. I had no intention of asking her to marry me or anything. She was good to talk to. Being around her relieved a lot of stress I was under. So we continued. It was okay for a while. Then it wasn't."

"What happened?" I asked.

"I really just couldn't get past the fact she had a husband. She even offered to introduce me to him so I'd know he really was okay with our arrangement. I don't know. I come from a really strict religious upbringing. I told you that. It just got to me. Then when she told me she had a kid, well ..."

"But Bryson wasn't Nathan Clay's son," I said.

"Didn't matter," he said. "They were a family."

"Who ended it?" I asked.

"There was never a specific end," he said. "We just kind of faded. I stopped calling her. She reached out maybe once or twice but I think she knew. She never put any pressure on me. There was no drama. I think she understood. Then, two cops showed up at the lab and took me in for questioning. I hadn't talked to Juliet in like a month at that point. I had no idea her husband had died, let alone been murdered. And now my life has been completely destroyed."

"They fired you over this?" Eric asked. "On what grounds?"

"They said it was cutbacks. But we've been busier than ever and we're short-staffed. I told you I'd been working sometimes eighty-hour weeks. It was all bull. The lab got bad press because of Juliet's arrest, and my name got printed in the news. Nobody cares that I was cleared. They gave me a nice severance package if I went quietly and signed a release, but in a few months, that'll be gone."

"I'm sorry that happened to you," I said.

"Sure. Whatever you say, lady."

"You're telling me you never discussed Juliet's marriage with her? After she initially disclosed it?"

"Not never," he answered. "But she made it pretty clear it was an off-limits topic. She said when she was with me, she was with me."

"Did you ever ask her if she was going to leave him?" Eric asked. "I mean, come on, man. You said you stayed in it for months after she told you about Nathan. You had to be curious."

"I asked her if things were okay," he said. "Look, she said her marriage was none of my business. That really got me. I just didn't want this guy to show up on my doorstep with a shotgun for something that I didn't cause. Plus, I was worried about her. Like if she wasn't being honest and he found out. Was he going to hurt her? Was she safe? So I did ask her that. She told me Nathan wouldn't hurt a fly. She also told me that they were never getting a divorce."

"Why?" I asked.

"She said their marriage worked for them. She knew other people wouldn't understand it. But they were happy. Anytime

I tried to bring it up, she shut me down pretty quick. So that was that. Like I said. I was fine with it for a little while. Then I wasn't, so I got out. Or tried to. Now it feels like this thing is going to follow me everywhere. And that's all I have to say. Your ten minutes are up. I've got your stupid subpoena. You can't keep me here. So I'm leaving."

He rose, threw a ten on the table, then stormed out.

I think my jaw was actually on the floor as I stared after him.

"Well," Eric said. "That was ... something?"

"I don't know what to make of it. I don't know if he helps or hurts."

We left the restaurant together. Eric walked me to my car.

"You think you'll use him if the prosecution doesn't?"

I dug my keys out of my purse. "I think I'll have to. I need him to do just what he did. Deny he ever gave that poison to Juliet."

"Yeah," Eric said. "Only the thing is ... I'm not sure I believe him. Do you?"

As I looked him square in the eye, I honestly had no idea.

Chapter 15

I HAD to give them credit. My inquisitors waited almost two full weeks before cornering me in a united front.

It was Saturday afternoon. In a few days, Juliet Clay would go on trial with the rest of her life hanging in the balance.

"It's a perfect day for pot pie!"

My sister Vangie blurted it as she and my brothers showed up on my doorstep. She foisted a huge baking sheet with a giant pie on top, carrots and peas spilling out of the bulging, latticed crust.

"Uh ... sure," I said. I barely got the door open before they all barreled through, none of them empty-handed. Joe carried a bag of rolls. Matty had another smaller baking sheet.

"Brownies?" I asked. "You actually made brownies?"

"I have skills you don't even know," Matty teased as he pecked me on the cheek in passing.

I peered out the door after them, but it was just the core three. That meant this was even more serious.

"Sure," I sighed. "Come on in. I've got nothing but time."

Vangie put the pot pie in the oven to warm it. Joe pulled plates out of my cupboard and set the table. Matty got the silverware and grabbed a stick of butter for the rolls.

There was no help for it. My siblings came here on a mission. I'd been the orchestrator of visits like this a thousand times. When Joe had marital trouble. When Matty had addiction trouble. And drama of all kinds seemed to follow Vangie everywhere.

Soon enough, we were at the table as Vangie sliced up and doled out heaping slabs of pot pie on each of our plates.

"I can get my own," Matty protested.

"You most certainly can't," she said, slapping his hand away. "You'll make a mess of it."

She wasn't wrong. Still, I covered my mouth to suppress my laughter.

We ate. It was delicious. I took my time, savoring every bite and stalling for time. It was an unspoken Leary rule. You don't interrogate someone during a meal. We saved that for dessert.

Later, as Matty pulled out the brownies, they started in.

"So," Joe said. I knew then he'd drawn the short straw. "Eric's back."

"Eric's back," I repeated, sinking my teeth into a moist corner piece. No way Matty had made these himself. It dawned on me then who might have. He saw my expression and acted quickly to try to distract me.

"Are you back together?" he asked. "What's he planning?"

I put my brownie down and dusted the crumbs off my fingers. "We're working together," I said. "He's stepping in in an investigative role on Juliet Clay's case."

The three of them absorbed my answer for all of ten seconds.

"What the hell does that mean?" Joe said. "Has he explained himself? Apologized for disappearing for six months?"

"I need a drink," I said. Without offering the rest of them anything, I went into the kitchen and poured myself a glass of Riesling. It was too cold to sit on the porch, so I picked a chair near the window. They all followed.

"Cass," Vangie said. "You went through the wringer with Eric. We're just concerned and wanted you to know we're here for you."

I eyed her. Then I laughed. They laughed with me.

Things got easier for a moment, but I knew that didn't mean I was off scot-free. "Listen," I finally said. "We're taking baby steps. This whole thing has been, well, weird, to put it mildly. If you're asking me if Eric and I have figured out where we stand as a couple or if we are still a couple, I don't have a good answer for you. I'm in the middle of a murder trial. We're focused on that."

"Cass," Vangie said. "Before Wendy died, Eric was getting ready to ask you to marry him. He asked me about a ring! I just do not get you. How are you not going crazy with questions for him? How are you not wanting to strangle him?"

"Because I needed space too," I said. "The last year has been a mess. He had his life upended. So did I. I appreciate your concern. All of you. But I'm fine. Really. I've got my personal life handled. I really do just want to focus on this trial. I'm perfectly content not having everything defined and labeled right now."

"Is he staying?" Joe asked. "Is he going back to being a detective? Would he even be able to? He's been on leave for the better part of the year."

"Where's he even staying?" Matty asked. "His house is for sale. Does he think he can stay with you?"

So much for my speech. None of them listened or cared about a word I said.

"I don't know, okay?" I said, practically shouting it. As cool as I wanted to play it, they all saw right through me. I had the same questions they all did. And yes, part of me wanted to strangle Eric, too.

"Look," I said, finding some Zen. "I meant what I said. I'm in trial starting Wednesday. It's a big one. Maybe one of the biggest in my career. It's going to be brutal and there's a good chance I'll lose. This time, there's more at stake than just my client's future. She's got a scared kid out there who doesn't have any other family. It's a lot of pressure. That needs to be my focus for the next couple of weeks. Regardless of our history, Eric's been a godsend on this case so far. I'm glad he's back."

I'd finished my wine and headed back to the kitchen for a second glass. That would be my limit today.

I'd left my phone charging on the counter. It lit up with an incoming text. Eric. We had plans to meet at my office with Tori to go over some last-minute trial prep. I'd asked him to sit in the courtroom for the duration and be a second set of eyes and ears for me.

"We still on for three o'clock?" the text read.

I answered with a thumbs up emoji then quickly flipped my phone screen-side down. Smiling, I turned back to Joe, Matty, and Vangie.

"Enough already," I said. Matty's brownie pan sat a few inches away. Screw it. I would have a second one of those too.

I didn't recognize the pan as anything Matty had at his place. Most of what he did have were things I gave him.

"These are really good, Matty," Vangie said, her mouth stuffed with her own brownie.

"While we're on the subject," I said, focusing on my little brother. "You want to fess up who actually made them?"

Matty feigned offence, slapping a hand over his wounded heart. "How dare you?"

Maybe it was my natural inclination to deflect, but I decided not to let him off the hook with humor. "Matty, I saw you. A few weeks ago, you dropped Tori off near the courthouse. She was getting out of your truck."

His smile dropped. "Sure. She asked me for a ride. I think she was having car trouble."

Oh no. He was flat-out lying. It meant things between them were more serious than I thought.

"Matty," I said gently. He'd taken a seat on a stool at my massive kitchen island. I leaned across and touched his hand.

"I saw you," I said. "You were together. It wasn't just a friendly favor. You kissed her. It was meaningful."

Vangie and Joe exchanged a look of shock. So he'd been keeping this secret from them as well.

"It's nothing you have to worry about," he said.

I picked up the brownie tray. "She made these, didn't she? Come on. Be honest. What are you doing?"

He crossed his arms in front of him, taking a defensive posture.

"How long has this been going on?" Vangie asked, hurt. The two of them were extremely close. I could understand him not wanting to tell me about his involvement with Tori, but to not confide in Vangie at least?

"It's new, okay?" he said. "She *did* have car trouble a few months ago. She was at the Pickle Jar with some friends, having dinner. I was there with some guys after work. I went out to the parking lot and gave her a jump. I followed her home because it was dark and that's a rough part of town. She invited me in and we got to talking. Then we kept talking."

"Then you asked her out," Joe said.

"She asked me out." Matty smiled. "I know I should have probably said something, Cass. But I like her. She's easy to talk to."

"Matty," I said. "She's essential to me. Miranda has more or less adopted her. You know all of that, right? If things end badly and ..."

"They won't," he said. There was something in my brother's eyes. His expression turned grave and my heart flipped.

"Holy crap," Vangie said, reading the same thing I had. "Matty, are you in love with Tori?"

His silence was all the answer we needed.

"Oh boy." Joe spoke for all of us.

I sank slowly onto a stool.

"She's worried about what you'll think," Matty said. "I wanted to tell you. But Tori wants to focus on this trial too. You don't have to worry, Cass. I swear. Nothing bad's going to happen."

The rest of us took a collective gasp. Matty had just tempted fate by uttering those words. No amount of rosaries or salt over the shoulder could undo it. Any Leary who proclaimed nothing bad would happen pretty much ensured that it did.

Chapter 16

TUESDAY NIGHT, ten p.m., I thought I was alone in the office. I liked it like this. Pure quiet. Only the soft glow of the lamp in the corner of my desk. From a side window, I could see the steeple of St. Cecelia's church. It was two blocks behind the courthouse. I could see that too.

Tomorrow morning, Juliet's trial would begin.

I had solid avenues for cross-examination. I had the glimmer of motives for other people wanting Nathan Clay dead. But was it enough for reasonable doubt?

I heard a thud. Something fell to the floor in the conference room that adjoined my office. I shut my laptop and went to the door.

Tori sat cross-legged in the middle of the floor, surrounded by mountains of files. Witness statements. Photographs. Multiple copies of every piece of evidence we expected the prosecution to introduce.

"You okay?" I asked. "I thought you went home?"

"Oh!" Tori scooted backward. My voice, startling her.

"Sorry." I smiled.

"I, uh ... I thought you went home, too. I just wanted to take a last look at everything. Just in case ..."

"You haven't missed anything," I reassured her. "You're ready. And they may not get to any of the Berriman lab witnesses until Friday. Possibly not even until Monday."

"But they'll put Trainor on first," she said. "That's what I'd do."

"You think she's going to slip up?" I asked.

"I don't know. Maybe ..."

"She won't," I said. "Amelia Trainor will make a solid, compelling witness."

"You have to get her to admit there's at least a chance the cancer was Clay's ultimate cause of death."

"I'll try," I said. "But very carefully. She's smart enough to know that's where I'm headed. I'm not going to get her to second guess her own autopsy findings."

"Then how?" Tori said, her expression pained. "How are we going to get those people to think Juliet's innocent? And don't give me the reasonable doubt spiel. It won't be enough if they think she really did it."

"Maybe," I said. "Maybe not."

Tori slowly rose from the center of her piles.

"How do you keep from feeling so nervous?"

"I don't," I said. "I am nervous. The day I ever feel cocky heading into a murder trial is the day I need to find a new line of work. But for better or worse, I know I have command of the evidence. My job is to raise as many questions in the jurors' minds as I can. And hope that's enough."

"If only she hadn't posted those videos," Tori said. "I honestly don't think we'd be here right now."

"Come on," I said. "It's time to go home. Neither of us will serve Juliet well if we show up on no sleep."

"Oh, I'm not sleeping tonight," Tori said. "No way."

"Need a ride home?" I asked.

Tori took a breath to say something, then stopped herself.

"You're not going home, are you?" I asked. No. Of course not. She was headed to Matty's.

"Cass," she said. "I know I should have told you about Matty and me. We were worried about how you'd react. But don't blame him. I told him to keep it to himself. He wanted to tell you straight off."

"I see," I said. "Why didn't you?"

"To be honest? I wanted to make sure it wasn't just some fling. At first it was. We went out for drinks a couple of times. We …"

I put a hand up. For the love of God, I didn't want the details. Part of me would always need to assume my little brother was just playing with Power Rangers in his bedroom.

"Right," Tori said. "Sorry."

"You're saying it's more than just a fling?"

Tori sat perched on the conference room table. "Yeah," she said quietly. "Cass, it is."

"Oh boy."

"Yeah."

"Matty?"

"Yeah."

"You and Matty?"

"Yeah."

"Are you?" I hardly wanted to say the words. "In love with him?"

Her face flushed a deep red. She tried to stop it, but her dimples showed as she smiled.

"Does he know?"

"It's new, Cass. We're just trying to figure it all out. Believe me. The last thing I wanted was to get serious about someone with this trial looming. I know you're counting on me. This is not going to be a distraction."

"Tori, stop. Do you think I think you can't walk and chew gum at the same time? For Pete's sake. It's not like I don't have plenty of my own love life drama. Before, during, and after trial."

Tori laughed. "Yeah. We're all kind of waiting until after next week. But Miranda, Jeanie, and I have questions for you on that front."

My turn to laugh. "I already got interrogated by my siblings."

"I heard."

We started walking downstairs together. She was heading to my brother's house. I wanted to ask her how often that occurred. Were they actually living together?

No. Not now. None of my business. She'd tell me when she was ready. And I couldn't grill her, then ask her not to grill me about Eric.

"It's good having him back," she said as if she could read my mind.

"Yeah," I said.

"You make a good team. You're ... happier. Lighter. When he's around. We all notice."

"Yeah." I smiled. "Good night, Tori. I'll see you in the morning. Bright and early. I'll meet you at the courthouse."

She nodded. "I'll be there. And Cass?"

"Yeah?"

"I'm glad you're on my side."

"You've become like a little sister to me," I said. It was true.

As Tori turned to leave, it hit me how hard things might get if my little brother screwed this one up.

Chapter 17

Juliet Clay nearly fell apart before the trial even started. They'd cleared an empty jury room for us so she could change out of her jail garb and into a cream-colored suit Jeanie had brought from Juliet's collection.

"Juliet," I said. "I want you to wipe all that off."

Jeanie had also brought Juliet's make-up. While I was off making final arrangements in the courtroom, Juliet applied it flawlessly. She looked like a supermodel with false eyelashes, cheekbones high and perfectly shaded. I'd honestly never seen make-up done that well.

"What's wrong?" she asked.

"It's too much. You have to project humility. You aren't auditioning for a movie."

"It's an audition, all right," she said. "My followers expect me to look a certain way, Cass. I know what I'm doing."

"Your followers? This isn't for them. This is for the twelve people sitting in that jury box."

"Make sure you seat as many men as you can," she said. "Women tend not to like me."

I reached in her make-up caddy and pulled out some wipes.

"Tone it down," she said. "You're going to have to trust me."

I handed her the cloth. Like a switch had been flipped, Juliet burst into tears. She doubled over, racked with sobs.

I didn't have time to coddle her. The bailiff had already knocked on the door to tell us we had five minutes before Judge Castor called her case. Five minutes before a potential pool of jurors would see her for the first time.

A minute later, Juliet pulled herself together. When she did, her eyes were swollen and red. Her perfectly applied make-up smudged, revealing blotches all over her cheeks.

"I'm ready," she said, her voice unwavering.

"What?"

"I'm ready." She pursed her lips and rose slowly. I had the unsettling feeling that I'd been very wrong about her. She'd known exactly what she was doing when she applied all that make-up.

I grabbed her and wiped away the worst of the mascara smudges. She let me. Then she followed behind me as the bailiff led us into the courtroom.

It took half the day to seat the jury. In the end, we had a good mix. Six men, six women. Mostly older. Voir dire had been challenging as most of the younger members of the pool had seen Juliet on social media. Our jury had never seen her videos, but they skewed more conservative. They might hold her unconventional marriage against her. But there was always a trade-off when it came to juries.

Juliet sat in the center of the defense table. Tori sat on her left, I on her right, closest to the prosecution's table. Since they had the burden of proof, they sat closest to the jury. Rafe Johnson was there, but took a back seat. He'd handed the chief litigator position to a younger associate prosecutor by the name of Charlotte Stahl. At twenty-eight, she was among the first of the next generation of lawyers to practice in Woodbridge County. She made me feel old.

"Are you ready to present your opening arguments, Ms. Stahl?" Judge Castor asked.

At sixty-nine, he was now the longest-serving circuit court justice in the county. As such, he'd just been elected to his final eligible term last week. He was also one of my favorite judges to appear in front of. He peered at Charlotte over his glasses and I had a feeling he was questioning his own, by comparison, ancient age as well.

Charlotte sprang up. She wore a black pantsuit and had a lustrous head of thick, black hair cut into a trim bob. She approached the lectern and faced the jury.

"Members of the jury, I'll have many jobs throughout this trial. For me, I feel my most important one is to introduce you to Nathan Clay, the victim in this case. I have to show you the grisly nature of how he died. Because he didn't die quickly. It wasn't a bullet to the head. Or a stabbing into a major artery that would have allowed him to bleed to death while he slept. Painful, still. But quick. No. Nathan wasn't given that mercy. Instead, he was given a poison so heinous, it literally rotted him from the inside out. Not over hours. Not even over days.

But for weeks. Day after day, he trusted his wife, Juliet, to take care of him. To be there for him. Instead, she cheerily delivered the instrument of his torture and death.

"Calculated. Cold-hearted. She planned. Researched. Conspired. Watched as the man who loved her withered away and suffered under her eyes. And then she recorded it for the world to see. Displayed it. Set it to music. Animated it. Members of the jury, over the course of the next few days, I'll show you everything Juliet Clay did. The evidence against her is staggering. There are mountains of every kind. Documents. Photographs. Videos. Witness testimony. And then there's Nathan Clay's own body. I can promise you, at the conclusion of this trial, you will have no doubt that the instrument of Nathan Clay's torturous death is sitting in the room with you. And I trust you will make sure she can never kill or breathe a breath of free air again. Thank you."

She buttoned her jacket and took her seat in front of her boss. Juliet was rigid as stone beside me.

"Ms. Leary?" Judge Castor said. "You're up."

Chapter 18

Dr. Amelia Trainor, M.E., took the stand immediately after I delivered my opening statement. I was good at defining the jury's role for them. It wasn't enough to feel bad that Nathan Clay died. It wasn't enough to hate Juliet Clay. It wasn't even enough if the prosecution proved Nathan died from thallium poisoning (an element I hoped to muddy with Dr. Trainor's testimony right out of the gate). It was only enough if the prosecution could connect every single dot beyond a reasonable doubt. Every. Single. One.

By the end of the first day of trial, Dr. Trainor fired the prosecution's biggest cannons. If we'd ended right there, even I might have voted to convict Juliet.

"Dr. Trainor," Charlotte said. "Were you able to determine Nathan Clay's cause of death?"

"Yes," she said. As coroners went, Amelia was a rock star. She delivered fat-free testimony the average juror could understand. She wore the same navy-blue suit she'd sported at every trial I had with her. Crisply pressed. A white scarf tied at her throat.

"What were your findings, Doctor?" Charlotte asked.

Amelia leaned ever slightly closer to her microphone. "The victim, Nathan Clay, died from cardiac arrest brought on by acute respiratory failure. In layman's terms, his lungs shut down and then his heart stopped."

"Were you able to determine a cause for this sudden lung failure?"

Amelia sat back. She had her clinical notes in front of her. Her full autopsy report was already entered into evidence. On the projection screen on the far wall, the jury gazed over a post-mortem picture of Nathan Clay.

He lay naked on Dr. Trainor's examination table. His opaque eyes stared blankly at the ceiling. His skin had a strange, reddish tinge to it though his lips were blue and pursed. His body lay forever frozen at the moment he struggled to draw his last breath.

"At first," she said. "There were no obvious clinical findings to support such catastrophic organ failure. No fluid on the lungs. No myocardial infarction."

"His lungs just stopped working?" Charlotte asked.

"To put it bluntly, yes," she said. "The victim did have some moderate plaque buildup and thickening of the arterial walls consistent with his age. But overall, his heart and lungs were in good shape."

"He was otherwise healthy," Charlotte asked.

"I wouldn't say that. Not at all."

"Why not?"

"Mr. Clay had a large mass in the head of the pancreas. It was malignant. It had metastasized to the lymph nodes in his groin and there were other smaller malignant masses in his small intestine."

"What does that mean?" Stahl asked.

"It means Mr. Clay had stage four pancreatic cancer."

Stahl waited a moment. Several members of the jury sat wide-eyed at the revelation. Beside me, Juliet began to cry. I put a hand on her wrist.

"Dr. Trainor, in your expert medical opinion, was Mr. Clay's cancer the cause of his death."

"No."

"Was it a contributing factor?"

"No."

"How can you be so sure?"

"Because Mr. Clay had toxic levels of thallium sulfate in his bloodstream."

"Is that something you normally test for when a person dies under suspicious circumstances?"

"Objection," I said. "Counsel's characterization is improper and assuming facts not in evidence."

"Sustained, Ms. Stahl," Judge Castor said. "The jury will disregard counsel's definition of Mr. Clay's death as suspicious."

Castor took an abrupt pause after the word suspicious. Almost as if he had to stop himself from adding the word yet.

"I'll rephrase," Charlotte said. "Why did you test for thallium poisoning, Dr. Trainor?"

"I didn't just test for thallium. I ran a toxicity screening to rule out a number of pharmacological causes for Mr. Clay's death. It was a combination of factors. First, the victim's family had reported Mr. Clay exhibited flu-like symptoms in the days prior to his passing. His symptoms became gastrointestinal. There was significant inflammation in Mr. Clay's esophagus that was consistent with a period of intense vomiting. His skin, as you can see in Exhibit 4, displayed a distinct reddish discoloration. You'll also see, if we can flip forward to Exhibit 6, there are the beginnings of a brownish discoloration at his hairline. When I ran a gloved hand over Mr. Clay's head, his hair began to fall out. Those are all classic symptoms of thallium toxicity."

"Could they be symptoms of anything else? Say, cancer treatment drugs?"

"Mr. Clay was not being treated for his cancer," she said. "The only prescribed drugs in his chart were Lipitor and Rhinocort for seasonal allergies. Additionally, I was contacted by Detective Blackfoot from the Woodbridge County Sheriff's Office. She was the lead detective assigned to this case. The police found a baggie containing a white powder in a cupboard at the victim's residence. They tested it along with a powdered chocolate shake mix they believed was given to the victim. The white powder tested positive for thallium sulfate. The shake mix had thallium in it as well. I analyzed the contents of Mr. Clay's stomach. Though it was mostly empty, there were traces of a partially digested brown mixture. That mixture was positive for thallium."

"Doctor," Stahl said. "Can you tell me how thallium kills? What makes it toxic to humans? In layman's terms, if you can."

"Sure," she said. "When ingested at high enough levels, thallium affects the body's nerve impulses. Essentially, the brain stops communicating with the body's other life-sustaining systems."

"Like the lungs, for example?"

"Yes," she said. "Most definitely. Respiratory paralysis is one of the hallmarks of thallium toxicity. It's also quite common to see neurological symptoms with thallium poisoning."

"What kind of neurological symptoms?"

"Fatigue at the outset. Mental confusion. Perhaps seizures."

"Dr. Trainor, do you have an opinion on how long Mr. Clay would have had to ingest thallium in order to rise to the level of toxicity?"

"Oh, that depends wildly," she said. "Thallium is extremely toxic to humans. It could take as little as one gram to kill an adult human."

"Based on the symptoms you observed in Mr. Clay, do you have a theory on how long it might have been since the first time he ingested the poison?"

"Objection as to form," I said. "Dr. Trainor did not treat the victim."

"Sustained. You may answer, Doctor."

"That's true," Trainor said. "I don't observe symptoms. But from my clinical findings, the reddened skin, discoloration at the hairline, symptoms reported from the victim's family, in my opinion, Mr. Clay likely began ingesting thallium within two to six weeks prior to his death."

"Thank you, Doctor," Charlotte said. "I have no further questions."

"Ms. Leary?" Judge Castor said.

"I have a few, thank you," I said. I stepped up to the lectern.

"Dr. Trainor, in your expert medical opinion, was Nathan Clay's cancer terminal?"

"Objection," Charlotte said. "Dr. Trainor was not Nathan Clay's primary physician."

"Doesn't matter," I said. "This witness is more than qualified to render an expert medical opinion on the severity of the disease process she found in Nathan Clay's body."

"Overruled, you may answer," Castor said.

"Well," Trainor started. "As I indicated on direct, the cancer was advanced. It had spread to his lymph nodes and intestines."

"Would his cancer have produced symptoms?"

"That's hard to say."

"Is it possible that the flu-like symptoms the victim experienced could have been caused by the tumor in his pancreas?"

"That's hard to say. Mr. Clay was not undergoing any treatment for his cancer. In most cases, it's the medicine used to treat cancer that causes the worst of a patient's symptoms, not the cancer itself. In fact, pancreatic cancer most often produces no symptoms at all until it's too far advanced to treat effectively."

"And Mr. Clay's cancer was advanced, you're saying?"

"Most definitely," she answered.

"It was going to kill him."

"If untreated, yes," she said.

"If untreated," I repeated. "Doctor, you've performed autopsies on many cancer patients, haven't you?"

"Yes," she said.

"Thousands, probably?" I asked.

"Probably, yes," she said.

"Do you think treatment would have saved Nathan Clay's life?"

"Saved it? Probably not. Prolonged it, perhaps. And if you're asking me how long he had, I can't tell you that."

"Dr. Trainor, in advanced stages of pancreatic cancer, what is the ultimate cause of death?"

"Ultimately?" she said. "Cardiac arrest."

"Thank you," I said. "I have no further questions."

"I just have one," Charlotte said. Judge Castor motioned her to the lectern.

"Dr. Trainor, is it possible Mr. Clay died of anything other than thallium poisoning?"

"Unlikely," she said.

"How can you be certain?"

"Well," she said. "With pancreatic cancer, patients generally go into liver failure. Mr. Clay wasn't in liver failure. He was in acute respiratory failure and as I indicated earlier, that was a direct cause of the neurological impact of thallium toxicity. He also had fatal levels of the drug in his system. There's no doubt about that."

"Thank you, I have nothing further, Doctor," Stahl said.

Amelia Trainor thanked the judge, then stepped down from the witness stand. I knew if given the case today, the jury would have voted to convict. And I wouldn't have blamed them.

Chapter 19

DETECTIVE SOFIA BLACKFOOT of the Woodbridge County Sheriff's Office would take the stand first thing on day two of the trial. I'd never tried a case against her before today but Tori and I had watched her testify in a rape case a few weeks ago to get a feel for how she played to a jury. The short answer? She was good. Respectful, direct, concise. A ten-year veteran of the detective bureau, I knew she was well liked in the prosecutor's office as well as the upper command of the sheriff's office.

"She'll probably take a command position herself someday soon," Eric said as he handed me his notes on her. He would sit behind me today as well during Blackfoot's direct. If anything came up I could use on cross, he'd be ready with another notebook.

"You gotta give me something," I said.

"Cass, she's clean," he said. It occurred to me he might not tell me anyway if he found something on her. Eric was fine running down background checks on witnesses. The idea of digging up dirt on a fellow detective, even from another department, didn't sit well with him. I understood.

I took my seat at the table as they led Juliet in. Today she sported a black suit, her hair still tied back. She had more color in her cheeks today, but had taken my note about not overdoing her make-up. She was coachable.

"I saw Bryson out in the hall," she whispered, her voice shaking. "Is he taking the stand today?"

"It's hard to say," I said. "But he won't be allowed in the courtroom, until after he testifies. Please tell me you didn't talk to him."

She blinked hard to stave off tears. "Of course not. He looks so thin, Cass."

"All rise!"

I put a calming hand on Juliet's sleeve as we went to our feet. Two minutes later, Charlotte Stahl called Detective Blackfoot to the stand.

Sofia Blackfoot was tall, broad-shouldered, and had a thick head of long black hair that she wore parted in the middle. In her early forties, she didn't have even a strand of gray. No easy feat for someone in her line of work these days.

Charlotte took her through her foundational testimony quickly. Sofia joined the sheriff's office after five years in the army. She'd served a tour in Iraq, then got her bachelor's degree in criminal justice. She made her way through the ranks in the usual way. Field ops, a stint in property crime, then sex crimes, and now she and two other detectives handled homicides that happened in county but outside the Delphi border.

"Detective," Charlotte said. "How did you come to be assigned to Nathan Clay's case?"

"Mr. Clay was found unresponsive by his teenage son on the evening of May 2nd at approximately nine p.m.," she said. "After calling 911, Mr. Clay was taken by ambulance to Windham Hospital. He never regained consciousness and was pronounced dead at six a.m. on the morning of May 3rd of this year. The attending physician contacted the sheriff's office when he suspected the cause of death was not by natural means."

"What does that mean?" Charlotte asked.

"Dr. Seymour met with me at the hospital and indicated Mr. Clay had exhibited some troubling symptoms that were consistent with ingesting poison. Reddish skin, and other discoloration. It is my understanding that Dr. Seymour had been unable to determine any immediate cause for Mr. Clay's respiratory failure. So I was called in to rule out foul play."

"When did you arrive on scene?" Charlotte asked.

"As I said, the victim was admitted to the hospital around nine on the evening of the second. Dr. Seymour called our office at approximately four a.m. The victim was still alive at that point, but had lapsed into a coma. I arrived at the hospital at 6:02 a.m., just a few minutes before Mr. Clay was pronounced dead."

"What did you do then?"

"I spoke with Dr. Seymour as a hospital social worker spoke with Mrs. Clay and her son. A little after seven a.m., I interviewed Mrs. Clay. She indicated she had no idea what had happened to her husband. That he was fine just hours before."

"Fine?" Charlotte asked.

"Yes. And that was inconsistent with what the son reported. He said his father had been ill for days. He'd been taking care of him. At that point, the coroner's office had been called and I knew we needed to get over to the scene. I secured a search warrant for the Clay home and served it on Mrs. Clay at the hospital. This was approximately nine a.m."

"Mrs. Clay was still at the hospital?"

"Yes."

"So in other words, she hadn't gone home since the night before when Mr. Clay was brought in?"

"That's correct. Which is also why I felt time was of the essence in obtaining the warrant and securing the scene. So I did."

"What, if anything, did Mrs. Clay say when you served her with the warrant at the hospital?"

"She was angry," Blackfoot said. "Confused. But she said she would cooperate with the warrant and gave us keys to the front door and to two locked spare bedrooms. And she told me where medication was kept within the home."

I scribbled a few notes. Juliet leaned in close. "Now why would I do that if I thought they were going to arrest me later?"

"Shh," I cautioned her.

"Detective," Charlotte asked. "What evidence did you find within the Clay home?"

"Objection as to form," I said. "It's up to the court to determine whether something is admissible evidence."

"Sustained," Castor said, though he seemed annoyed at the interruption.

"Detective," Charlotte started over. "What did you find at the victim's home?"

"We collected all the medication in the home, searched the victim's bedroom and bathrooms. There was a green blender bottle sitting on the bedside table where Mr. Clay had been found unresponsive. There was perhaps a quarter of a cup of a brown, chalky liquid still in it. Mrs. Clay indicated that it had belonged to her husband. We collected that for analysis as well as a small can of shake mix found in the kitchen."

Charlotte introduced photographs taken at the Clay home. The blender bottle sat on a nightstand, a red-and-white paper straw sticking out of it. Another photo showed the shake mix in its can, sitting on a shelf in the pantry.

"Detective," Charlotte said. "What else did you find in the kitchen of the victim's home?"

"When we moved the can of shake mix from the pantry, Officer Kiefer noticed a small section of contact paper was sticking up on the back of the shelf."

"Where was Officer Kiefer in relation to you?"

"He was standing right beside me. His job was to photograph the items as we collected them. In Exhibit 19, you can see the can of shake mix as we found it when we opened the pantry.

In Exhibit 22, you can see the yellow shelf paper dislodged in the back of the shelf."

"Your Honor, can we let the record reflect that the witness is pointing to a section of shelf paper that's pulled up away from the back of the shelf in Exhibit 22?"

"So noted," Castor said.

"What did you do next, Detective?"

"I used my pen to move the section of contact paper because as you can see in the photo, there is a corner of clear plastic sticking out behind it. It looked like a baggie."

Charlotte introduced a small, sixty-second video taken from Officer Kiefer's phone. It showed the detective probing the section of loose paper with her pen. When she pulled it away, a small sandwich bag with white powder in it could be seen.

"Detective, I'd like to show you what's been marked as Exhibit 24. Do you recognize it?"

"I do."

"What is it?"

"It is the small baggie containing a white powdery substance that Officer Kiefer and I observed and then collected at the Clay residence on May 3rd at one p.m."

With a chain of custody established, Judge Castor allowed the exhibit in.

"Detective, did you then later have that substance analyzed?"

"We did."

"And can you tell us the results of that analysis?"

"Yes," Detective Blackfoot said. At that point, Charlotte Stahl introduced the lab results positively identifying the white powder as thallium. The results from the blender bottle on the bed were also positive for thallium.

"Detective, what investigative steps did you take next?"

"I attempted to re-interview Mrs. Clay. It was about this time she attempted to return to the residence with her son. When I approached her, she asked that her lawyer be present so all questioning ceased. Understand that at this point, I didn't have the lab results back on the white substance. The doctors at the hospital suspected thallium but it was unconfirmed. Along with my team, we continued canvassing. I interviewed Mr. Clay's law partner as well as their neighbors."

"Then what happened?"

"Mr. Gorney, the victim's law partner, informed me he suspected Mr. and Mrs. Clay were having marital difficulties. He directed me to speak with Donovan McNamara."

"Did you?"

"I did."

"Who is Mr. McNamara?"

"Mr. McNamara and the defendant were involved in a romantic relationship at some point prior to the victim's death. Around that time, the lab results came back on both Mr. Clay and the items we collected at the residence. Along with the autopsy report, of course. They all confirmed the cause of death was thallium poisoning."

"At what point did you begin to suspect Mrs. Clay?"

"I always suspected Mrs. Clay as she lived in the home with the victim. Her son indicated that she used to prepare the shakes for him."

"What else, if anything, did Bryson Ballard tell you about his mother's relationship with his stepfather?"

"Bryson was reluctant to speak with me. He was understandably upset," Blackfoot said. "I asked him if his parents fought a lot. He said that they did."

"Did Bryson give you any opinion as to who he thought might have poisoned his father?"

"Objection," I said. "This is improper hearsay."

"Ms. Stahl?" Castor said.

"Your Honor, I'm asking the detective what investigative steps she took. Bryson Ballard's opinion would have a direct impact on Detective Blackfoot's next steps."

"Sustained," Judge Castor said. "You can ask her that way. But Bryson Ballard's statement isn't admissible at this point."

"Detective," Stahl continued. "Did Bryson Ballard tell you anything about fears his father had prior to dying?"

"Objection!" I rose again. "Your honor, Bryson Ballard is available to testify. If Ms. Stahl wishes to question him, she can. Same basis for my objection."

"Sustained."

"Detective," Stahl said, flustered. "Who else did you interview in your investigation into Nathan Clay's death?"

"I also interviewed two neighbors who made me aware of social media videos Mrs. Clay posted in which she can be viewed making the shakes for Mr. Clay and feeding them to him."

For the next hour, the jury got to watch Juliet's videos. She appeared first in a black leotard, fresh from a workout. She had her hair pulled back in a ponytail as she bounced into the home office where a much heavier Nathan Clay sat in front of his laptop.

"Hey, baby," video Juliet Clay practically sang. "Today's the day, everyone. Time for Nate to join the healthy revolution."

"Just give me the damn thing," Nate muttered in the video, but he was smiling up at Juliet, clearly turned on as she pranced around in front of him. He took the blender bottle and started drinking.

"Here we go!" Juliet said. "Check back with us tomorrow!"

Day after day, Juliet brought Nathan his shakes. It began three months before his death. After about six weeks, she had him get on the scale and recorded it.

Week by week, she documented his weight loss, all while Nate rolled his eyes and came off as a lovable curmudgeon to his hyperactive blonde, fit wife.

The last video was from a week before he died. He'd lost forty pounds in three months. "They work, people!" Juliet sang. Nate came out wearing a tee shirt and a pair of jeans. Smiling. Twirling Juliet around in a romantic little box step. At this point, he knew he was dying. Maybe not from poisoning, but it would come up in the timeline that he'd already been told he had pancreatic cancer. The comments under the video had all been positive. Nate had a following of his own.

Only now, the town knew his hidden pain and sadness. It made you want to reach through the screen and tell them to stop. I'd been successful pre-trial in keeping more than half the videos out. But every one that showed Juliet either preparing Nate's shakes or handing them to him made it in.

Beside me, Juliet fell apart. "Nate," she whispered. "Oh Nate."

"Detective," Charlotte said as the last video ended. "You said you were able to speak to the victim's neighbors?"

"I was," she said. "But before that, we had a record of two different domestic disturbances out at the Clay home. The complainants heard shouting and breaking glass during the first. During the second, Mr. and Mrs. Clay were involved in an altercation on their front lawn."

"Were you able to identify which neighbors those were?"

"Yes. The glass-breaking incident was reported by their next-door neighbors, the Snows. Phil and Lisa Snow. The second disturbance was reported by their neighbors across the street, Kim and T.J. Humphrey."

"You spoke with both?" Charlotte asked.

"Of course."

"Okay. I'll not ask you what they said. They're here to testify later. But Detective, you requested an arrest warrant against Mrs. Clay at some point, did you not?"

"I did."

"Can you explain to the jury what the basis of that warrant was?"

"I had the physical evidence collected at the scene. We had a definitive cause of death as thallium poisoning and the positive analysis for that substance in Mr. Clay's shakes. I had video evidence of Mrs. Clay preparing and giving those shakes to Mr. Clay. Her son confirmed that for me as well. I have witness statements from neighbors, his stepson, and Mr. Clay's law partner in which the defendant was heard threatening the victim's life on multiple occasions. Finally, the warrant on Mrs. Clay's password-protected laptop revealed numerous searches on different kinds of poison and their effects on the human body. There was also a search on a murder case where thallium was used on a family in Florida by a disgruntled neighbor. I believed, based on those factors, I had probable cause to arrest Mrs. Clay for the murder of her husband."

"Thank you, Detective," Charlotte said. "I have no further questions. Your witness, Ms. Leary."

With Julie still sobbing quietly at the table, I took my place at the lectern.

Chapter 20

"Detective Blackfoot," I started. "You never really ruled out any other suspects in Nathan Clay's murder, did you?"

"Excuse me?" she said.

"What I mean to say ... isn't it true that Juliet Clay was the target of your investigation from the outset?"

"I take issue with your characterization."

"How so?" I asked.

"To the extent you're implying I targeted your client; that's false."

"But you don't deny that your investigation was always focused on Mrs. Clay, isn't that right?"

"Juliet Clay was the primary suspect from the beginning, yes," she said.

"Because you found thallium in the home," I said.

"Among other things, yes. There was never any doubt that Nathan Clay died of thallium poisoning, counselor," she said.

"Never any doubt," I repeated. "Not even when you learned Mr. Clay had terminal cancer?"

"He didn't die of cancer," she said.

"You're sure? You never explored the possibility that Mr. Clay succumbed to either the cancer ravaging his body or complications stemming from that?"

"Dr. Trainor's autopsy was conclusive, as far as I was concerned," she said. "Nathan Clay died of acute thallium poisoning."

"Let's talk about that for a minute. Thallium isn't something one would normally have lying around the house, is it?"

"No. It's been banned for commercial use in this country since the 1980s, I believe."

"So isn't it true that thallium, in its raw, powdered form, isn't something you can just go pick up at the farm supply store?"

"That's true, yes."

"And isn't it also true that you can't prove how the thallium you found got into the Clay house, can you?"

"We believe the defendant obtained it from a lab in Brighton, Michigan."

"You believe?" I said. "But there's no evidence of that, is there?"

"I don't see how it matters," she said. "The fact is the thallium *was* in the Clay household. Regardless of how it got there, Juliet Clay had access to it."

"Any number of people had access to it, isn't that right?"

"I'm sorry?"

"Well, it wasn't locked up when you found it, was it?" I asked.

"No. As I testified earlier, it was in a cupboard. But it was hidden behind shelf paper. If I hadn't been specifically looking for it, I probably wouldn't have spotted it."

"You questioned Ted Gorney, didn't you?"

"The victim's business partner? Yes. I did."

"You're aware that Mr. Gorney often came to visit Mr. and Mrs. Clay, isn't that right?"

"I asked him when the last time was he saw Nathan Clay. He visited the house a few weeks before Nathan died."

"I see," I said. I made a few notes. "You testified that you confiscated Mrs. Clay's laptop."

"Yes."

"You testified that her laptop was password protected."

"It was, yes," she said. "It also had a fingerprint identification option. Just like her phone."

"But sitting here today, you can't say whether anyone else might have had access to her passwords, isn't that right?"

"I cannot, no."

"Detective, did you interview any of Nathan Clay's clients?"

"I didn't, no," she said.

"In fact, you don't even know who any of Nathan Clay's clients are, do you?"

"Objection, relevance?" Charlotte said.

"Ms. Leary?"

"Your Honor, this witness has testified that she never entertained the possibility of another suspect in this case. I believe it's perfectly within my rights to explore how thoroughly she interviewed other witnesses in this case or people who might have had a motive to harm Nathan Clay."

"I'll allow it," Judge Castor said.

"Detective Blackfoot, during the course of your investigation, did you ascertain whether Nathan Clay had any grievances filed against him with the State Bar?"

"I'm unaware of any," she said.

"You never bothered to find out," I said.

"Objection," Charlotte said. "Asked and answered."

"I'll move on," I said. "Detective, did you ascertain whether Ted Gorney had any grievances filed against him with the State Bar?"

"I'm not aware of any, but I do know there were no pending malpractice cases filed against Mr. Clay or Mr. Gorney," she said.

"But you didn't even think to get a copy of Nathan Clay's active client list, did you?"

"I reject the premise of the question," she said. "I had no probable cause to pursue that information."

"You never asked Mr. Gorney whether he knew of any clients that might have an axe to grind with Nathan Clay, did you?"

"He wouldn't have told me even if he knew," she said.

"Didn't ask, or didn't know?"

"He didn't offer that information, no," she said.

"Didn't offer it. So you took everything he told you at face value?"

"Your Honor!" Charlotte said.

"I'll rephrase," I said. "So if I understand your testimony and what's written in your report. Your investigation of Ted Gorney consisted of a single interview with him, isn't that right?"

"I interviewed him, yes," she answered.

"Thank you," I said. "I just have one more thing I'd like to explore. Detective, you've recently put in for a promotion to lieutenant, haven't you?"

"Objection, relevance!" Charlotte became exasperated.

"I'll get there in two questions, Your Honor," I said.

"See that you do," Castor said.

"Detective?"

"Yes," she said. "But I too fail to see what that has to do with this investigation."

"It's fair to say that the Clay murder is the most high-profile case you've ever investigated, isn't that right?"

"Well," she said. "If by that you mean there are a lot of internet warriors spouting opinions about it, then yes."

I paused as I paced in front of the lectern, then turned back toward it. "Since you mentioned the internet. Ms. Clay never tried to hide the fact that she encouraged her husband to try the diet shakes she was selling, correct?"

"I would say not. She was all over the internet, preening and crowing about it," Blackfoot said. Her stoic demeanor melted away. She gestured wildly as she spoke.

"She seemed proud of it, didn't she?" I asked.

"I'd say she was flaunting it, that's for sure," Blackfoot said. "Putting it all out there."

"Right," I said. "And the tumbler you found containing thallium-laced shake, where was that again?"

"It was right by the defendant's bedside," she said. "His fingerprints and her fingerprints were all over it, as I stated in my report and testified earlier today."

"Right. Out there in the open on the bedside," I said. "And where was Mrs. Clay when you were conducting your search warrant?"

"She was still at the hospital. She rode there in the ambulance with her husband."

"Her son called 911, correct?"

"Yes."

"So she'd been in the house with the victim before that call was made, as far as you were aware?"

"Yes."

"Interesting," I said. I hoped the jury was thinking along my same lines. I knew when to quit when I was ahead. "Thank you, Detective, I have no further questions."

Charlotte deferred redirect and Sofia Blackfoot left the stand. She'd been solid, but not nearly as solid as Amelia Trainor. I could only pray that the jury could start to see the cracks in the case like I did.

Chapter 21

JUDGE CASTOR WAS ON A ROLL, letting Charlotte Stahl tear through as many witnesses as she could before breaking for the day. Juliet barely caught her breath from Detective Blackfoot's testimony before Lisa Snow took the stand. Juliet wrote three words in bold letters on the notepad between us.

"She hates me."

Lisa's rubber-soled shoes squeaked as she walked up to the witness box. She had freshly dyed hair in a color I can only describe as maroon. When the bailiff asked her to raise her hand to be sworn, Lisa's nerves got the better of her and she tried to shake his hand instead. It broke the tension among the jury a bit. They laughed with Lisa as she took her seat and adjusted the microphone.

"Mrs. Snow," Charlotte began. "Can you tell me how you knew the victim, Nathan Clay?"

"He was our neighbor. My husband, Phil, and I live directly next door, to the east of the Clays."

"And how long has that been?"

"Going on twenty years," she said.

"So you knew Nathan Clay even before he married the defendant?"

"Oh yeah. Um. Yes. We built our houses in that subdivision right around the same time. We knew Nathan a little before that, actually. He did some work for Phil's brother, Kurt. Kurt's a pipe fitter and he got hurt at work. Nathan handled his worker's comp claim. So we knew Nate a little bit back then. He settled the case for Kurt. Kurt was really happy so they stayed friends and had Nathan and his wife over for drinks when we were there. That was maybe twenty-five years ago."

"Okay. Thank you for that," Charlotte said. "If I can fast forward a bit. Did you have occasion to interact with Nathan and Juliet Clay socially as well?"

Lisa Snow squirmed in her seat. Her pleasant expression darkened. "It's a very social neighborhood," she said. "We have block parties. All of our kids went to high school together. For years, before Nathan married Juliet, his house was the social hub, I'd say. We live on the cul-de-sac and Nate had the big pole barn behind his house. We're right in the center of the subdivision."

"You said his house used to be the social hub. Did that change?"

"Yes," she said.

"When?"

"After Nate married Juliet."

"Do you know why?"

"Look, we're a tight-knit group, and everyone loved Alison. We were sad when she left, but we really tried with Juliet. She was just harder to get to know."

"Were you friendly with Juliet Clay?"

"I tried to be," Lisa answered.

"Mrs. Snow, what was the problem?"

Lisa let out a great sigh. "Look, what goes on in someone else's marriage is their business. I don't judge. But Juliet was a big flirt. She would wear these skimpy workout clothes and throw herself at all the other husbands. It got to be an issue."

"How so?"

"I caught her sitting on Phil's lap at the Halloween potluck two years ago. She had her hand between his thighs. Phil was feeling no pain at the moment. He'd had several beers and somebody was passing around fireball shots. So I walked in and saw them together and we had words."

"You and Juliet?"

"Yeah."

"What words?"

"I told her to stay away from Phil."

"What did she do?"

"She laughed it off and told me I was overreacting."

"Then what happened?"

"Well, I'll admit tempers were pretty hot. But I wasn't the only one who saw what happened. The Humphreys were there too. Kim and T.J. They live across the street from the Clays and us. Kim told me ..."

"Objection," I said. "Calls for hearsay."

"Mrs. Snow?" Judge Castor said. "Please refrain from testifying about things that were said to you by others. Continue, Ms. Stahl."

"Mrs. Snow, what did Kim and T.J. Humphrey do after the incident you described?"

"You said I can't say what she told me?" Lisa protested.

"But you're permitted to tell the jury what Mrs. Humphrey did."

"Oh," Lisa said, still looking confused. "Well, she threw a drink on Juliet. It was quite the scene. The party broke up after that and it was the last time we had one over at the Clays. We started having them on the other side of the neighborhood at the Kowalskis, Christy and Dan's. Juliet came once but nobody would talk to her. There were always rumors flying around about her and other husbands in the neighborhood. I don't care for gossip, but after what I saw on Halloween with her on Phil's lap, I started to wonder."

"Mrs. Snow, was that the only problem you had with the Clays?"

"I didn't have problems with them," she protested. "I had no issues with Nathan at all. It just made me sad that after he married Juliet, we saw him less and less. The Halloween party was really the last straw. But it had always been awkward when Juliet was around."

"How so?"

"She was a flirt," Lisa explained. "And I don't know, she just always tried too hard. Before the thing with Phil, I tried to be a good friend to her. I tried to tell her to just lighten up a little."

"How did she respond to that?"

"Not well," Lisa said. "I learned Juliet Clay had a really wicked temper. She yelled at me on the front lawn. Yelled isn't even the word, actually. She screamed at me."

"What did she say?"

"I'm allowed to say that?" Lisa asked.

"Yes," Charlotte responded.

"She said we were all just a bunch of fat, jealous crones."

It was hard to hear. I debated objecting. Beside me, Juliet stiffened. But Lisa Snow was laying out her main weakness as a witness without even realizing it.

"Mrs. Snow, I'd like to direct your attention to the evening of March 14th of this year. Do you remember what happened that day?"

"I do," she said, raising her chin. "Listen, we were always hearing shouting coming from the Clays' house. They seemed to fight all the time. And these were violent fights. We'd hear glass breaking. Doors being slammed. Phil and I just kind of put up with it. I felt so bad for Bryson. My kids were grown and flown by the time Juliet moved in with him, but he was always welcome over at our place. I made sure he knew that. There were a handful of times I saw him sitting out on the curb while Nathan and Juliet were going at it. I invited him to come over and hang out with Phil in the garage or whatever. Phil was handy, Nathan wasn't. So Phil was always at the ready with some project or another and he'd have Bryson come over to help him work on it. You know. To get him out of the house."

"Objection," I said. "The witness is unresponsive."

"She's right," Judge Castor said. "Mrs. Snow, please answer the questions you're asked."

"Oh, sorry," she said. "I forgot what it was."

"Mrs. Snow," Charlotte said. "What happened the night of March 14th?"

"Well, Bryson wasn't home. He'd just got his license and his car was gone. Thank God. But we were sitting in the backyard. It was one of the first really warm spring days. Peaceful. Well, Juliet pulled up and we saw her run into the house. The screaming started really quickly after that. It went on for at least a half an hour. I'd about had it by then. Phil had tried to talk to Nathan so many times about keeping it down. It didn't work. So, I finally decided enough was enough. I called the sheriff's department. And I wouldn't have done that, but we saw Nathan go out into his backyard and he was holding a bloody cloth to his temple. Juliet came out and threw a dish at him. It shattered all over the patio. I called the cops."

"Did you ever talk to Nathan or Juliet Clay about the incident?"

"No," she said. "We pretty much didn't speak to them at all anymore. We wanted peace and quiet and Nathan just wasn't the same guy anymore. We tried to be good neighbors. That was it."

Juliet scribbled furiously beside me. I made a subtle sideways gesture with my hand. She put down her pen.

"Thank you," Charlotte said. "I have no further questions."

"Ms. Leary?" Judge Castor said.

"I just have a few. Mrs. Snow? It's fair to say you hate Juliet Clay, isn't that right?"

"What?"

"You can't stand Juliet Clay, can you?"

She pursed her lips. "She is not a quality person, in my opinion."

"Are you still friendly with the former Mrs. Clay?"

"What? Well, we talk sometimes, yes."

"In fact, you were willing to testify on her behalf in her divorce from Nathan if it came to that, weren't you?"

"I suppose so," she said.

"And other than the dish you saw Juliet throw, you never saw her being violent to Nathan, did you?"

"He had a bloody towel to his head!"

"But you don't know how he received that wound, do you?"

"She was throwing things. That's what I saw. And I told you, we heard things being broken all the time when they fought."

"But you don't know if Juliet was the one throwing them or breaking them other than that one dish, correct?"

"I know she had a temper, I told you that."

"She yelled," I asked.

"Yes."

"Did Mr. Clay yell too?"

"I told you, we heard them both screaming."

"Got it. And did you ever hear arguments coming from the house when Nathan Clay was married to Alison Clay?"

"From time to time," she said. "I mean, no marriage is perfect."

"Of course not. Now, isn't it true that despite your dislike of Juliet Clay, you actually bought diet shakes from her yourself, didn't you?"

"I was trying to be nice," she said.

"How much did you buy?"

"I don't recall."

"Was it more than a hundred dollars' worth?"

"Maybe."

"Is it possible it was more than six hundred dollars' worth?"

Her nostrils flared. "Yes."

"You also subscribed to her social media channels, didn't you?"

"Yes."

"Thank you," I said. "I have no further questions."

Lisa Snow practically sprinted off the stand when Judge Castor dismissed her. Juliet stared her down while the jury watched it all.

They might just think she was the jealous, disgruntled neighbor Juliet told me she was. Or they might hate Juliet for the same reasons Lisa seemed to. It was open to interpretation. But Charlotte's next witness would make that much harder for me to argue

Chapter 22

T.J. Humphrey was a giant, lumbering man with hands the size of dinner plates and dark-brown eyes.

His testimony mirrored Lisa Snow's on the main facts. He lived across the street from the Clays and knew them socially. He and Nathan had been friendly, borrowing each other's power tools when the need arose, though most of the time, T.J. would have to go over and repair whatever Nathan had tried to initially fix on his own. It was a running joke between them. Just like Lisa Snow had said, Nathan Clay was not handy around the house.

"Mr. Humphrey," Charlotte said. "What was your relationship with Juliet Clay?"

It was then T.J. withdrew into himself. I looked at Juliet. She'd gone stiff as a board again, her eyes misting with tears.

My spine started to tingle. Something was wrong. We were about to get hit. Hard.

"We had an affair, okay?" T.J. said. "I'm not proud of it, but I slept with her."

"Objection," Tori shouted, rising to her feet.

Judge Castor looked puzzled for a moment, assuming T.J. was my witness to cross. Because he was.

"Counsel?" Castor said.

"This is irrelevant," Tori said, realizing she'd waded into deep waters without a life jacket.

"The witness's relationship with the defendant is relevant," Charlotte said.

"Overruled," Judge Castor agreed.

Tori sank back into her seat. Her face had gone white. I kept mine neutral. I couldn't let the jury deduce this was the first time I was hearing this fact right along with them.

"We had a brief affair," T.J. explained. "And I mean brief. Like over one weekend last year."

"Who initiated that affair?" Charlotte asked.

"It was mutual," T.J. said,

"But you were friends with Nathan Clay," Charlotte said.

"Yeah," T.J. said, dropping his head. "Juliet told me Nathan was okay with it. She said their marriage was open. I'm ashamed to admit it, okay. But she was young and pretty, and I was attracted to her. But immediately afterward, I felt awful."

"Why?"

"Because if her marriage with Nate was open like she said, mine wasn't. Anyway, it was just over one weekend when Kim, my wife, was gone. So was Nate. But then it was over. I didn't talk to Nate or Juliet for a long time after that. Not until …"

"Until when?"

"Last Christmas. Juliet and Nathan hosted a party and they invited us. I thought it was going to be for the neighborhood. It wasn't. It was just a bunch of people from Nate's work. Kim was furious. She didn't want to be there. At the time, she didn't know about Juliet and me. I wouldn't have gone but Nate asked me. Actually, he begged me. It was awkward as hell and ended with Kim calling the cops."

"What happened at the party, Mr. Humphrey?"

"Juliet and Nathan got into a big fight. I don't know what started it. But she was accusing him of ruining everything for her. I heard her say that over and over. She said you never support me. You want to keep me down. You don't want me to ever have anything that's just mine."

"What did Nate do?"

"He just stood there and took it. He looked miserable. Just awful. Everyone started to clear out then. Including us. It was like Juliet didn't even remember there were other people around. She just lit into him."

"Then what happened?"

"We went home. Things were quiet for a little bit then we heard shouting outside. I looked out the window and Nate and Juliet were on their front lawn. She was throwing his clothes out there at him. She said I'll kill you. I'll kill you in your sleep. A few minutes after that, the cops showed upI pulled Kim away from the window and a little bit after that, everything died down."

"Did you ever talk to Nathan or Juliet about that incident?"

"I talked to Nate a few days later. He was out shoveling snow and so was I. I wanted to just avoid it but he came up to me and apologized for everything. He was embarrassed."

"Mr. Humphrey, what did Mr. Clay tell you?"

"Objection," I said. "Calls for hearsay."

Castor gave me a stern look. I knew he didn't like what he thought was the tag-team approach Tori's earlier objection presented. "Sidebar," Castor said.

When Tori rose, I motioned for her to stay seated.

"Your Honor," I said. "This witness cannot testify to things the victim told him."

"He told him he thought his wife would kill him one day," Charlotte snapped.

"And you can't offer that up for the truth," I said. "That's exactly what hearsay is and this doesn't fall under any exception. He can't say it. Period."

Castor sighed. "I'm inclined to agree. Are you handling the cross of this witness or what, Ms. Leary?"

"I am," I said.

"Fine," Castor said. "Let's continue."

Charlotte went back to the lectern. Unable to ask her killer question, she ended her direct examination of T.J. Humphrey.

I knew my job was to get him off the stand as quickly as I could.

"Mr. Humphrey?" I said. "Were you interviewed by the police in connection with this case?"

"I was," he said.

"And in your statement you never mentioned this alleged affair with my client, did you?"

"It didn't come up," he said.

"Didn't come up. Your neighbor was dead. You knew they suspected it was murder, and yet you didn't feel this information was worth sharing?"

"Look," he said. "I hadn't told my wife about it. And no, I had no idea they were thinking Juliet was involved."

"You told them you heard her scream across the lawn that she was going to kill him. That's what you just testified to, correct?"

"Correct."

"But now you're trying to get everyone to believe you didn't know the cops were looking at Juliet as a suspect. Is that correct?"

"I didn't know what they wanted exactly, no."

"You hadn't told your wife about your alleged affair, had you?"

"No," he said, his face turning red. "I said no."

"In fact, you concealed it from her, didn't you?"

"I didn't tell her. She knows now though. I told her how I was going to testify."

"Ah," I said. "But you conveniently withheld that from the police."

"Do I need a lawyer here?" he asked the judge.

"Your Honor," I said, fuming. "I have no further questions for this witness."

And with that, we were mercifully done for the day.

Chapter 23

"I NEED a few minutes with my client before you take her back," I said to the deputies as they cuffed Juliet, preparing to take her to her holding cell across the street.

"I'll find somewhere," Eric said to them. They stared after him with pure disdain as he exited the courtroom. To them, he was working with the enemy. Me.

Juliet trembled, making the metal cuffs rattle around her wrists. She held back tears of either rage, sadness, or fear. I couldn't tell which. Maybe it was all of them.

A moment later, Eric came back. "Jury room 4 is open. The clerk said you can have it for the next half hour."

"We won't need that long," I reassured the deputies. Reluctantly, they led Juliet across the hall as Eric held the door open.

"Find me when you're done," he said. "I'll walk you back to your office."

"Thanks," I said. "Tori, why don't you go on ahead?"

"Cass, I'm sorry," she whispered. "I don't know why I got so jumpy today."

"We'll talk later," I said. "But don't worry about it."

I didn't want to say any more in front of the deputies or Juliet. She took a seat at the empty jury table and buried her face in her hands.

"I'll just need fifteen minutes," I told the female deputy. "Thanks for doing this."

I could have arranged a meeting under the normal course at the jail, but this was easier. I waited for the deputies to close the doors behind them as they took sentry just outside.

Gripping the back of a chair, I looked at Juliet.

"You lied to me," I said.

"I didn't lie," she said, letting the tears flow. "I've never lied."

"You're gonna split hairs with me? You're smart enough to know withholding a pretty critical fact from me is the same as lying. You should have told me about your history with T.J. Humphrey. You had an affair. Did Nate know?"

"Of course he knew," she said. "And it was nothing. It wasn't even an affair. It was a lost weekend. If that. He came to me for marital advice. It became pretty clear the guy didn't know how to take care of his wife, um, sexually. We got to talking. One thing led to another. If you ask me, I did Kim Humphrey a favor. If he did even one of the things I showed him on her the next time they, well ..."

"You know what?" I said. "I don't even care about the details. They are meaningless. What matters is I had to hear about it for the first time right along with the jury. That cannot happen."

"What difference does it make!" she yelled. "You tell me. Yeah. T.J. and I had sex. I think it was only once."

"You think?"

"Nate knew!" she said.

"Him knowing isn't the same as him approving," I said.

"Fine," she said. "So what would you have done differently today if I'd told you about T.J. and me? I told you the truth, by the way. He was just my neighbor."

"That may be how you feel, but it's clearly not how T.J. feels."

"I knew you wouldn't understand," she said. "That's why I didn't tell you."

Vitriol dripped off her words. It was as if a mask Juliet had been wearing slipped. Her eyes narrowed, her lips curled into a bloodless smirk. It made her look almost ghoulish. Then, just as quickly, she recovered. She tilted her chin, giving me an almost regal pose. She was pretty again. Composed. Professional.

"Juliet, it's been a long day. And if I'm being honest, a pretty bad one."

"You got your point across to the jury," she said. "I don't think they have any doubt that Lisa, Kim, and T.J. hate my guts. Of course they're going to say bad things about me. As far as they are concerned, I'm the town witch. They're only too happy to see me burned at the stake. You can argue that later, right? In our closing?"

"Yes," I said, though I wasn't sure what good it would do. The damage was done if the jury chose to believe the neighbors.

There was a knock on the door. Our time was up. Juliet looked panicked again.

"All right," I said. "I need some time to think and to prepare. And you need to prepare. Charlotte Stahl is more than likely going to put Bryson on the stand tomorrow. Are you ready for that?"

She blanched. "I want to see him. Can I talk to him before tomorrow?"

"Absolutely not," I said. "Jeanie is with him." I stopped short of saying everything would be all right. It probably wouldn't. But underscoring that wouldn't help anything right now.

"Just try to get some sleep," I said. "More than any other day, I'll need you to keep cool in the courtroom tomorrow. If the jury senses that you're trying to influence Bryson from the defense table ..."

"Influence him?" she shrieked. "Cass, he's my son. This has destroyed him. In spite of everyone else's opinion of me, my son still loves his mother. At least I hope he does. But he loved Nate too. This is killing him. Of course he's influenced by me sitting there while they put him through this."

"I mean signaling him," I said. "Bryson needs to know you can handle all of this. As hard as it is for him, he's also trying to manage your emotions. So keep them in check. Can you do that?"

"Yes," she said. Another knock on the door.

"I have to go," I said. "I've still got some work to do tonight to get ready. You'll be all right."

I didn't know if I'd meant that as a question or a statement. Juliet gave me a slight nod. I grabbed my leather bag and left her.

Eric was waiting for me on the courthouse steps, his expression dour. We walked down the steps in silence. It wasn't until we reached the crosswalk that he spoke.

"You know they hate her, right? The jury?"

We got a walking signal and stepped off the curb.

"Yeah," I said. "They can hate her for cheating on her husband. It doesn't mean they'll believe she killed him."

"Yeah," he agreed. "Maybe. You made some points when Blackfoot was on the stand."

"Which ones?" I asked. I was being at least partly sarcastic.

"They're gonna ask themselves why she did some of the stuff she did. Taping herself, giving Nate those shakes. Not even bothering to hide the thallium powder really. Those aren't the acts of a guilty person. Unless she's a really dumb guilty person."

"Does Juliet strike you as dumb?"

He paused. We'd reached the alley next to my office.

"No," he said. "She strikes me as the opposite. She can be cold and calculating. Manipulative. Narcissistic, for sure. But not dumb."

"So why would she do it?" I asked. "Why would she kill the guy? She could have her affairs. If he cared, he didn't make her stop. He didn't file for divorce. Didn't throw her out of the house."

"That's it then," he said. "The crux of your defense? She hasn't acted guilty?"

"I've won cases on less," I said, smiling. Eric stared hard at me for a moment. I hadn't meant it as a reference to his recent past. If he took it that way, he let it go. His gray eyes began to twinkle and his face broke into his trademark smirk. I couldn't help that it sent a tingle shooting straight to my toes. Then, Eric upped the ante and leaned in to kiss me.

It was quick. Almost chaste. But it was the first time he'd done it in a very long time. Like always, the air went out of me. I took a step backward to catch my breath.

"I'll see you tomorrow," I said. "It's going to be a pretty big day."

"The kid," he said. "Juliet's boy?"

I nodded. Eric pursed his lips and shook his head. "Tough spot for him to be in. I don't envy you having to cross-examine him in front of his mother."

"Thanks," I said. "So bring me some good news. Where are you on Gorney?"

Eric's brow went up. "I need a day. Maybe two."

"What?" I said, my hopes lifting. "What do you know? Eric, please, I need a break."

"I need a day or two. And you need to not know my methods. You think Stahl's going to rest before the weekend?"

"Boy, I was hoping not to cut it that close."

"I'll have something," he said. "I just can't promise what."

"You think it'll be enough to neutralize Bryson Ballard's testimony tomorrow?"

Eric's expression turned to stone. I couldn't read him.

"Cass ..."

"I know. I know. It all depends on how he holds up on the stand tomorrow."

Eric nodded. And I knew tomorrow would be the pivotal day in the trial of Juliet Clay.

Chapter 24

THE COURTROOM FELL DEADLY silent as Bryson Ballard took the stand first thing after lunch the next day. The last few months had aged him far beyond his teenage years. He sported a fresh haircut from a real barber. He wore a gray suit with a red tie that I knew Jeanie probably helped him get just right. But he took halting, shuffling steps as he made his way to the witness box. Juliet gasped beside me as Bryson turned and swore to tell the truth.

"He's a man," she whispered. "Where's my little boy?"

"Mr. Ballard," Charlotte started. "How are you related to the defendant, Juliet Clay?"

"She's my mom," Bryson said. He sat with hunched shoulders, reminding me of a turtle trying desperately to slip his head into his protective shell.

"Can you explain your relationship with Nathan Clay? How long had you known him, that kind of thing?"

"He is ... was ... my stepdad. But I'd been calling him Dad for years. He and my mom got married when I was eight, I think. Seven or eight."

"So they'd been married almost ten years?"

"Yeah. Um. Yes."

"Bryson, what was your home life like?"

"What do you mean?"

"I mean, how would you describe your parents' marriage?"

Bryson shrugged. "I don't know. Okay, I guess."

"Did they fight a lot?"

Bryson looked nervously at the jury.

"Objection," I said. "Foundation."

"Sustained. Rephrase your question, Ms. Stahl," Judge Castor said.

"Bryson," Charlotte said. "Did your parents get along?"

"Sometimes," he mumbled.

"They only got along sometimes? What about the rest of the time?"

"Do I have to talk about this?" he asked.

"Yes," Charlotte said. "I know this is difficult, Bryson. But yes. You do."

"Can you repeat the question?"

"You said your parents only got along sometimes. So I'm asking you, what was it like between them the rest of the time?"

"It's okay," Juliet whispered. She fought back tears as she tried to lock eyes with her son. He avoided looking at her, perhaps afraid he'd fall apart if he did.

"My mom is ... I don't know how to say it so it doesn't sound bad. People get the wrong idea about her."

"Bryson," Charlotte said. "If you could just answer the question."

"Yes," he said. "They argued a lot."

"What do you mean by a lot? Once a week? Twice a week? Every day?"

"Sometimes every day," he said. "Sometimes not for weeks or months at a time."

"What would happen when they argued?"

"There was a lot of yelling. Sometimes they'd throw things."

"Who did the yelling?" Charlotte asked.

"My mom, okay? She yells. She loses her temper and yells."

"What would set her off?" Charlotte asked.

"Lots of things. Nothing. Everything. I don't know. Look, you have to understand my mom. She came from nothing. She got kicked out of her parents' house when she was fifteen. She was on her own after that. And my dad, my real dad, he was a jerk, okay? Really, really bad. He would hit us. Her mostly, but me too. My mom is just ... she's a fighter. When we moved in with Nate, it was the first time we had anything. A nice house. She wasn't worried about paying the bills all the time or getting evicted."

"That must have been really hard for you to deal with growing up, Bryson. But I'd like to direct your attention to the last few months before Nate died. Can you do that for me?" Charlotte asked.

"What do you want to know?" Bryson said.

"When your parents fought," she said. "Did your mother ever threaten Nate?"

Bryson looked down at his lap. "Sometimes," he whispered.

"Bryson," Charlotte said. "How did your mother threaten Nate?"

"People say things they don't mean when they're upset," he said.

"What did she say, Bryson?"

Silence.

"Bryson, do you remember a fight your parents had in March of this year? It got so bad the neighbors called the police, didn't they?"

"Yeah," he said. "But I wasn't there for that part."

"When did you come home?"

"I came home as the police were leaving. They asked my dad to get a few things and stay somewhere else that night."

"Do you know why?" she asked.

"I think it was just so they'd cool off."

"Do you remember telling anyone else about that incident?"

"What do you mean?"

"Well, isn't it true you discussed that incident with Shane Waters?"

I froze. Bryson had never mentioned talking to anyone about his parents' fight.

"Maybe," Bryson said.

"Who is Shane Waters?" Charlotte asked.

"He's in my class. He lives down the street."

"Bryson, after your father came home on March 15th, did your parents argue again?"

"They were still mad at each other," Bryson said.

"Tell me what your mother said to Nate when he came home. Tell me what you told Shane Waters you heard."

"I lost my temper," Juliet whispered to me. "She's making it into something it wasn't!"

"Shh," I said, then stood up. "Objection, Your Honor. Foundation."

"Ms. Stahl," Judge Castor said. "If you want to ask this witness about his direct observation, go ahead. Meandering around what he said to other people isn't the way to go here."

"I understand, Your Honor," Charlotte said. "Let me rephrase."

"Please do."

"Bryson," Charlotte said. "Did your mother say anything to your father when he came back the morning of March 15th?"

"She said a lot of things," Bryson said.

"What did she say that shocked you so much you felt compelled to repeat it to a friend?"

"She said she'd kill him, okay?" Bryson shouted. "But she didn't mean it. It's just a thing people say."

"Can you recall exactly what she told your father?"

Bryson gritted his teeth. "She said she'd kill him if he ever tried to file for divorce."

"Thank you," Charlotte said. "Bryson, let's talk about the weeks before Nate died. How was his health?"

"He got sick with the flu."

"What were his symptoms?"

"He was just run down. He worked from home a lot."

"Was that unusual for him?"

"It was."

"Did you ever become concerned about his health?"

"He'd lost a bunch of weight in the months before he died. I knew my mom got him on those shakes. They were working. He looked great. He felt great. Then he didn't. He started sleeping a lot. His stomach was bothering him. I found him in the bathroom a couple of times, throwing up. And his color didn't look good."

"Do you know if he sought medical treatment?"

"He told me he went to a doctor. Because I asked both him and my mom. They both said he was seeing a doctor or had seen a doctor. My dad said it was the flu. I believed him."

"Bryson," Charlotte said. "Was there ever a time when you began to believe your father's illness was more serious than the flu?"

Bryson closed his eyes. It looked like he was trying to teleport himself anywhere else.

He opened his eyes. "Yes."

"Why?"

"Because he wasn't getting better. And I could tell my dad was scared. He just ... he wasn't himself. He was in a lot of pain."

"Did you express your concerns to him?"

"Yes," Bryson said.

"When?"

"The day before he died. He was in bed all the time by then. I mean, he could barely get up to pee. I had to help him. I begged him to let me take him to the hospital. He wouldn't go."

"Did you tell your mother about your concerns?"

"Yes," he said.

"But she didn't take him to the hospital?"

"He wouldn't go. He was stubborn."

"What did your father say to you when you spoke to him the day before he died?" she asked.

"Objection," I said. "Your Honor, to the extent counsel is asking this witness to testify about statements the decedent made, this is hearsay."

"Your Honor," Charlotte said. "May we approach?"

Castor motioned us forward. He covered his hand over his microphone. "Let's have it, counselor," he said to Charlotte.

"Your Honor, if you'll allow me, the statement this witness will repeat falls under MRE 804 as a hearsay exception as a dying declaration."

"Your Honor," I said. "The witness just testified that this conversation took place well before Nate Clay actually died."

"If you'll allow me some leeway," Charlotte said. "I'll get there."

"See that you do," Castor said. "The objection is overruled for the moment."

"You can't …" I started. Castor gave me a steely-eyed stare.

"I said for the moment," he cautioned me. "Let's get on with it."

My pulse racing, I went back to the defense table. Juliet's face had drained of color.

"Bryson," Charlotte began again. "What did Nate Clay say to you the morning before he died?"

Tears rolled down Bryson's face. "He told me he knew he was going to die."

Beside me, Tori rifled through the police report. She slid it across to me. I didn't need to look down. I knew it by heart. This wasn't what Bryson said to the police. He'd told them Nate had said he wasn't sure if he would get better. That was a chasm of difference where evidentiary rules were concerned.

"How did he say it? What were his exact words, if you recall?"

"He said, I know I'm dying."

"He never said that before," Juliet whispered.

"What else did he say, Bryson?" Charlotte asked.

"He said, I know I'm dying. He said, I know I'm gonna die, Bryson. Something's wrong. Be careful of your mom." Bryson choked out his words.

"Be careful of your mom," Charlotte repeated. "Not look out for your mom? Not take care of your mom?"

"He said be careful of her, okay?" Bryson said.

"Did you ask him what he meant by that?"

"No," he said. "I was just listening. Talking took a lot out of Dad by then."

"Did he seem delirious to you? Fevered?"

"No," Bryson said. "Just tired. Weak and tired."

"You talked about other things too? What were they?"

"He asked me about my golf game. I'd played with friends the day before."

"So he knew exactly what day it was?"

"Yes."

"Where was your mother during this conversation?"

"Out," he said. "She had a lunch date or something."

"In fact, that's why your father called you in, isn't it?"

"Yes," Bryson said. "He said he wanted to talk to me before my mom got home."

"He said he knew he was dying," Charlotte repeated. "He knew something was wrong, and that you were to be careful of your mother. What else did he say, Bryson?"

"Your Honor," I said, fuming. "I'd like to renew my objection. This is hearsay."

"Come on back," Judge Castor said. We approached the bench.

"Your Honor," Charlotte said. "The exceptions are clear under 804. The declarant must have a settled expectation of death, actually die, and the statement is being offered in the trial for the resulting homicide. It's well-settled law. I've made my proffer."

"She's right, Cass," Judge Castor said. "Your objection is overruled. You'll have your chance to cross-examine."

I bit my tongue to keep from blurting out that it would be far too late by then. We headed back to our tables.

"Bryson," Charlotte said, delivering her coup de grâce. "What else did your father say after he told you to be careful of your mother?"

"He said she's done something?" Bryson was full-on crying now. "Mom, I'm so sorry."

"It's okay," she mouthed. "I love you, baby."

"Your father told you that your mother did something. Did he say what?"

"No," Bryson said. "He just said I know your mom did something. Then she came home. That was it."

"Thank you, Bryson," Charlotte said.

"He needs a break," Juliet whispered in my ear.

She was right, only I couldn't give him one. I could not let his testimony marinate in the jury's mind as is.

"I need you to trust me," I said to her.

"Listen to me," she said through tight lips. "Leave him alone. Don't hurt that boy. He's in enough pain already. This isn't his fault. If he lied before, he was just trying to protect me."

"I have to do my job," I said.

"Ms. Leary?" Judge Castor called out.

"One moment, Your Honor," I said.

"Let him go," Juliet said. "Get him out of here. Quickly."

On that, we were in agreement.

"Bryson," I said. "Just to clarify, you said your father wasn't acting like himself in the few days before he died, was he?"

"I said that," Bryson said. "And he wasn't."

"It wasn't his habit to work from home?"

"No. Not at all. Not until the last few weeks before he died."

"You testified that you tried to get your father to go to the hospital, is that right?"

"Yes," he said. "I offered to take him there."

"Were you the only one trying to convince him to go to the hospital?"

"No," Bryson said, his face brightening. "No. My mom was on him all the time, too. She begged him to go. She's the one who first told me to work on him about it."

"What do you mean?"

"I mean like I said. Nate was really stubborn. He did a lot of personal injury cases, including medical malpractice. He didn't really trust doctors. My mom thought maybe he'd listen to me if I asked him to go."

"Did she offer to take him to a doctor?" I asked.

"Yes," he answered. "A couple of times."

"Did they fight about it?" I asked.

"Yeah," he said. "But he wouldn't go."

"You didn't question your father about what he thought your mother did to him?"

Bryson looked to Charlotte, then the jury, then at Juliet. "No."

"You didn't call the police then, did you?"

"No."

"You never questioned your mother about what Nate said, did you?"

"No."

"In fact, you never even told your mother what he said, isn't that right?"

"I didn't tell her, no."

"You were questioned by the police, too. After Nate died. You didn't tell them what you claim Nate said, did you?"

"I don't know what you mean."

"Isn't it true that your statement to the police was only that Nate told you Juliet would be the death of him?"

"I might have. Yeah. I think maybe that's what I said."

I paused. Was it better to grill and challenge him more about how he characterized Nate's alleged statements? Or was it better to do as Juliet wanted and get him the hell out of here? His testimony was a problem. At the same time, he'd just given me a huge hook for my closing argument. If I impeached his statement about Nate's so-called dying declaration, I risked losing that hook.

Juliet was still crying and looking at her son, agony written all over her face. She didn't seem angry at all. Over and over she mouthed, I love you.

It was a gamble. A huge one. But for now, Juliet's pain spoke louder than anything I could get out of Bryson on cross.

"I have no further questions. But I'd like to reserve the right to recall this witness."

"So be it," Judge Castor said. "Ms. Stahl? Any redirect?"

"No, Your Honor," Charlotte said.

With that, Bryson stepped off the stand. As he walked back out of the courtroom, he seemed broken, defeated, and more like the little boy he still was.

Chapter 25

I HAD no time to talk to Juliet after Bryson left the stand. Charlotte was back up at the lectern, calling her next witness.

"I have to talk to him," Julie scribbled on a note. She slid it across the table. I put my hand over it so no one else could read it. I carefully flipped it over.

"The state calls Ray Meisner to the stand," Charlotte said.

"Not now," I whispered to Juliet. "Just hang in there."

Ray Meisner was a bald, stout, compact guy who had a Conor McGregor-like strut as he made his way to the witness stand.

"Mr. Meisner," Charlotte said, after he identified himself to the jury. "How were you affiliated with the victim in this case?"

"He was a client," Meisner said. "I was his accountant and financial advisor."

"How long did you work with Mr. Clay in that capacity?"

"Fifteen years," Meisner answered.

"So well before he married the accused, Juliet Clay?"

"Yes," he said. "Nate and I were fraternity brothers so I'd known him for, I think, thirty-five years."

"As Mr. Clay's accountant and financial advisor, what services did you perform for him?"

"Well, I did Nate's taxes. Both personal and business. I also handled his investment portfolio."

Charlotte went through a series of questions with Meisner, describing the various assets Nate held. It was dry, dull testimony and it perplexed me why she hadn't called him earlier in the trial.

"Mr. Meisner," she finally asked, "What was Nate Clay's net worth right before he died?"

"Before he died? Well, he had half a million dollars in the bank. Cash on hand. That was spread over three different accounts. General savings. Money market. A checking account. The house on Ford Street was paid off. It's a unique lot so it's a little tougher to peg fair market value, but the house was conservatively worth another half a million dollars. He had a stock portfolio worth roughly three hundred thousand dollars. His 401(k) was over a million dollars. Then there was the value of his practice. He and his law partner operated as a true partnership. That was a thorny issue between us."

"How so?"

"Well, I was concerned about this very thing. When Nate died, the partnership automatically dissolved. So it's my understanding everyone's still trying to sort out what, if anything, Nate's estate is owed."

"Okay," Charlotte said. "So I'm clear, you're saying Nate Clay was worth in the neighborhood of two million dollars plus potentially the value of his share of the law practice?"

"Roughly, yes," he said.

"Were there any life insurance policies?"

"Oh yes," Meisner said. "You asked me his pre-death value. Nate also had a two-million-dollar life insurance policy."

"Who was the beneficiary of that policy?"

"His wife, Juliet Clay," he said.

"And who stands to inherit the remainder of Mr. Clay's assets?"

"That's murkier," he said. "Nate had a complicated estate plan. The life insurance went to Juliet. Though that's tied up now because of this matter."

I wrote a note and tore off a sheet of paper to take with me to the lectern.

"What about the rest?" Charlotte asked.

"Nate had a living trust. He left a lot of his assets to various charities. The rest, around a million dollars' worth, is in a trust to benefit his widow and their son Bryson."

"So I'm clear," Charlotte said. "Your testimony is that Nate's estate plan plus his life insurance provided for a payout close to two million dollars to Juliet Clay upon his death. Is that right?"

"That's rough numbers. But yes."

"Thank you," Charlotte said. "I have no further questions."

"Ms. Leary?" Judge Castor said.

"Mr. Meisner," I said. "You mentioned some murkiness regarding the disposition of law firm assets upon Nate's death, isn't that right?"

"It is. Unfortunately, Nate and his law partner were in the habit of deciding things by verbal agreement."

"So it's likely that if Nate's estate and his partner, Ted Gorney, can't come to an amicable agreement, there could be litigation?"

"I don't know. It's possible, yes."

"So you're saying Mr. Gorney has a financial interest in firm assets."

"Most definitely," he said.

"In other words, Ted Gorney stands to benefit financially since Nate died?"

"Objection," Charlotte said. "Asked and answered."

"Your Honor, I'm simply clarifying Mr. Meisner's answer in layman's terms."

"Overruled," Castor said. "The witness may answer."

"Yes," Meisner said. "It's fair to assume that Ted Gorney will get some kind of buyout or a payout since Nate died."

"Mr. Meisner," I said. "Are you familiar with so-called slayer laws?"

"Objection," Charlotte said. "This witness is an accountant, not a lawyer. He's not a legal expert."

"Your Honor," I said. "This witness is qualified as a financial expert who has already testified about his intimate knowledge of the decedent's estate plan. I asked him if he's familiar with slayer laws. I didn't ask him to render a legal opinion. That said, in his profession, Mr. Meisner is likely responsible for understanding, interpreting, and complying with any number of laws that pertain to the disposition of one's property upon death."

"You've made your point, counselor," Castor said. "The objection is overruled. You may answer, Mr. Meisner."

"Can you repeat it?" Meisner asked.

"Are you familiar with Michigan's slayer law?"

"Yes," he said.

"You've also had occasion to explain it to clients within the various and lengthy financial disclosures you go over with them when they open accounts, correct?"

"I'm not a lawyer. Like Ms. Stahl said, I don't give legal advice."

"What is the slayer law as you understand it, Mr. Meisner?" I asked.

"Basically, murderers don't get to inherit from people they murdered," he said.

"What about life insurance policies?"

"It applies to that too, as far as I'm aware," he said.

"So, if Mrs. Clay is convicted of killing her husband, she won't get a dime from his estate, will she?"

"That's probably true, yes," he said.

"Mr. Meisner, you also had occasion to counsel Juliet Clay about financial matters, didn't you?"

"I did, yes. Nate asked me to."

"Did Mrs. Clay have any wealth of her own?"

"Recently? Yes. But only very recently. She'd started making money in ad revenue from her social media channels."

"What was her net worth prior to Nate's passing?"

"She had about a hundred thousand dollars in the bank. She'd bought some stocks that did well. Her portfolio is worth about three hundred thousand. So, she had her own money. Yes. And she'd just signed a deal with the manufacturers of a diet shake that we were really excited about. We were projecting it would net her half a million dollars over the next three years."

"But that deal got pulled when Nate died, didn't it?"

"Of course," he answered.

"Thank you," I said. "I have no further questions."

I went back to my table. Juliet's face was still blotchy from crying during Bryon's testimony.

"Mr. Meisner," Charlotte said. "That diet shake deal. Do you know why Mrs. Clay was offered it?"

"Her online videos were really taking off. She had over fifty thousand followers and it was growing. Her videos were getting watched millions of times."

"Which videos were those?"

"She went viral posting videos of Nate drinking those shakes and losing weight," he said.

"Thank you. I have no further questions." Charlotte stayed at the lectern as Ray Meisner strutted through the courtroom and out the door.

"Ms. Stahl?" Judge Castor said.

"Your Honor," Charlotte said, looking straight at the jury. "At this time, the prosecution rests."

Juliet gasped. The jury stayed stonily silent and unreadable.

"All right," Castor said. "It's four o'clock. We're adjourned until Monday morning."

The bang of his gavel echoed across the marble floor as Juliet collapsed in tears.

Chapter 26

THERE WAS nothing I could do for Juliet. I had a few last-minute motions to tie up with the judge before I could present my defense Monday morning.

"Tell him it's okay," Juliet managed to get out as the deputies prepared her for transport back to the jail. "Tell Bryson Mom loves him and it's okay."

"I'll do what I can," I said. "Just hang tight. If we need to meet before Monday, I'll let you know."

With that, they led her out. I made my obligatory motion for a directed verdict but was denied, as I expected. The judge felt Charlotte had presented enough evidence to put the case to the jury.

"How long do you think you'll need for your side, Ms. Leary?" Castor asked.

"Two, three days at most," I said.

Castor nodded as he wrote notes on a pad of paper. "All right. So we can get this to the jury no later than next Thursday. Let's try to stick to that, counsel. No surprises."

"Yes, Your Honor," Charlotte said. She gathered her things and left the courtroom ahead of me. I made my way out of the service exit, on the off chance there might be a local reporter or two waiting in the wings. I wanted nothing to do with them.

Tori had already headed back to the office. When I got there, I found her and Jeanie waiting for me in Jeanie's office. Jeanie rushed toward me, face ashen.

"I heard," she said. "Bryson just left. He was in pretty bad shape. I told him to go home. How much damage do you think he did?"

"Well," I said, plopping my messenger bag onto an empty chair. "He pretty much told the jury Nate Clay believed Juliet killed him."

Jeanie sank down into her winged leather desk chair.

"Did he tell you that, Jeanie?" I asked.

"How did that get in?" she asked.

"Dying declaration," I said. "Bryson said Nate said he knew he was dying. Castor decided it was immediate enough in time to when he actually died to meet the standard."

I wanted to punch something. I wanted to scream.

"What are you going to do?" Jeanie asked.

"I'm ready with the Berriman lab guys," Tori said.

"I'm not sure I'm calling them," I told her. Her shoulders slumped in disappointment. "There might not be a need. Charlotte didn't call Donovan McNamara. She appears to be abandoning the argument that Juliet got thallium from him or that lab."

"Why would she do that?" Tori asked.

"Because she doesn't need it," Jeanie answered. I nodded.

"She's proven there was thallium in the house," I said. "She's proven that it was in the shakes Nate drank and has strong evidence Juliet might have spiked them with it. It doesn't matter how she got the stuff."

"Risk reward," Jeanie said. "I'm sorry, but it's what I'd do if I were Charlotte. Why open the door to letting you parade a bunch of scientists through claiming the stuff didn't come from them? There's a chance the jury starts looking for other holes in the case."

"So what are we going to do?" Tori asked, dismay heavy in her voice. The Berriman lab techs would have been her chance to shine. She'd spent weeks prepping.

At the moment, I truly didn't have good answers for any of them. All this time I'd assumed the autopsy evidence was my biggest problem.

"He's trying to do the right thing," Jeanie said.

"Jeanie, he never told you those specific words? He said Nate said *I know I'm dying. I know your mother did something*?"

Jeanie rubbed her temples. "Cass, you know I can't tell you what we discussed. He's my client. But if I thought there was this kind of problem, I never would have honored Bryson's wish to ask you for help. He doesn't want his mom to go to jail."

"I know," I said. Though I didn't really believe it anymore. Why on earth hadn't that kid told Jeanie or me what he said on the stand today?

"How's Juliet?" Tori asked. "She was about to collapse when I left."

"They got her out," I said. "She told me to make sure Bryson knows she loves him. She's pretty torn up worrying about him feeling guilty."

"You sure that's it?" Jeanie said. "You think maybe it's more she now realizes she's about to get caught?"

"All of a sudden you think she's guilty?" I asked, my temper flaring. Even as it did, I knew it wasn't Jeanie I was mad at. I was mad at Juliet. I was mad at myself.

"Sorry," I recanted. "Have I been an idiot this whole time? Have I let my ambition cloud my judgment?"

"Okay," Tori said. "Just because Charlotte doesn't think she has to explain where the thallium came from, doesn't mean it's not still a huge question. You can't just head down to Menard's and pick up a can. It came from somewhere."

"I don't know," I said, shaking my head, which started to throb. "I really don't know. The bad news is now the jury gets to sit with all of this over the weekend. That's why Charlotte rested. It was smart. It's what I would have done. I need sleep. I need a drink. I need to just ..."

"Yeah," Jeanie said. "Just go on home. You can come at this fresh tomorrow. I don't want to leave Bryson alone too long. I'll deliver Juliet's message. It'll help."

"Is he staying with you this weekend?" I asked.

Jeanie nodded.

"Good. I may need to talk to him again. But first, I need to come up with a new game plan for Monday morning."

I had an unanswered text on my phone from Eric. I read it now.

"Meet you at your place first thing in the morning. Got some news you're going to like."

I waved my phone in front of me. "Just pray Eric has something good to tell me."

I left Jeanie and Tori and headed for the lake.

Chapter 27

SLEEP WOULDN'T COME. Instead, I paced. A single glass of wine turned into three quarters of a bottle but even that didn't dull the edge of my spinning brain.

I sat in the back bedroom I'd converted into a home office. On the large forty-inch monitor, I played Juliet's social media videos on a loop.

Juliet bouncing around in spandex as she mixed a shake. That first video where she brought one to Nate and sat on his lap as he rolled his eyes and took it from her. Two months later as she recorded him stepping on a scale wearing only boxer shorts.

She caught him just waking up. In one video, she burst in on him while he was taking a shower. Half the draw of her content was the grumbling, put-upon reactions of Nate as he realized the camera was on him. He was the lovable curmudgeon with the sexy wife. Like Al Bundy. Or every other TV dad Ed O'Neill ever portrayed.

"Come on, baby, you know what time it is," she said in one video. This was two weeks before he died. Nate sat in his home office, staring at his computer monitor.

"You shake for me, I'll shake for you," Juliet said in a breathy, Marilyn Monroe-esque voice. Nate looked up, his eyes sunken, his skin hanging from his gaunt face. It took on new meaning now that we knew he was really dying. To Juliet's unsuspecting viewership at the time, it just looked like a miraculous weight loss.

"You go first," Nate said, his voice raspy. He rested his chin on his fist, the glow of his monitor casting him in blue.

Juliet leaned forward and shook her breasts off screen. You could see her shadow in the monitor behind Nate's head. Then, the shake appeared. Nate grabbed it and drank.

"You in there?"

I jumped. Eric stood in the doorway. He still had a key to my house and permission to use it.

"What time is it?" I asked. I'd drawn the shades hours ago.

"Eight o'clock," he said. It was then I noticed Eric came bearing two paper coffee cups from the bakery down the street.

"Bless you," I said, my brain still buzzing.

"You been up all night?" he asked, taking a seat on the small couch I kept in the office.

"Apparently so," I said, peeling the plastic lid off my cup and blowing off the steam.

"Tori called me," he said. "She clued me in on Bryson's testimony."

Behind me, Juliet's videos still played. In this one, she caught Nate in his home office again. He had his head on his desk. His computer monitor flashed the LexisNexis logo before flipping to his beach scene screensaver.

"I don't want to talk about it," I said. "What's your good news? I need it."

"Well, it's less good in light of what Bryson had to say. What the hell, Cass? You interviewed him. Blackfoot interviewed him. He actually testified that Nate said he knew Juliet had done something?"

"Pretty much," I said.

"You couldn't impeach him?"

"His testimony wasn't inconsistent with his police statement," I said. "It was just more detailed on the witness stand."

"How convenient," Eric said. I didn't like his tone.

"You think he made it up?"

"I just question the timing," he said. "And so do you."

"He's a kid," I said. "A traumatized kid. He was afraid."

"Except he changed his story to Charlotte. No way she fishes for that without already knowing what she was going to catch. She's new, but she's not stupid. And she's got Rafe Johnson coaching her. I just don't like it."

Behind me, the last of Juliet's videos played. In it, Nate was still in his home office, stretched out on a leather love seat with a file open on his chest. Juliet had caught him sleeping. With his readers perched on the end of his nose, he moaned when she came forward with yet another shake.

"Poor bastard," Eric said. He left the couch and came closer to my computer monitor. "He worked until the day he dropped. That's what I came to tell you about."

"What's that?"

"You were right about Gorney. There was trouble in the firm. Gorney had a growing list of disgruntled clients. One in particular was getting ready to file a malpractice claim against him."

Eric froze the screen and cocked his head to the side. He tried to enlarge the image of the file Nate was holding. "That can't be. That'd be too easy."

"What do you know?" I asked.

"Talbot? Taylor? I can't make out the tab on that file. Can you? Anyway, there was an insurance settlement that went missing. Client's name was Russ Taylor. It was an auto-neg case. Wrongful death. Three hundred grand. Gorney's cut was a third of that. Only Taylor's family never got paid their two thirds. They were going to come after him."

"Were? They never pursued it?"

"No," Eric said. "That's the thing. A few months before Nate died, Taylor's family dropped the whole thing. They signed a release."

"Wait a minute," I said. "You said it was just against Gorney. Why wasn't Nate on the hook too? Gorney's story is he brought in the clients and Nate did the litigation side. Any med mal lawyer worth their salt would have come after both partners and the firm."

"That's the thing that got me curious," Eric said. "Nate's never mentioned in the pleadings they were going to file. And as far as I can tell, they never retained a lawyer of their own."

Eric pulled a folded stack of papers out of his back pocket and handed them to me. It was an unfiled civil complaint and a single page release of liability. The would-be plaintiff was named Mary Taylor.

"Mary Taylor? How did you get a hold of pleadings that were never filed? How did you ... no. You know what? I don't want to know."

"Yeah," he said. "Believe me. You don't. But don't worry. Like I said, there weren't any lawyers involved on Taylor's side. Those documents came off a website. Anyway, I went digging in the probate court. An estate was opened by Taylor's mother, Mary. I tried getting her on the phone. She hung up on me. I went out to her address of record and the neighbor said she's not living there anymore. I'm trying to figure out what happened to her. But when I showed the neighbor a picture of Nathan Clay, she recognized him. Said he'd been out to talk to Mary Taylor once or twice right after Christmas. That release was dated February 1st."

"You think Nate had something to do with smoothing things over for Gorney? Why? They weren't exactly on the greatest terms before Nate died. I sensed a lot of tension when I talked to Gorney. He didn't exactly volunteer any of this."

"I'm not surprised," he said.

"Why didn't Sofia Blackfoot look into it?"

"Why would she?" Eric said. "I don't even think I would have. The evidence against Juliet has always been pretty damning. Taylor was a client of Gorney's, not Nate's. There's no paper trail tying any of these negotiations to Nate. This wouldn't have been remotely in the investigative ballpark."

The caffeine hit. My brain was on fire.

"Can you use it?" he asked.

"I don't know. I know if I were Charlotte I'd fight like hell to keep it out for all the reasons you just said. Juliet didn't know anything about it. Gorney was asked repeatedly if he knew anyone else with a reason to hurt Nate or the firm. Their secretary was also questioned. This Taylor matter was never brought up by anyone. I've got to know. How did you get it?"

"You sure you want to know?"

"I want to know a little," I said.

"Did some poking around online. Got into some neighborhood Facebook groups. Tracked down anyone who ever gave Gorney or Nate a bad online review and went digging from there. The rest, well, I'll just keep some of my tricks to myself."

"All the negativity was against Gorney? You didn't find anything linking this Taylor case to Nate?"

Eric shook his head. "No. Nothing. I wouldn't have even bothered to look into Gorney if you hadn't asked me to. There's really no obvious trail leading to Nate off Taylor's case."

I rose and started to pace. "Unless he was getting ready to turn on Gorney," I said. "If he had something on him. And Gorney found out. Or if Nate was trying to protect his own ass from Gorney's misdeeds, it would give Gorney a motive to keep Nate quiet."

"I don't have proof of that," Eric said.

"But you'll get it," I said. "You're not done trying to find Mary Taylor, are you?"

"It's the longest of shots, Cass. Just because Ted Gorney had an enemy or two, like you said, there's no clear path to Nate's murder."

"Except Gorney lied about it," I said. "And both he and Nate kept the whole thing off book. Not even their secretary knew. It's weird. It's at least worth a conversation with Mary Taylor. See if you can find any of her family."

"It's a common name," he said. "Might take a while."

"Time is the one thing I don't have, Eric. Can you do it?"

"Yeah," he said, smiling. And I knew then he'd already been working on it. He was just as jazzed about the potential lead as I was.

His smirk melted me. Maybe it was the jolt of caffeine or lack of sleep, but I bolted across the floor and took Eric's face in my hands. As he stared at me wide-eyed, I kissed him hard and deep.

His hands went up, encircling my waist.

"You're back, aren't you?" I asked.

He smiled. "Well, when you put it that way."

"Wait here," I said. "Or wait wherever. I need a shower. And a toothbrush. Then we have some work to do!"

For the first time in days ... weeks ... I felt a glimmer of hope for Juliet.

Chapter 28

"Ms. Leary? Are you ready to proceed?"

"I am, Your Honor," I said. Monday morning, at nine a.m. We'd reached the fourth day of trial. My turn. I had every belief that if Juliet's case went to the jury last Friday, she'd have been convicted. Full stop.

I took a breath, straightened my back, and called my first witness for the defense.

"The defense calls Doctor Melvin Broyles to the stand."

At eighty-five, Dr. Broyles was one of the oldest doctors still in practice in the entire state. But you wouldn't know it by looking at him. He had a youthful spring in his step and didn't appear to have lost a strand of hair. He'd gone pure white in his forties so most of his long-time patients said he'd looked the same their entire lives.

We got through his credentials quickly. He got his medical license fifty-eight years ago. Board certified in internal medicine. He'd treated Nathan Clay from the cradle to the grave.

Once I had him qualified as a medical expert, I led him into the meat of his testimony.

"Dr. Broyles, how would you describe Nate Clay's overall health up until the end of last year?"

"He was in good shape," Broyles said. The man was an absolute freak of nature. He didn't even wear readers as he reviewed his clinical notes. "His cholesterol was higher than I wanted so he was taking medication to lower that. His blood pressure was good. He had arthritis in his knees and that was beginning to cause him some pain and mobility issues, but we were managing it with over-the-counter medication. I was working up to convince him to try cortisone shots for that. But my main concern with him was his weight."

"How much did he weigh in December of last year?" I asked.

Dr. Broyles referred back to his notes. Charlotte and I had already stipulated to their entry into evidence.

"Nate was two hundred and ten pounds on December 21st of last year. At his height that edged his BMI into the obesity category. I didn't like that so we discussed some strategies for getting that under control."

"When did you see him clinically again?" I asked.

"In early February of this year. He came in complaining of stomach pain and fatigue. Upon physical exam, his gallbladder felt bigger than it should have. I ordered an ultrasound and didn't like what I saw."

"Which was?"

"He had a mass in his abdomen. I referred him to an oncologist."

"Do you know what came of that?"

"After a CT scan and biopsy, he was diagnosed with stage four pancreatic cancer. It had spread to his lymph nodes."

"When was this definitive diagnosis made?"

"On March 10th of this year."

"Dr. Broyles, in your expert medical opinion, what is the prognosis for an individual with that diagnosis?"

"Well, it, of course, depends on a lot of factors. But it's ninety-nine percent fatal within a five-year period. And most patients diagnosed that late in the game don't live much more than six months, in my experience. Pancreatic cancer is what's called a silent killer. In most cases, it doesn't start producing symptoms until it's well advanced, as it was in Nate's case."

"Did you remain in communication with Nate's oncologist?"

"We consulted, yes. But I have to tell you, Nate didn't follow up with his treatment."

"And what course of treatment was available to Nate? What did you recommend?"

"Dr. Halsey, the oncologist, recommended a course of radiation and chemo to shrink the tumor. Nate's condition wasn't curable, but it was treatable."

"In your professional opinion, was Nate Clay terminal?"

"Yes. If you mean was it likely the cancer was going to kill him. Yes. Not only was it likely, it was imminent. But I believe we could have prolonged his life. People with stage four pancreatic cancer can live with it for years in some cases. With treatment."

"What treatment did Nate receive for it?"

Dr. Broyles let out a frustrated sigh. "None."

"Excuse me?"

"I said none. Nate opted not to pursue any medical treatment for his condition. He didn't want it."

"Did he tell you why?"

"Nate's grandfather died of the same thing. He had a rough go of it and Nate didn't want to go through the same thing."

"Dr. Broyles, isn't it true that Nathan Clay knew he was going to die of pancreatic cancer?"

"Objection," Charlotte said. "Calls for speculation."

"Your Honor," I said. "Dr. Broyles was recommending a course of treatment. Nathan Clay's reasoning for accepting or rejecting that treatment is relevant. To the extent Mr. Clay told the doctor about those reasons as it relates to treatment decisions they made together, it's highly relevant and not speculative."

"Well," Judge Castor said. "I agree you can ask the doctor what Mr. Clay told him regarding said reasoning. Rephrase and I'll allow it."

"Dr. Broyles," I said. "What did Nathan Clay tell you regarding his reasoning for rejecting any treatment that might have prolonged his life?"

"He said he knew he was a lost cause. That was the phrase he used. He asked me point-blank if I thought this thing was going to kill him. I told him yes, eventually."

"So in other words, Nate Clay knew he would die of pancreatic cancer and you agreed."

"In a manner of speaking, yes," Dr. Broyles said. "But I'm not saying I agreed with his treatment decision."

"In fact, you had him sign a waiver, didn't you? You made him acknowledge that his decision to forgo treatment was against your sound medical advice."

"Yes," Dr. Broyles said.

"When did Mr. Clay sign that acknowledgement? If you recall."

"He had his last office appointment with me on April 1st of this year."

"Doctor," I said. "Do you recall discussing with Mr. Clay how long he might have left to live if he didn't pursue the treatment options recommended?"

"Yes," Dr. Broyles said.

"And what did you tell him?"

"Objection," Charlotte said. "This is hearsay."

"Your Honor, discussions between Dr. Broyles and Nathan Clay were held for the purposes of proper diagnosis and treatment of a medical condition. They fall well within the hearsay exceptions."

"I'll allow it. Overruled," Judge Castor said.

"I was very worried about Nathan," Dr. Broyles said. "Very worried. He knew this was a terminal condition. I knew it. Without letting us go in and try to shrink that primary tumor, he didn't have long."

"Does that mean weeks or months?" I asked.

"Not many months," he said. "I told him three months at the most. Possibly less."

"So you're telling us that on April 1st of this year, it was your medical opinion that Nathan Clay would be dead within three months or less?"

"That's correct," he said.

"And in fact, Nathan Clay died a few weeks later, isn't that correct?"

"Yes."

"So you weren't surprised by that?"

"No."

"In fact, you believed Nathan died as a result of complications from pancreatic cancer, isn't that right?"

"That's correct. But April 1st was the last time I saw and examined him."

"Dr. Broyles, during your appointments with Nathan Clay, did he ever express concerns he had about issues at home?"

"We talked about what he was going to tell his family. Nathan was adamant that he didn't want them to know how sick he was."

"And that was a concern to you?" I asked.

"Yes."

"Why is that?"

"Because patient outcomes can largely depend on their support systems. If spouses know what to look for, that can make a difference. And you can't really quantify the emotional support of a family when you have a terminally ill patient."

"Did you counsel him to tell his wife and family about his diagnosis?"

"I did."

"And what was his response?"

"He said he didn't want to worry them."

"Did you press the issue?"

"I did. I offered to have his wife come in with him so we could discuss it all together. I was hoping maybe she could convince him to pursue treatment. Nate refused. As far as I know, he hadn't told his wife as of April 1st, the last time I saw him."

"I see," I said. "Doctor, is it standard practice to ask your patients questions about their mental health when they come in for checkups?"

"There are standard questionnaires we're required to give, yes."

"And among those questions, it's standard to ask about issues within the home, correct?"

"What do you mean?"

"Well, you ask your patients if they have enough food to eat, right?"

"Yes."

"And you ask them whether they feel safe in their home, correct?"

"We do, yes," he said.

"Did Nathan Clay express any concerns about domestic violence within the home?"

"No, he didn't."

"Did he indicate that he was afraid for his safety within the home on his April 1st appointment?"

"No, he didn't."

"Did you have any concerns about Nathan Clay's safety within his own home?"

"Well, of course I worried about him getting sick and weaker. I wanted to make sure he would have proper in-home care because I knew his condition would decline. At some point, he was going to have issues eating. And possibly become weak enough he'd have problems getting out of bed. So yes. I was concerned about arranging for home care. I suggested hospice."

"And what was his response?"

"He refused. He said he had everything under control."

"So you never felt that Nathan Clay was afraid of his wife?"

"That didn't come up, no," he said.

"Doctor, can you describe what kind of symptoms a person with end stage pancreatic cancer would experience?"

"You'd have a lot of digestive symptoms. Vomiting, diarrhea, bloating, loss of appetite."

"Could there also be neurological symptoms?" I asked.

"Sure," he said. "Though the gastrointestinal symptoms would be the worst."

"What kind of neurological symptoms might you see?"

"Well, anytime you're dealing with someone at the end of life like that, they can become altered. Confused. That kind of thing."

"I see," I said. "Thank you, Doctor, I have no further questions."

"Ms. Stahl?" Judge Castor said.

Charlotte was quick.

"Doctor, have you had a chance to review the medical examiner's report on the death of Nathan Clay?"

"I have, yes."

"Do you have any reason to believe Dr. Trainor's conclusions are erroneous?"

"I don't know what you mean?"

"Well, first off, it's true that you didn't examine Mr. Clay in the weeks before he died, did you?"

"I didn't. My records speak for themselves. As I said, our last visit was April 1st."

"Dr. Trainor testified that Nathan Clay died from acute thallium poisoning, not complications from pancreatic cancer, isn't that right?"

"That's what she found, yes."

"And sitting here today, you have no reason to conclude otherwise, do you?"

"Well, as I said, I didn't examine Nate after April 1st. So as far as that goes, I'd defer to Dr. Trainor, as she did the postmortem."

"And you were interviewed by her as she prepared her report, weren't you?"

"She called me, yes."

"And you provided her with your medical records on Nathan Clay, correct?"

"Well, yes. That's standard in a case like this."

"A case like what, Dr. Broyles?"

"In a homicide where there's a coroner's inquest," he said.

"Again, so the record is clear. You concur with Dr. Trainor's determination that Nathan Clay died of thallium poisoning, not pancreatic cancer."

"Objection," I said. "The doctor has already answered the question. The postmortem examination is beyond the scope of his knowledge."

"Overruled," Judge Castor said. "The witness may answer."

"I have no reason to go against what Dr. Trainor found," he said. "But like Ms. Leary said, I didn't do the postmortem. I'm taking Amelia's word for it."

"Thank you," Charlotte said. "I have no further questions."

I deferred redirect and Dr. Broyles stepped down.

"Call your next witness, Ms. Leary," Judge Castor said.

"Your Honor," I said. "The defense calls Theodore Gorney to the stand. And I'd like permission to question him as a hostile witness."

Chapter 29

THIS WAS A RISK. A big one. On cross-examination, Ted Gorney could do damage if the judge didn't rule my way. I stepped back up to the lectern as Ted practically stormed his way to the witness box. When he turned to face me, I swear his eyes gleamed with satisfaction. He'd been waiting for this. He felt he had a story to tell. Two words flashed in my mind.

Oh crap.

"Mr. Gorney," I said. "You and Nathan Clay were business partners, weren't you?"

"Yes," he said.

"How long have you known him?"

"Almost twenty-five years."

We got through the background information easily enough. Ted stuck to what he'd told me earlier. They knew each other from law school. When the opportunity arose for Ted to need a law partner, he approached Nate. Good. No controversy there. I went to the court records.

"Mr. Gorney, isn't it true that you've filed a claim against Nathan Clay's estate?"

"Yes," he said.

"What is the substance of that claim?"

"Well, we were partners. Generally speaking, we split firm profits in half. I'm only asking for there to be an accounting and that I get my fair share."

"Your fair share," I said. "Ballpark? How much money is that?"

"I don't have a solid number. It would be fifty percent of net profit, not gross. We've got overhead. Court costs and other fees that have to be paid off the top before we get to the profit split. That all has to be figured out."

"I understand," I said. "But I asked for a ballpark figure. Roughly speaking, how much do you think you're owed from Nate's estate?"

"I don't know exactly."

"You filed a claim. A written pleading in the probate court. How much were you asking for?"

He shifted in his seat.

"It was a million dollars, wasn't it?"

"It could be," he said. "Again, we'll need a final accounting. I filed the claim to protect my interests."

"Of course," I said.

"Mr. Gorney, isn't it true that prior to Nate's death, you and he were having issues with how your business was being run?"

"I don't know what you mean."

"Well, isn't it true that Nate Clay approached you about dissolving your partnership?"

"We never dissolved the partnership," he said.

"That's not what I asked. But now that you put it like that, Nate couldn't file for formal dissolution because he died, isn't that right?"

"Death dissolves the partnership, Ms. Leary. Maybe you've forgotten what you learned in law school."

I smiled. There he was. I wanted the jury to see Ted Gorney the way Nate might have.

"Fine," I said. "Did you have a formal partnership agreement with Nate?"

"No," he said.

"In the absence of that formal agreement, how would your business be split in the event of one partner's death?"

"Fifty-fifty under the law," he answered.

"Got it," I said. "Mr. Gorney, how much money did you bring into the partnership last year?"

"What?"

"I mean, of the two million dollars you're claiming in estimated partnership assets ... of which you're asking for half ... how much of that comes from business you brought into the firm?"

"That's hard to say."

"Well, let me ask it another way. What was the biggest settlement your firm handled last year?"

"We had a medical malpractice case against a plastic surgeon that settled."

"Right," I said. "Maxine Forest, right? Whose client was that—yours or Nate's?"

"We're a partnership," he said. "And I can't confirm or deny the identity of a client."

"How many times did you personally meet with Maxine Forest?"

"I can't answer that. It's protected by privilege."

"It was zero, wasn't it? And Nate Clay was the attorney of record, right?"

"Yes."

"If you reviewed your time slips, how many hours did you spend working on Maxine Forest's case? I mean, you personally, not the firm."

For all he knew, I had the records in front of me.

"Nate was lead counsel," he said.

"And yet you're asking for half of the settlement proceeds?"

"We were a partnership," he said.

"Fine," I said. "Isn't it true the Forest settlement split was one of the reasons Nate Clay wanted to dissolve your partnership?"

"We never dissolved the partnership!" he barked.

"Right," I said. "Because Nate died first."

"Objection," Charlotte said. "Your Honor, this is getting ridiculous."

"Your Honor, I don't think that's grounds for an objection under the rules of evidence."

"Overruled," Castor said. He gave me a withering look that told me he was starting to lose patience.

"Mr. Gorney, did you represent a Mary Taylor in a wrongful death claim she had regarding her son?"

Gorney's eyes flicked to Charlotte. She was busy taking notes.

"I can't answer that," he said.

"You can't," I repeated. "Are you sure about that?"

"Where did you get that information?" he said.

"I'm the one asking the questions, Mr. Gorney."

"Objection," Charlotte said. "That information, even if it were relevant, is protected by attorney-client privilege."

"Sustained, Ms. Leary," Castor said.

I knew I'd lose that one. But Gorney was rattled. Mission accomplished.

"Mr. Gorney, the Forest case wasn't the only one that caused problems between you and Nate Clay, was it?"

"We weren't having problems," he said.

"Mrs. Taylor accused you of mishandling a settlement you negotiated for her, didn't she?"

"Objection," Charlotte said. "Counsel is trying to ask the same question under a different premise."

"Sustained. Ms. Leary, you are not permitted to ask this witness about clients. And you know that. Move on."

I was stuck. The Taylor case was never filed in court. It was an out-of-court settlement so I had no paper trail to go on other than what Eric brought me. If he couldn't find Mary Taylor and get her to cooperate, we were sunk. I needed more time. I needed to talk to Mary Taylor myself and find out what Nate Clay was doing talking to her.

"Mr. Gorney," I said. "When was the last time you saw Nate Clay?"

"I visited him a few weeks before he died."

"You went to his home, didn't you?"

"Yes."

"You were inside the house?"

"Yes."

I left it there.

"What did you go there to discuss?" I asked.

"We talked about a lot of things. I knew Nate wasn't feeling good so I went to check on him. He hadn't been in the office for a week or so, which wasn't like him."

"Did he express any concerns about his health or safety at that time?"

"I told him I thought he should go to the doctor. He blew me off."

"Is that a no? He never expressed concerns for his safety?"

"No."

"Did you know Nate had cancer?"

"No," he said. "God, no."

I tried one more line of attack.

"Were you aware Nathan Clay met with a Mary Taylor earlier this year?"

Gorney stared blankly at me. Let him think I'd already spoken to Mrs. Taylor. Let him wonder what else I had.

"Objection," Charlotte said. "Whether this Taylor woman was a client of this witness is privileged. The court has already ruled on that. And Mr. Clay's privilege survives his death."

"Sustained." Castor practically shouted it. Another dead end.

"In your statement to the police," I said. "You never mentioned any issues you were having with disgruntled clients, isn't that right?"

"That's right," Gorney said.

"Detective Blackfoot asked you if you had any information about who might want Nathan Clay dead? Isn't that right?"

"She asked me if he had any enemies. I told her Juliet and Nate were having trouble. Everyone knew that."

"So you never volunteered any information about potential malpractice claims you had or liability exposure of the firm's?"

"There weren't any," he said. "I told the detective the truth and I can tell you, I resent the implication that any of this had anything to do with me. That woman, your client, is an evil, manipulative ... well ... I won't say the word. She berated Nate, emotionally abused him ..."

"Your Honor," I shouted over him. "The witness is unresponsive."

"He's her witness!" Charlotte jumped up. Judge Castor banged his gavel. The four of us were shouting over each other.

"Mr. Gorney," Judge Castor said. "You know better. You too are an officer of the court. Knock it off. Ms. Leary? Move on."

"Your Honor," I said. "I have nothing further for this witness."

Charlotte was already at my shoulder, ready to pounce. Given the go-ahead by Castor, she did just that.

"Mr. Gorney," she said. "Have you had occasion to observe the defendant and Nathan Clay together socially?"

"Of course," he said. "Nate wasn't just my partner. He was my friend. I was there at their wedding. I was his best man, as a matter of fact. I tried to maintain a friendship with Juliet too because I was close to Nate."

"Mr. Gorney," she said. "Did you ever become concerned about Nathan Clay's safety?"

"His safety? Physical safety?"

"Sure. Let's start there."

"Well, the two of them, Nate and Juliet, would have horrible arguments. Juliet never cared who heard. I overheard them in

Nate's office going at it. They were arguing over money. He had her on an allowance because she blew through money like Nate grew it on trees. She had a hell of a temper."

"Did you ever overhear Juliet Clay threaten to harm her husband?"

"Yes," he said, his voice dripping with hate. "It was at a Christmas party at Nate's house. They got into a fight over something. They were in the back bedroom and I was headed there to get my coat as I was about to leave. I saw Juliet try to hit Nate. He grabbed her wrist. And she screamed at him, I'll kill you."

"Thank you," Charlotte said. "Nothing further from me."

"Any redirect, Ms. Leary?"

"Yes," I said.

"Mr. Gorney, you've never liked Juliet Clay, have you?"

"Excuse me?"

"In fact, you hate her, don't you?"

"Look what she's done," he said. "Nate was my friend."

"Your friend," I said. "But that didn't stop you from making a pass at Juliet at the same Christmas party, did it?"

Silence.

"You tried to kiss Juliet Clay, didn't you?"

"That was a misunderstanding," he said. "There was mistletoe."

"You grabbed her buttocks and tried to kiss her and she rejected you, didn't she?"

"It was a misunderstanding," he said.

"But you don't deny it," I said.

His face was ashen. If he could have killed me with a stare, I'd be dead. I only hoped the jury could see the full force of it like I did.

"Thank you," I said. "I have no further questions for this witness."

As Ted Gorney stepped down, Judge Castor adjourned us for the day. Juliet waited until Gorney and the jury were gone.

"He did it. Didn't he? My God, Cass. This whole time. He's lying about everything."

"We'll see," I said. "There's still a lot of trial left." But not enough. I got nowhere with the Mary Taylor information.

As the deputies escorted Juliet out, Tori and I made our way out of the courtroom.

"Wow," Tori said. "Cass, I think she's right. Do you really think Ted Gorney ..."

"You little bitch!"

The voice came from my left. One second, I was walking toward the stairwell. The next, Ted Gorney blocked my path. He came out of nowhere.

"You think you scored points?" he said, spit flying. "Lady, I'll have your license for that."

"I'm going to need you to get out of my face," I said. I put an instinctive arm out, pushing Tori behind me.

"Your client is a lunatic," he said. "She killed Nate and you know it. You're nothing but a scum bottom feeder. And I'm not going to take this lying down. I'll sue your ass for slander. I'll make sure you never practice law again. I'm going to ..."

A blur of movement to my right. Eric came down with the force of a freight train, pushed Ted Gorney into the wall, and held him there with an arm bar to the throat.

"You touch her, you get in her face, you so much as talk to her again ..."

"Eric, stop!" I said. "Let him go. Move along, Gorney. Don't dig yourself in any deeper."

He was scared. To the point I wouldn't be surprised if he needed to change his suit after this. Eric's nostrils flared as he snorted like a bull. I put a hand on his arm.

"Come on," I said. "You can walk me back to my office."

Two of the courthouse deputies came running. Eric pushed Gorney again, but let him go. He straightened his jacket and turned to me.

"You okay, Tori?" Eric asked, though he kept his eyes locked with mine.

Breathless, she nodded. I took Eric by the hand. We left a terrified Ted Gorney behind us as we made our way to the stairs.

Chapter 30

I OUTLASTED everybody else but Eric. Tori had gone home hours ago. Miranda too. I sat in the conference room staring at the whiteboard. It was nine o'clock before anyone remembered we hadn't eaten dinner. The carnage of our pizza box sat in the center of the table now.

"You putting her on?" Eric asked. He'd found Jeanie's stash of Bud Light in the fridge downstairs. He pointed the neck of his bottle at the board. Juliet's face smiled down from her picture I'd taped to the top.

"How can I?" I asked.

"I don't know," Eric said. "It's just ... they want to hear from her. I can see it on the jury's faces. They watch her more than any of the witnesses that have taken the stand so far."

"Yeah?" I said. "And how do you think she's playing to them so far?"

"Honestly? Pretty terrible. Until that kid took the stand."

I rubbed my forehead. The makings of a monster headache throbbed behind my left eye.

"Jeanie says he's been an absolute wreck since," I said. "He killed us, Eric. Castor never should have let that hearsay testimony in."

"Appealable error?" he asked.

"God," I said. "I don't want to think that far. Everyone warned me. Rodney Reid set this train wreck in motion and his incompetence is going to stick to me."

"Why did you take this case, Cass?"

It was the first time he had asked me. Eric set his beer down and looked me in the eye.

"Do you think she's guilty?" I asked.

He chewed the inside of his mouth, weighing his answer. "The thing is," he finally said, "she did everything a guilty person would do. The arguments. The threats. The boyfriends. The poison in the cupboard. The damn shakes. The videos."

We'd watched those again too. The monitor beside me was frozen to Nate Clay's side-eyed smile as he sat at his home office desk. Juliet was just off screen, handing him a chocolate shake.

"But that's the thing," Eric said. "Juliet is a pain in the ass. She's insecure. Jealous. Narcissistic even. Manipulative. Only she's not ..."

"Dumb," I finished his sentence for him. Staring back at my monitor, I tried to read something in Nathan Clay's frozen eyes. He was thinner here. It was one of the last handful of videos Juliet had posted of him. She'd interrupted him while he was working. The blue-and-red logo of his LexisNexis screen flickered behind him on his own monitor.

"I'm sorry you couldn't do anything with the Taylor lead," he said.

"I was grasping at straws," I said. "Hoping the mention of her name would rattle Gorney enough to get him to acknowledge something about it. Even if it was just a denial that he did anything wrong. I want to talk to her, Eric. Any luck finding her?"

"Not yet," he said. "Russ Taylor had no kids. His mom was his only family. He worked for himself making fishing lures, if you can believe that. Had an online business so I can't even track down any coworkers. He had an ex-wife. That's all I could find out. Divorced seven years ago. Beatrice Morelli. I'm trying to figure out where she lives now."

"An ex he hasn't been with in seven years? Who had no interest in the wrongful death claim and probably hasn't seen her mother-in-law Mary in God knows how long?"

"You're not the only one grasping at straws. Do you want me to keep after it?"

I sighed. I knew the practical answer was no. But that's not what I said. "If there's something to it. Even if it's to show Gorney lied to the cops about trouble between him and Nate. Or an enemy they made. It might help me during closing."

"Yeah. I'll stay on the hunt."

"This case is costing you too," I said to Eric. He took another sip of his beer, not answering me at first.

"Blackfoot," I said. "I saw the looks she gave you after she testified. That they all gave you. You haven't made any friends in the sheriff's office working with me on this one."

"I never had a lot of friends in the sheriff's office to begin with. That's just the way the game is played," he said. "Delphi P.D. versus Woodbridge County. It's been that way forever and it'll be that way long after I'm gone."

"But they see you as sleeping with the enemy," I said.

Eric flicked his eyes back to mine. The question in that look sent heat straight down my spine.

"It's just an expression," I countered, but couldn't suppress a nervous smile. I knew I was blushing. It was a line we'd never crossed. Not while Eric was still technically married to Wendy. She'd been comatose for months before I ever came back to Delphi. And now ... she was gone.

"Yeah," he said. "But I suppose sometime soon we need to quit dancing around that particular issue."

"I like having you here," I said. "I'm glad you're home. You are home, aren't you?"

He didn't answer. He just kept his steely gray eyes locked with mine. He was looking for something. Some truth. Some admission on my part.

"I'm glad you're glad," he finally said.

"Did you find what you needed in North Carolina?" I asked.

I thought he'd give me a typical non-answer. Avoid. Joke.

"Some of it," he said, surprising me.

"They offered you a job out there. You never told me whether you were going to take it." This was the crux of it. The crux of us. Was he here to stay? Or was his helping me with Juliet's case some attempt to let me down easy? A peace offering before he left again for good. I realized I wasn't ready for his answer. Not yet.

"What about Delphi? It's been almost a year since you took your leave. Can you go back? Do you want to go back?"

"Well, I ..."

"Because this?" I said, pointing to the white board. "It's been good. I couldn't have done what I did with Gorney without your help."

"You making me a job offer?" he asked.

My heart thundered in my chest. My head throbbed.

"Yes," I said before really thinking about it. But once I had, I was all in.

"Yes," I said again, quieter. "I can't pay you a lot. Yet. But you've got your pension. And with you here, you know, as my permanent private investigator, I think I could take on more clients. Well-paying clients. Jeanie and Miranda have been on at me forever to bring in more help. It wouldn't just have to be criminal cases. Jeanie would have a lot on her plate that could use ..."

"Cass," he said. "Slow down. Take a breath. Think about what you're saying."

"I am," I said. "I have. And it could be good for you, too. I worry about you. Even before Wendy and everything that happened. Your job has worn you down. You could make a change. You could have a life!"

He smiled. "What about you? Your job wears you down too. When are you going to take a break?"

There was something else. Our careers had always put us at odds with each other up until now. Me, a criminal defense lawyer. Him, a homicide detective.

"It seems like we've both got a lot of decisions to make," he said. "I just don't know if now is the best time to make them."

He switched his gaze to the computer screen behind me. Nathan Clay was staring at us.

"Right," I said, turning back.

"I know I don't want that," he said.

"What?"

"That." He pointed to the screen. "Never mind the how of it. The poor guy never retired. Worked until the day before he died. I mean, the literal day before he died."

Eric had a stack of exhibits in front of him. Among them were the phone and computer dumps the forensics team had done. Eric was right. Nathan Clay had logged billable hours two days before he died.

I looked at the screen. I looked at the stack of paper.

"She would have spent him to death even if she wasn't the one who poured that poison into his drink," Eric said, sighing.

I couldn't take my eyes off the monitor. A familiar tingling sensation snaked through my nerve endings.

Something. There was something.

I grabbed my mouse and enlarged the screen. I tried to focus in on the monitor over Nathan Clay's shoulder.

"Cass?"

"Hang on," I said.

I tried to make out the words printed under the LexisNexis logo.

"What is it?" Eric said.

Without breaking my stare from the screen, I reached back and grabbed the computer forensic report.

I tilted my head to the side, squinting, struggling to make out the name of the case Nathan Clay had up on the screen behind him. "Eric," I said. It felt like my heart had melted right out of my chest. I hadn't seen it before. I'd never bothered to look. Neither had Detective Sofia Blackfoot.

"Eric," I said again.

"Shit," he muttered. "I know that look."

"I'm going to need you to serve a subpoena for me," I said, picking up the forensic report. "And first thing in the morning, I'm going to need to put Bryson Ballard back on the stand."

Chapter 31

"You can't do this," Juliet said as we sat at the defense table. We had a few precious moments before Charlotte made her way back into the courtroom and Judge Castor took the bench.

"I'm going to need you to trust me," I said.

"Well, I don't. Not when it comes to my son. He's been through enough, Cass. I don't want him traumatized anymore."

"Do you understand what happens if that jury decides you're guilty?"

"I didn't kill Nathan."

"It won't matter," I said. "You'll spend the rest of your life in prison if the prosecution gets its way. The rest of your life. You're thirty-five years old. You've been in jail since this whole thing started. We're talking about state prison. For fifty or sixty years, if you live that long. And if you do, you'll make the record books for one of the longest terms of any female inmate."

Her eyelids flickered. She flinched as if I'd slapped her. For the first time in all the weeks I'd known her, it seemed like she began to grasp what I was saying. What she truly faced.

"All rise!" The bailiff's booming voice caught me off guard. Charlotte Stahl rushed into the courtroom, buttoning her jacket as she came.

Judge Castor came out of chambers and climbed up to the bench. A moment later, he called the jury back in. I was sweating. Beside me, Juliet looked about ready to faint.

"Ms. Leary," Castor said once everyone was in place. "Are you ready to call your next witness?"

"Yes, Your Honor," I said. "The defense recalls Bryson Ballard to the stand."

Charlotte looked puzzled. She turned and whispered something to Rafe Johnson who sat behind her. He made a downward gesture with his hand. To me, it read like "you can handle this, whatever game she's playing."

No games. Just one of the biggest risks I'd maybe ever taken in the middle of a murder trial.

Bryson came into the courtroom, looking even more puzzled than Charlotte. I knew Jeanie had brought him. Of course, I couldn't tell her anything about what my plans for him were. She was almost as worried for him as Juliet was.

"Mr. Ballard," Judge Castor said. "You understand you're still under oath?"

"Yes, sir," Bryson said. He wore a light-blue polo shirt today and tan dress pants. His hair was getting too long again. He gave his mother a weak smile as I stepped up to the lectern.

"Bryson," I said. "Thank you for coming back today. I know this has been an ordeal for you."

"It's okay," he said. "She's my mom."

"Yes," I said. "Your mom. And you understand what happens if she's convicted of this crime, don't you?"

"What? Of course."

"The judge just reminded you that you're still under oath from when you testified the other day. So you know that means there are penalties for not telling the truth?"

"Of course," he said again.

"Okay. Good. Bryson, I want to ask you about what you said on the witness stand the other day. When Ms. Stahl asked you about your conversation with your stepfather a day or two before he died. Do you remember her asking you about that?"

"Sure," he said.

"So let's go back to that time, the few days before your stepfather passed. You were concerned about him, weren't you?"

"Yes."

"You saw that he wasn't feeling well."

"Yes."

"Did you ask him to see a doctor?"

"Yes."

"Did he?"

"No. I'd say two or three days before he died, I don't think he could have made it to one by himself."

"You or someone would have had to take him?" I asked.

"Yes."

"Or you or someone would have had to call an ambulance?"

"Yes."

"Why didn't you?"

"What?"

"Did you offer to drive him to the hospital?"

"Yes. I think so."

"Two days before your father died, do you know if he was able to get out of bed by himself?"

"He tried," Bryson said. "He was really weak. He couldn't keep anything down."

"He was vomiting?"

"Yes."

"You saw him vomiting?"

"Yes."

"Do you know if your mother saw him vomiting that day?"

"She wasn't in the room when I saw it, no."

"Do you know if she ever saw him vomiting?"

"They had separate bedrooms by then. So I'm not sure what she saw."

"Bryson, you've indicated your stepfather wasn't able to get out of bed unassisted toward the end. So how did he get to the bathroom?"

"He didn't always get there."

"When the police searched the house, you're aware they went into your stepfather's bedroom, isn't that right?"

"That's right."

"Forgive me, I know what I'm about to ask you is indelicate, to say the least. But I'm curious. The police didn't report finding any evidence that your stepfather threw up in the bed or on the floor, or anywhere other than in the bathroom. The room was for the most part clean. Did you know that?"

"I think so, yes."

"You were the one helping your father to the bathroom, weren't you?"

"Yes."

"You were also the one cleaning up after him, weren't you?"

"Yes."

"You did that three days before he died?"

"Yes."

"You did that two days before he died?"

"Yes."

"And you were taking care of him the day before he died?"

"Yes. He was my dad. He needed me. I was taking care of him."

"But you never called a doctor, isn't that right?"

"He didn't want one. He insisted."

"Objection," Charlotte said. "This has all been asked and answered the last time this witness took the stand. Counsel isn't covering any new ground."

"Agreed, Ms. Leary. Do you have a point with this?"

"I do, Your Honor," I said. "That's a promise."

"Get to it quickly," Castor warned me.

"Bryson," I said. "The police found spots of blood near the bathroom toilet. Your dad threw up blood, didn't he?"

"Yes."

"And you saw it. You were there. You were the one that helped him clean part of that up, weren't you?"

Bryson's eyes filled with tears. Sweat broke out on his brow.

"Yes," he cried.

"You saw your father cough up blood. You helped him to the bathroom, but yet you didn't call for an ambulance?"

"I wanted to. I begged him to let me. He said he didn't want it."

"Bryson, I need you to remind me what else your father said about his illness."

"He said I know I'm dying. He said I know I'm gonna die, Bryson. Something's wrong. Be careful of your mom. He told me he thought she'd done something to him."

Heart thundering in my chest, I picked up the transcript I'd ordered from last week's testimony. "Bryson, when Ms. Stahl asked you for your stepfather's exact wording, do you remember what you answered?"

"I said the same thing. I said my dad told me I know I'm going to die. Something's wrong. Be careful of your mom. He told me she'd done something to him."

"He said I know I'm dying. He said I know I'm gonna die, Bryson. Something's wrong. Be careful of your mom. Yes. That's exactly what you said. Word for word. Just like you did right now."

"So?"

"We spoke in my office just before I agreed to represent your mother. Do you remember that?"

"Yes."

"But you didn't tell me this, did you? When I asked you what you knew about your stepfather's illness?"

"I don't remember what I said," he said.

"And you never said those exact words to your current lawyer, Jeanie Mills, did you?"

"Objection!" Charlotte said. "Ms. Leary really loves to ask about privileged communications, apparently."

"Sustained," Castor said. "Be careful, Ms. Leary. I won't warn you again."

I took a breath and started again. "But you remembered word for word what you claim your father said the day before he died. You used the same language. Each time. It's very specific."

Bryson's eyes flicked from the jury to Juliet, then to the judge. He was looking anywhere but at me.

"Bryson, who told you to use that specific wording?"

"What?"

"You saw your father cough up blood but didn't tell anyone about it?"

"I told you. My dad insisted. He said not to call anyone."

"And you always did what your dad told you to do, didn't you?"

"I don't ..."

"You followed his instructions explicitly, didn't you?"

"I didn't. I mean ... I was ..."

"Bryson, your father told you what to say, didn't he?"

Bryson looked at the floor.

"He told you what to say in court, didn't he?"

Tears rolled down his face.

"Your Honor," Charlotte rose. "Counsel is badgering the witness."

"I've asked a question," I said. "The witness has yet to answer."

"Mr. Ballard," Judge Castor said. "Can you answer Ms. Leary's question?"

"I don't remember it," Bryson said quietly.

"Bryson," I said. "Nate Clay, your lawyer stepfather, he told you exactly what to say when the police or the prosecutor questioned you, didn't he?"

"He knew what she'd done!" Bryson shouted. "He knew what she'd done. He wanted to make sure she paid."

"Oh, baby," Juliet sobbed. "Bryce."

"Bryson," I said. "You're telling me that your stepfather coached you on what to say if you took the stand?"

"He knew what she'd done," he kept repeating.

"But he didn't call the police himself," I said. "He didn't call for a doctor?"

"He knew what she'd done," Bryson said. "You don't understand. You don't know what she's like. What she put him through. What she put all of us through. He knew what she'd done and he wanted to make sure people would listen to what he had to say."

"Bryson," I said. "What did your father really say to you the day before he died?"

The boy was lost. He looked at Charlotte. The judge. His mother. The jury.

"What did you father tell you to say, Bryson?" I repeated. "The truth. You are under oath."

He let out a sob. Buried his face in his hands. Finally, he looked up.

"He told me I had to make sure they knew he knew he was going to die."

"Why?"

"He said I had to be clear that he knew he was about to die."

"He coached you," I said. "He told you exactly what to say in the event you were questioned in court?"

"Yes," Bryson said, weeping. "He knew what she'd done. He told me when I get up here, I should make sure to say he knew he was going to die. They have to be sure he knew he was going to die."

"So he never said to you, I know I'm going to die. He told you what to say if you spoke to the police or took the stand. Because he knew his statement might not be admissible if you didn't say that, isn't that right?"

"Yes," he said.

"Thank you, I have no further questions."

Charlotte made a point of shrugging her shoulders for the jury. She passed me on the way to the defense table.

Juliet practically collapsed against me. "He hated me," she whispered. "Nate turned my own son against me."

"So I'm clear," Charlotte said, through a haughty laugh. "It's still your testimony that Nathan Clay knew he was going to die, correct?"

"Yes."

"And it's still your testimony that your father believed your mother had done something to make him sick, correct?"

"That's what he told me, yes."

"Then I have no further questions, either. Thank you, Bryson."

With that, we broke for lunch. Bryson practically sprinted out of the courtroom, refusing to look at Juliet.

The kid had lied under oath and withheld information from the police. I still felt he knew more than he was saying. But I was running out of time to prove it.

Chapter 32

"THERE's a name for what you are!" Spit flew from Charlotte Stahl's mouth as she accosted me heading out of court. Juliet would stay in holding while I figured out my next move.

"I don't have time for this," I said, whirling around to face her. "And if I find out you had anything to do with coaching that kid on what to say ..."

"Coached him?" Charlotte said. "You think you did damage just now? If anything, you let him bolster what he said on direct. Nathan Clay knew that woman was trying to kill him. Your client is going down, Cass."

"I meant what I said," I said. "I'll be holding your office accountable."

"Cass." Rafe Johnson stood at Charlotte's left shoulder. "You're going to want to be careful what you say."

"Get out of my way," I said. Adrenaline raced through me. Rafe and Charlotte called after me but I was done with them. They could hurl all the threats they wanted but it was their office that needed to scramble. Eric was on my heels carrying a manila file folder. As I walked up the front steps to my office, the door flew open and Jeanie stood there, red-faced, eyes blazing fire.

"What the hell are you doing?" she yelled. Miranda scooted out from behind her desk and locked the door behind us. The Leary Law Group was closed for the day.

I stormed into Jeanie's office. Eric stood in the hall, watching the spectacle as Jeanie flew in ahead of him.

"What the hell are you doing?" she yelled again. "You ambushed that kid. Behind my back. You basically accused him of perjury. I'm his lawyer."

"Jeanie, I did my job. A job *you* asked me ... no ... begged me to take on."

She plopped down in her chair. "He's a wreck. You have no idea what this thing has done to that boy."

"Jeanie," I said. "You weren't in the courtroom ..."

"That's the problem!" She cut me off. "You should have given me a heads-up. You exposed that kid to criminal liability. He should have had a lawyer in there."

"He didn't ask for one," I said, then immediately wished I hadn't.

"It was a cheap trick. You hung that boy out. And if I know anything about her, you acted against your own client's wishes. You want to try telling me Juliet was on board with that? Christ, Cass. Even if Bryson smothered Nathan Clay right in front of her, she wouldn't want you going after him."

"That's not your call," I said. "And if I had even the slightest inkling that Juliet and Bryson were colluding, I'd be off this case and so would you. I get you're mad at me. But you're madder at that kid. You just don't want to admit it. He didn't tell you the whole truth either."

Jeanie stared out the window. She was still pissed off, but she knew I was right.

"Jeanie, I'm sorry you're angry. I swear, I'm not out to get Bryson Ballard. If it makes you feel any better, Rafe and Charlotte think his testimony helped them more than what he said on direct. I think they're crazy, but there it is."

"I can't talk about this anymore," she said. "I've got to figure out where Bryson is and how I can help him. And I need you out of my face for a few minutes."

I smiled. "Fair enough. I love you, Jeanie."

Deciding to quit before she actually started throwing things at me, I backed out of the room and grabbed Eric by the sleeve. The two of us escaped to the recesses of my upstairs office. Tori was already waiting in the conference room for me. She closed the door behind us.

"I don't understand what's going on?" she said, keeping her voice down. The conference room was directly above Jeanie's office. "Why would that kid lie? How the heck did you figure out he had?"

"He hates his mother as much as everyone else seems to," Eric said. "I don't know how I didn't pick up on that before. Think about it. He's been dragged through every bad relationship she ever had. She's a narcissist. She made scenes at school functions, and couldn't get along with the other parents. She's an embarrassment to him. With Clay, the kid finally has some stability. And by all accounts, Nate Clay was even-tempered. Mellow. Affable. If things were starting to go south between Juliet and his stepdad, why wouldn't he want to hitch his wagon to Clay?"

I sat down and kicked off my heels. My feet were killing me. My brain was killing me.

"Nothing about this case makes sense to me anymore," I said.

Tori took up one of my habits. She paced in front of the whiteboard. "You think Nathan told Bryson what to say in case he died? How did you get there?"

I opened my laptop. I'd taken a screen capture of the video I'd watched over and over last night. I turned the screen to Tori.

"Take a look at what's on Nate's monitor in this video. This one was taken three weeks before he died."

"A Lexis search," Tori said. "So what?"

"Look harder," I said.

Tori tilted her head to the side. "People v. Bradfield?"

"It's a seminal hearsay exception case," I said. "You want to have a crack at which one?"

She shook her head. Still confused. "Dying declarations. Nate Clay was researching what conditions a murder victim's statement would have to meet in order for the person who heard it to be able to testify about it."

"I still don't get it," she said. "You actually think Nathan was coaching Bryson how to get around a hearsay exception at the trial for his own murder?"

"Bryson as much as admitted that's exactly what happened," Eric said. "But why? If Nate really believed Juliet was poisoning him, why wouldn't he just call the police? Or an ambulance? Why go to all the trouble prepping Bryson to be able to testify when he could have just done it himself to the cops?"

"Because maybe he was laying the groundwork," I said.

"You think that's even going to work?" Tori said.

I stared at the whiteboard. Now that the trial adrenaline started to wear off, a screaming headache rose up in its place.

"I think Charlotte Stahl had a point," I said. "If she's got any skills as a closer, she'll make the jury see it as even stronger evidence that Nathan believed Juliet was killing him. I'm going to need more to prove what I think was really going on. A whole lot more."

Eric had taken a seat opposite me at the table. The file folder sat in front of him. Our eyes met and he slid it across to me.

"Please tell me this is going to make me happy," I said.

Eric arched his brow. "I don't know."

"What's that?" Tori asked. She came around the table and stood at my shoulder.

"I had Eric serve a subpoena on Lexis."

"But we have the forensics on Nate Clay's phone and computer already," Tori said.

"The only thing his computer records showed was the amount of time Nate spent on any given website. We've got his google searches, emails, things like that. But his Lexis searches only showed up as time logged on their site, not the details of the actual searches. Blackfoot didn't dig deeper because she didn't know what she was looking for. There's nothing unusual about a lawyer with a home office spending four hours a day logged into a legal research website. It's the searches themselves I needed."

"So you subpoenaed Lexis," Tori said.

I combed through the pages. In the two- and three-week span before Nathan Clay died, he searched hundreds of cases on the admissibility standards for statements constituting a dying declaration.

"I'll be damned," Tori said. "He knew what Bryson needed to say in order to survive a hearsay objection at trial."

"Yeah," I said.

"I know this case," Tori said, pulling apart a single page. "U.S. v. Shepherd. It was part of a law school exam question I took. The declarant told a nurse she believed her husband had poisoned her with mercury."

I kept flipping through the pages.

"What are you looking for?" Eric asked.

"A client identifier," I said. "Usually when you log in to do a particular search, it asks you to type in the client's case you're working on. That way it gets properly billed."

"He could have made that up though," Tori said.

"Maybe," I said. "But we could at least cross-reference it and see if there's any pattern. Or see if Clay actually billed a particular client for these searches."

"There," Tori said. "Morelli. The hearsay cases he's assigning to a client named Morelli."

Eric sat bolt upright.

"What?"

Eric opened his phone and scrolled. "Beatrice Morelli," he said. "I told you, that's the name of Russ Taylor's ex-wife."

"Have you found her?" I asked.

Eric pulled up something else on his phone. "I have an address. It's out in farm country. I was going to pay her a visit."

"You think it's the same Morelli?" Tori asked.

"I don't know," I said. "But I think it's time I had a talk with her."

"I'll go with you," Eric said. "I've got a bad feeling about this. The woman thinks she's out over a hundred grand she's never going to see again. Who knows what Gorney told her about Nate."

"Fine," I said. "But we better find her fast. I've got to put on my next witness in less than twelve hours."

Chapter 33

Eyes clouded with cataracts peered at me through a gap in the crooked storm door. The Morelli residence sat on forty acres of farmland off old U.S. 12.

"Ms. Morelli," I said for the fifth time. "We're just here to ask you a few questions about Mr. Gorney. I'm sorry to be so blunt, but time is of the essence."

"I've seen you before," she said in a brittle voice. She wasn't looking at me though. She was looking at Eric.

"It's nice to meet you, ma'am," Eric said, in his most charming, mid-western drawl. If he had a hat, he'd have tipped it toward her.

"Save it, hotshot," she snapped. "You're a cop. I don't like cops."

Eric's face fell. "I'm not on duty today, ma'am. This isn't an official visit. I'm just working with Ms. Leary on one of her cases."

"I said I know who you are," she said. "You ask me, you're a lousy detective." She started to laugh. Her eyes filled with tears. Eric and I exchanged a look. The woman was cracking up.

"Ms. Morelli?" I said.

She laughed even harder. "If you're looking for Bea, you'll probably find her playing with her damn horses. Them she'll talk to. Can't even get her to give *me* the time of day."

With that, the woman slammed the door in our faces.

"You sure we have the right place?" I asked Eric. He pulled up an app on his phone. It showed a map with an overlay of property lines with their legal owners.

"Says Beatrice Morelli owns this plot," he said. He turned his phone toward me so I could confirm it. We stepped off the porch together and started walking back toward the car.

"Let me see that again," I said, taking his phone. It showed a satellite image of the property. I peered closer. Behind the house, through the woods, there was a barn.

"She said Bea would be out playing with the horses. You think?" I showed him the phone screen. Eric scanned the horizon. In the distance, we heard a horse whinny.

"Shit," he muttered. "I don't like the idea of rolling up on someone if they don't know I'm coming. Not if I don't have a SWAT team in front of me."

"You think Beatrice Morelli is going to shoot you?" I joked. Five minutes later, I ate my words.

As we drove around the farmhouse and back through the dirt trail, a woman with flaming red hair burst out of the barn door carrying a shotgun.

"Whoa!" Eric yelled through his open window, slamming the car into park. He put his hands up. I did the same.

"You got a warrant?" the woman yelled.

"You got a permit?" Eric yelled back. "I could arrest you for brandishing even if you do."

"You're the one trespassing," she said. "And I know my rights."

"Ms. Morelli," I said through the other open window. "My name is Cass Leary. I'm here to talk to you about your late husband, Russ Taylor."

"Cass," Eric warned.

Keeping my hands elevated, I stepped out of the car.

"She's just as nutty as the old lady," Eric muttered. "But you're even worse!"

"Shh," I cautioned him. As I approached, Beatrice Morelli lowered her weapon.

She was trim, muscular, wearing a fitted flannel shirt, jeans, weathered riding boots, and a silver belt buckle.

"My ex is dead," she said. "If you're here from the insurance company, it's his mother you want to talk to."

"I've tried that," Eric said. "Do you know where we can find Mary Taylor?"

Bea Morelli cocked her head to the side. "If you came from the house, you already did."

Eric and I looked back up at the house together in confusion. "That was your ex-mother-in-law?"

"That's Ma," Bea corrected. "Technically, yes. I kind of got custody of her in the divorce."

"Ms. Morelli," I said. "I've got questions about Ted Gorney, for starters."

"Ted Gorney's a snake," she said. "If he ever steps foot on this land, I'll put holes in him."

She leaned her shotgun against the barn door. Eric was at my side, his own weapon holstered. Bea Morelli clocked it though.

"You I don't like," she said, echoing her ex-mother-in-law's statement. "But I like lawyers even less than cops. What the hell do you want?"

She turned and headed back into the barn.

Eric shook his head. He had a look in his eyes. A warning. If things got any weirder, he was liable to fling me over his shoulder and march back to the car.

"Relax," I whispered. "What could possibly go wrong?"

I followed Bea into the barn. Just as Mary Taylor said, Bea had a brush in her hand and proceeded to use it on a large black mare in the nearest stall. The horse eyed me with a dubious brown eye, snorted, then stomped her front hoof.

"Don't come any closer," Bea said. "Fancy'll kick you."

"Fair enough," I said. "Ms. Morelli, I understand you had a malpractice case against Ted Gorney. He was your mother-in-law's lawyer?"

"He's a crook," she said, still brushing Fancy.

"She never filed a case," I said. "I understand Nathan Clay, Mr. Gorney's law partner, came to talk to her and they settled. But would you mind telling me what happened?"

Bea stopped brushing. She tossed her brush in a nearby bucket and turned to me, arms crossed.

"Russ, my husband. He was a real prick. Best thing he ever did was get hit by a drunk driver. He used to beat her, his mother. Did you know that?"

"No," I said. "I didn't. But the settlement? I understand that drunk driver's insurance company paid her a sum of money …"

Bea stopped brushing the horse.

"Ms. Morelli, did you know Nathan Clay, Mr. Gorney's partner? Your mother-in-law claimed Ted Gorney made off with that settlement money. Is that what happened?"

"Boy," she said as she picked up a pitchfork. "He said someone might come asking. You want to know what he told me to do?"

"He? Who are we talking about? Nathan Clay?"

"When was the last time you spoke with him?" Eric asked.

Bea paused, scowling at Eric. Then, with cat-like quickness, she tossed her pitchfork straight at him. Eric caught the handle just in time.

"You wanna ask me dumb questions? Then make yourself useful. Hay bale's over there. Put some down in that stall."

Eric narrowed his eyes at me. I widened mine and gestured toward the open stall. Shaking his head, he grumbled and started doing as Bea Morelli instructed.

"Nathan Clay," I said. "You're aware I represent his wife, aren't you?"

"They're nuts," Bea said. "They're all nuts and thieves. Good riddance to him too."

"Ms. Morelli," I cut her off. "Your mother-in-law signed a release of liability absolving Ted Gorney from her legal malpractice claim. She was paid off, wasn't she? Did Nathan Clay make good on that claim on Ted Gorney's behalf?"

"I think I'm done talking. I told him what would happen if another lawyer so much as stepped foot on this property. Don't make me make good on my threat. Yes. He paid my mother-in-law's claim. But don't think he was some hero. He was just trying to save his own skin, too. We'd have sued them both."

"Wait a minute," I said. "You're telling me Nathan Clay came to see you? He came here? You spoke with him? Do you remember when that was?"

Bea brushed past me and headed for her wall of tack. She grabbed a saddle and headed back to Fancy's stall. She heaved the thing on Fancy's back.

"A couple of times, yes," she said. "Asked me not to sue the firm. Begged me, if you want to know the truth of it. He said he was trying to work things out with Ted. He asked me the same questions you are. How much does Gorney owe me?

How the hell didn't he already know that? They were partners!"

"In name only," I said. "At least that's the story Ted Gorney is telling."

"That's what he said. He said Gorney was his friend and he meant well but that he got into trouble. Gambling. I told him that wasn't my problem. I just wanted my money. I don't trust any of them."

"When did Nate Clay come visit you?" I asked.

"It was cold. Real cold. January or February. Didn't wear the right shoes. Ruined his stupid loafers coming to meet me out here."

"Did you make him shovel hay too?" Eric asked.

"Damn right I did!" she yelled. This time, I saw a small smirk on Bea Morelli's face. I tried to hide my own.

She finished saddling Fancy. "Clay fronted the money for Ted Gorney," I asked.

"Ma didn't give a crap where the money came from. As long as she got what was hers," she said, leading Fancy out of her stall. "I'm sorry Clay up and croaked. But at least he had the decency to do it after his check cleared."

"Nathan Clay paid off Ted's debt?" I asked.

"You slow or something? Yeah," she said. "I still think the Attorney Grievance Commission should know what Gorney did. You lawyers all stick together though. Ma said it wasn't worth the bother."

"Gah!" Eric yelled. "You've got mice or something out here. There's shit all over the place."

"Son of a ..." Bea tied Fancy to a post and went to Eric's stall. "Damn barn cat. He's useless. You hear that, Bosco? You're a useless freeloader!"

Eric propped the pitchfork against the wall and walked back to my side. Bea was on a tear, swearing and yelling, calling out for Bosco the barn cat. She stormed past us and headed out to the pasture looking for him.

"What in the hell was that?" Eric muttered. "She's a loon!"

"Why in the world was Nate Clay paying her off though?" I asked. "There was no love lost between him and Gorney at the end."

"Maybe it was like she said. He was just worried he'd get sued too or caught in the crossfire with the State Bar," Eric said, dusting off his hands on his jeans. "Who knows?"

I walked toward the open barn door. Bea was still shouting after the cat. I passed Fancy on the way. There was a small bucket of apples hanging on the wall. I reached for one and fed it to Fancy, flat-handed. I reached for another.

It was then I noticed the shelf on the back wall.

"Cass," Eric said. He saw what I saw. The hairs stood up on the back of my neck.

"Is that ..." I started. I handed Fancy another treat, then went to Eric's side.

"He came out here," Eric said.

"Two or three times, Bea said."

Bea's shouts grew fainter as she ran around the barn. I pulled my cell phone out and snapped pictures of the containers on the shelf.

"That was rat poop," Eric said. "In the stall. She has a rat problem."

"Eric," I said. "Can you call Sofia Blackfoot?"

He already had his cell phone out.

"What the hell are you two still doing here?" Bea shouted as she came in through the other side of the barn. "I'm done talking. Go back to whatever rock you just crawled out from under."

I turned to her, my jaw still half on the floor. "I'm afraid I can't do that, Bea. I'm afraid you're not done with lawyers for a while yet."

Chapter 34

BEATRICE MORELLI TOOK the witness stand in a storm of flying red hair, clacking four-inch heels, and blazing hatred shooting from her eyes.

"Your Honor," I said. "I'd like permission to treat this witness as hostile."

"You're damn right I'm hostile," Bea said. "I let you people onto my property. I should have blasted you right off with a 12-gauge."

I cleared my throat as Judge Castor banged his gavel.

"Ms. Morelli," Castor said, reading her name from his copy of the subpoena. "You're here under court order. I expect you to show due respect. Yes, Ms. Leary. You may proceed under the hostile witness rule."

Charlotte fumed at her table. She'd lost a sidebar motion to bar Bea's testimony. Though Castor made it clear, I was on thin ice.

"Ms. Morelli," I said. "Members of your family engaged the law firm of Ted Gorney and Nathan Clay, isn't that right?"

"Biggest mistake ever," she said.

"That's a yes."

"Yes."

"Can you tell me the nature of that representation?"

"Objection," Charlotte said. "This witness can't be compelled to testify against matters protected by the attorney-client privilege either."

"Your Honor, I believe this witness is privy to the nature of the representation the firm provided to her family member. There's no privilege as it attaches to her. Even if there was, she's the one who has the right to waive it."

"Overruled," Castor said. "Proceed, Ms. Leary."

"Ms. Morelli, once again, will you tell me what your family member hired Mr. Gorney's firm to do?"

"My ex-husband was killed in a car accident," she said. "Mr. Gorney was supposed to get us our money from the insurance company."

"Did he?"

"Well, that's a matter of opinion," she said.

"In what way?"

"Oh, he got the money for my mother-in-law. He just never forked over her share of it."

"You're saying Mr. Gorney embezzled funds from your mother-in-law?"

"Yes." She said it with the same intonation as if she were a rattlesnake. "He stole Ma's settlement money from when my ex-husband, her son, died."

"And you believe Ted Gorney absconded with it, is that right?"

"I don't believe it. It happened."

"Okay," I said. "And you met with Nathan Clay, his law partner, about your complaints, didn't you?"

"Yes."

"But before that, Mr. Clay called your mother-in-law, didn't he?"

"Yes. She didn't want to talk to him. The whole thing was too damn upsetting. So much so I moved her in with me because she was broke. She needed that money he stole to live off of."

"Did you ever speak to Mr. Clay yourself?"

"Yes."

"When was this?" I asked.

"After the first of the year. January, I believe."

"Where did you meet?"

"He wanted to come out to the farm. Told me specifically not to meet him at his office. He didn't want Gorney to know about it."

"Objection," Charlotte said. "This witness's claims about what the victim may or may not have said about their meetings are hearsay."

"Sustained," Castor said. "Ms. Morelli, I'll need you to refrain from testifying about what Mr. Clay may have said unless instructed otherwise."

Her face lit up. "Great! Then I guess you don't need me here." She started to rise.

"Sit down, Ms. Morelli!" Judge Castor snapped. "You don't move unless you hear me say you're dismissed. Continue, Ms. Leary. But get to the point."

"Did you meet with Nathan Clay?"

"Yep," she said.

"How many times, do you recall?"

"Three or four times," she said. "He kept coming out to the farm. It was weird."

"What did he come there to discuss? You can tell me the topic of your meetings."

"The topic was his good-for-nothing, lying, cheating partner. I think he wanted to make sure I didn't hold him responsible for what Gorney did."

"And you kept agreeing to meet with him out at the farm, isn't that right?"

"Agreeing? Well I didn't shoot him, if that's what you mean. He kept showing up."

"Your mother never filed a claim against Mr. Gorney or his firm, did she?"

"Nope."

"Why not?"

"Because his partner paid us off. Wrote Ma a check."

"You're saying Nathan Clay gave your mother-in-law her settlement money on Mr. Gorney's behalf?"

"And then some," she said.

"What do you mean?"

"I mean, he paid her what she was supposed to get from the insurance company plus more on top of it."

"For what reason?"

"To keep us quiet, I suppose," she said. "Ma signed a paper for him saying she'd never sue or talk about it. I took her to the bank to cash the check."

"And it was Mr. Clay who came out to the farm to discuss all of this, not Mr. Gorney?"

"I'd have shot Ted Gorney if he so much as stepped a toe on my land."

"Is that a yes?"

"Yes. It was Clay who came out. Only Clay."

I introduced an enlarged photograph of Bea's farm. She identified the main house and the barn behind it where we'd met. Then, I introduced interior shots of the horse stables.

"How many horses do you have out there?" I asked.

"Six," she said. "I used to run a boarding service but got sick of that. After Russ and me divorced, it was too much to deal with on my own."

"You've got barn cats out there too, don't you?"

"Objection," Charlotte said. "Is she serious with this? This witness's pet ownership isn't relevant. And it's a waste of time."

"I'm getting there, Your Honor, if you'll just give me a moment."

"So get there, Ms. Leary," Castor said. "The witness may answer."

Bea Morelli sat with her chin on her palm, rolling her eyes at all of us. "What am I answering?"

"Ms. Morelli, it's true you've got a couple of barn cats out there, don't you?"

"Two or three of them, yes. Useless little fu— Good-for-nothings."

"What are the cats supposed to be good for?" I asked.

Bea tapped the microphone and made a great show of leaning into it. She spoke slowly as if I were hard of hearing or addled. Clearly, she thought I was both.

"Cats kill mice and rats," she said. "Rats like barns. Rats are dirty varmints who must die."

"But you said your barn cats are useless. Do you mean they don't kill their fair share of rats and mice?"

"Not hardly."

"So how do you keep the rats and mice out of the barn?"

"Trap 'em," she said. "Poison 'em."

I pulled another photograph out. "Ms. Morelli, can you identify this picture?"

"That's the back shelf in my barn," she said. I handed a copy of the photograph to Charlotte. She ripped it out of my hand. It took her a second, but I relished watching as her eyes widened.

"Objection!" she shouted. We headed to a sidebar. I showed the judge the photograph.

"The witness just authenticated the photo," I said. "You going to try arguing this isn't relevant?"

"Ms. Stahl," Judge Castor said. "You might want to rethink your objection. Ms. Leary, are you sure you know what you're doing?"

He didn't get it. Charlotte stared hard at the photo. She seemed confused. Judge Castor thought my little photo would help her more than Juliet.

"Overruled," he said. "But get to it, Cass."

"Yes, Your Honor," I said. I went back to the lectern. "Ms. Morelli, can you describe what's in this photograph?" Behind me, Tori clicked her mouse and pulled the larger copy of it up on the projector for the jury to see.

"That's where I keep my pesticides," Bea said. "Up on that high shelf."

"Right next to that ladder there?" I asked.

"Yes."

I had Tori click to a blow-up, isolating two containers on the far right of the shelf. Their skull-and-crossbones poison labels filled the screen.

"Can you tell me what I'm looking at?" I said to Bea.

"Rat poison," she said. "You can't get that stuff in the States anymore. My granddad used to get it. Works fifty times better than the crap the tree-huggers want us to use these days. Bunch of fat-head lawyers telling real people what to do. Screw that."

"Ms. Morelli, what is the main ingredient listed on these cans of rat poison?"

"Thallium," she said.

"And how many times was Nathan Clay out on your farm?"

"Three or four times," she said. "I already told you that."

"And you met him in the barn, didn't you? Just like you did with me and Detective Wray the other day, isn't that right?"

"Yeah," she said. "I made him muck out stalls every time, too. He was better at it than you two were."

"He noticed the rat poison on those shelves too, didn't he? I mean, they're hard to miss with those ominous symbols on them."

"Objection," Charlotte said. "Now Ms. Leary is testifying."

"Ask a question, Ms. Leary," the judge said.

"We talked about the rats," she said. "I pointed out the containers."

"You pointed out the containers of thallium to Nathan Clay?" I asked.

"Yeah. He seemed real interested in it. Asked a lot of questions."

"Objection," Charlotte said. "Your Honor, to the extent this witness is about to testify about what Nathan Clay said or didn't say, it's improper hearsay. The court has already ruled in our favor on this."

"She's right, Ms. Leary," Castor said. "Watch your step."

"Ms. Morelli," I said. "Did you give Nathan Clay some of that poison?"

"He asked me for some. Yes. Said he had mice in his garage."

"And did you give him thallium?"

"A couple of scoops of it, yes," she said. "Put it in a baggie. He put it in his briefcase."

"A baggie," I said.

"Yes," she said, speaking slowly again as if she thought I needed her to. "A. Baggie."

"Do you recall when you gave that baggie of thallium to Nathan Clay?"

"Told ya he came out three or four times. I gave it to him the last time he came out. It was after Ma signed the papers and took his check. Sometime in April. Early April."

I showed her the prosecution's photograph of the baggie of thallium found in Juliet's cupboard.

"Does this look like the baggie you gave Nathan Clay?"

Bea cocked her head to the side. "Could be. Looks like one of mine. I like the little slide zipper closures like that one has. Not the ones you have to press to close."

"Ms. Morelli, have you ever met Juliet Clay, the defendant?"

"No. Can't say I have. I saw some of the videos she posted though. Somebody showed me. I'm not a fan."

"You're not a fan of Juliet Clay's?"

"I'm not a fan of social media in general."

"Got it. To your knowledge, has Juliet Clay ever been on your property?"

"Never seen her in person before today," Bea answered.

"The times Nathan Clay was on your property, did he always come alone?"

"Yes."

"He never brought his son, Bryson Ballard?"

Behind me, Juliet gasped.

"Not that I recall," she said. "I mean, I never searched his car or anything."

"Was Ted Gorney ever on your property?"

She screwed up her face, considering the question. "No. I told you. I'd have shot him. I used to take Ma to meet in his office.

He didn't do house calls. For what he owed her, he should have."

"Thank you, Ms. Morelli," I said. "I have no further questions."

"Ms. Stahl?" Judge Castor said.

"Ms. Morelli," Charlotte said. "Do you keep your barn locked?"

"It has a latch on the outside," she said.

"So it's locked from the outside, not the inside. In other words, theoretically, anyone could just walk up to it, unhook the latch, and go right on in."

"They could try," she said. "I've got alarms all over the place."

"Do you have security cameras?" she asked.

"Don't need 'em," Bea said. "If something trips that alarm, it's something or someone who isn't supposed to be there. It sends a signal to the main house. It'd take me all of thirty seconds to grab the 12-gauge out of the back closet and fire a warning shot."

"But surely you don't keep the alarm on all the time," Charlotte said. She was digging a hole.

"I keep it on when I'm not in the barn."

"But let's say you went off to ride one of your horses. You don't keep the alarm on when you've gone for a ride, do you?"

"Not usually."

"So there are, in fact, times when the barn isn't locked. During broad daylight, even."

"I suppose."

"And someone else inside the house could turn off the alarm, couldn't they?"

"You mean my mother-in-law? She doesn't touch it."

"But she could. If she wanted to."

"Yes," Bea said. "But she doesn't."

"Did you know Nathan Clay's death was ruled a homicide?"

"I heard a rumor he died. Only good lawyer is a dead one, as far as I'm concerned."

"You never went to the police with the information you just testified to?"

"Why would I?"

"You expect us to believe you didn't know Nathan Clay died of thallium poisoning?"

"Don't know, don't care what he died of. Not my business."

"You never saw fit to tell this story to the police?"

"If they'd have come out and asked, I'd have told them, I suppose. Nobody asked."

"The story of Nathan's murder has been on the news. In the papers. You expect us to believe you didn't know about it?"

"Don't expect you to believe anything. I mind my own business. I wish everyone else would get out of mine."

Then, Charlotte stopped digging. "Thank you," she said. "I've got no other questions."

"Ms. Leary?"

"No, Your Honor," I said.

"Fine," Castor said. "Now, Ms. Morelli. You are dismissed."

Bea rose. She stormed off the same way she came in, never bothering to meet my eyes as she went.

"Your Honor," I said. "I'd like to recall Detective Sofia Blackfoot to the stand."

Chapter 35

DETECTIVE BLACKFOOT's testimony took all of ten minutes. Calling her was a risk, but one I was willing to take. I had a stack of printouts from Nathan Clay's Lexis searches.

Along with the affidavit the company record keeper provided, they were self-authenticating. Blackfoot was free to refer to them.

"Detective," I started. "As part of your investigation, you had forensics run on Nathan Clay's computer, didn't you?"

"Yes," she said. "As I already testified."

"Let me direct your attention to your report detailing Mr. Clay's computer activities in the six weeks before he died. How much time did he spend on the LexisNexis website?"

She looked at her notes. "He was logging in a couple of hours every day."

"What is LexisNexis, if you know?"

"It's a computer-assisted legal research site. Lawyers use it to look up case law, statutes, and other legal resources like that."

"In your report, what types of cases or statutes was Mr. Clay searching in those six weeks?"

"What?" she said. "I can't tell you that."

"Why not?"

"Because the search we did will only tell us how long he's logged into that site. It's not like Google where you can see the actual search strings and terms."

"So how would you go about finding the actual LexisNexis search strings for Mr. Clay's searches?"

"If you didn't have Clay's login credentials, you'd need a subpoena from LexisNexis."

"Did you have Mr. Clay's login credentials for LexisNexis?"

"No," she said.

"Did you subpoena LexisNexis for the details on Mr. Clay's searches in the weeks before he died?"

"No."

"Detective, I'd like you to take a look at the documents I've handed you. They've been admitted as defense twenty-seven. Can you tell me what they are?"

"The top page looks like a subpoena," she said through tight lips.

"To whom?"

"To LexisNexis," she said.

"Can you turn the page please? What are these records?"

"They appear to be a search history for an account held by Nathan Clay on LexisNexis."

"What date appears at the top?"

"April 17th," she said.

"And the time stamp?" I asked.

"Two forty-five p.m."

"Detective, I'd like to refer you to State Exhibit 83." At my cue, Tori played the tape of Juliet bringing a diet shake to Nathan as he sat at his computer. She froze it at the spot where Nathan's screen was visible in the background.

"Detective," I said. "What search did Nathan Clay perform on April 17th at 2:45, according to the records you're holding?"

"You want me to read from it?"

"It's an admitted exhibit," I said. "Yes. I'd like you to read from it."

"Dying Declarations," she began. "MRE 804. And then there is a list of cases underneath that."

"Can you tell which of the cases Mr. Clay selected from those that popped up?"

"It says People versus Bradfield."

"Detective, can you read what's on the computer screen behind Nathan Clay in the video admitted as State Exhibit 84?"

"It says U.S. versus Shepherd."

"So that's consistent with the subpoenaed records you're holding?"

"Yes," she said.

"Turn the page again," I said. "Can you tell me how many searches there are on the topic of dying declarations?"

She thumbed through the printout. "There are at least a dozen searches. A few hundred cases."

"What is the date range of the report?"

"It's the week of April 17th through the 24th," she said.

"How many hours of research? You should find a total on the last page," I said.

She flipped to it. To her credit, she didn't blink. She didn't argue. She just read what was in front of her.

"Fourteen hours and fifteen minutes."

"Fourteen hours and fifteen minutes," I repeated. "Who is the client identifier on this report?"

"I'm sorry?"

"At the top of every page, who is listed as the client this research was done on behalf of?"

"It says Morelli," Blackfoot said.

"Morelli," I repeated. "Detective, did you question Ted Gorney about any potential grievances or malpractice matters he or Mr. Clay might have had against them?"

"I did."

"And he said there weren't any, correct? That's what you wrote in your report?"

"It was."

"You were in the courtroom today when Beatrice Morelli testified. Have you ever spoken with her?"

"No."

"Did you ever speak to a Mary Taylor?"

"No," she answered.

"And so you never went out to Ms. Morelli's farm, did you?"

"No."

"No," I repeated. "And you never bothered to subpoena Mr. Clay's LexisNexis records even though you knew he'd spent over fourteen hours logged into their site in the weeks before he died. In fact, it was more than thirty hours, wasn't it? The fourteen was just on research for Morelli, according to that report."

"It's not unusual at all for a lawyer to be using Lexis on their home computer, Ms. Leary," she said. "It would be unusual if they weren't."

"Got it," I said. "You were conducting a murder investigation. And yet you didn't feel it worthwhile to find out how the victim was spending his time in the weeks before he died?"

"That's completely false."

"Thank you," I said. "I have no further questions."

"Ms. Stahl?" Castor asked.

Charlotte rose. "Detective, what type of cases did Nathan Clay handle, if you know?"

"He was a personal injury lawyer," she said.

"Do you know if he handled wrongful death claims?"

"He did," she said. "Car accidents, mostly."

"Have you ever been at the scene of car accidents?"

"Of course," she said. "Many times."

"Do victims of car crashes sometimes talk before they die?"

"What? Yes? Of course."

"Your Honor." I rose.

"Your Honor," Charlotte said. "I have no more questions for Detective Blackfoot."

"You may step down, Detective. Ms. Leary, you may call your next witness."

My heart was a steady drum beat. I rose, walked to the lectern, and gripped the sides. I had one more witness. I needed to ask her just one more question. I recalled the M.E., Dr. Amelia Trainor, to the stand.

Dr. Trainor had been pulled from her office. She still wore her lab coat and was quite a bit more frazzled at being hauled back to testify with barely a warning. So, I got right to the heart of what I needed from her.

"Dr. Trainor," I asked. "Is there an antidote for thallium poisoning?"

"Yes."

"What is it?"

"There is a chemical compound commonly known as Prussian blue that should be administered along with activated charcoal if thallium poisoning is suspected."

"Prussian blue," I repeated. "How does it work?"

"It interrupts the way thallium is metabolized by the digestive system."

"So if I'm clear, if a person is known to ingest thallium, the protocol would be to administer Prussian blue?"

"Yes."

"If Nathan Clay were given this treatment when he first presented symptoms, might he have survived?"

"I wasn't his treating physician," she answered.

"All right, then hypothetically. If a person showed up at the hospital with thallium poisoning, there is a life-saving treatment available to them, is that correct?"

"Well, it depends on the level of toxicity and a number of other factors, but theoretically, yes. There is a treatment for thallium poisoning if medical intervention is sought in time."

"Thank you," I said. "I have no more questions."

When Dr. Trainor left the stand, I turned to the judge. "Your Honor," I said. "The defense rests."

A rumble went through the jury. The judge banged his gavel.

"All right," Castor said. "How long do you need for rebuttal, Ms. Stahl?"

She was on her feet. "None," she said, her tone smug.

"Fine," Castor said. "So let's plan on closing arguments after lunch. The jury is dismissed."

When I turned to face Juliet, she was beaming. I made a sideways gesture with my hand, reminding her to cool it in front of the jury. She thought we'd won. But I knew I may have just handed the jury the rope with which to hang her.

Chapter 36

"I don't understand," Juliet said. I looked at her. Really looked at her. She'd lost maybe twenty pounds since the first day I met her and she'd been thin to begin with.

"We have an hour," I said. "Charlotte isn't going to put on a rebuttal case."

"What does that mean?"

"It means she feels she's put on a strong enough case in chief and doesn't think there's anything to clean up before this case goes to the jury," Tori said.

"She didn't prove anything," Juliet said. "We'll win, won't we? Nate was lying to everyone. I told you that. Everyone wants to think he's some saint. Or a martyr now or something. He was a controlling, manipulative jerk," she said.

"You need to prepare yourself. That's exactly what Charlotte Stahl is going to tell the jury about you. You've kept your cool in there for the most part. You won't like Charlotte's closing. You can't react to it. Stare straight ahead. Write me a note if you need to, but don't draw attention to yourself. The jury will be watching you closely, just as they have all along."

"This is ridiculous," she said. "You can't think those people will make a decision on whether I'm a murderer from my facial expressions."

"I think it's impossible to know what a juror will fixate on. So we don't give them anything more. We're in the home stretch, Juliet. Just hold on."

There was a soft knock on the door. We'd tucked ourselves away in the unused jury room of another judge.

"They can't be ready for us yet," Tori said. Eric poked his head in. "Cass, can I see you for a minute?" The two deputies assigned to Juliet stood right across the hall. I left her with Tori and stepped out.

"How are you holding up?" he asked.

"I want this over. So does she. What's up?"

"Probably nothing, but I kind of called in a favor with the department. I didn't want to tell you, but I had a patrolman watching Jeanie's place."

"What?"

"Well, not so much Jeanie's place. But Bryson Ballard."

"He's been staying with her?" I said. "Is she okay? Eric, what's going on?"

"He's AWOL," Eric said. "Jeanie lined him up with a job interview at the State Park. He was supposed to be there at eleven and he never went."

"There could be a thousand reasons for that," I said.

"Yeah, except there's one really obvious one. The kid's scared. Depending on how this verdict comes down, the sheriff may have more questions for him. They're lying low."

"Which is crap," I said. "We've given them plenty of reasons to reopen this case."

"I'm just telling you what I know. I'm going to find the kid. First up, I plan to pay a visit to Jeanie. I wanted you to have a heads-up."

"Because she's liable to rip your head off," I said. "Do you want me to go with you after I'm done here?"

He looked back toward the closed door. "I think you've got your hands full here. I'll stay in touch by text. It's just …"

"What aren't you telling me?"

He had deep lines on his forehead. "Eric, what?"

"Jeanie's car's gone too. I think she might have driven Bryson out of town."

"They're on the lam?" I said, nearly shrieking it.

"I'll let you know," he said.

"I can't even … She wouldn't. For God's sake."

Eric met my eyes. We said it together. "She would."

"Look," he said. "I'll stay on top of this. You do your thing in there. Hopefully by this evening, the jury will have this case."

"Right," I said. "And thank you. I don't know if she'll talk, but there's a good chance Miranda was Jeanie's co-conspirator if she's up to something. You might want to roll by her place too."

"Got it," he said.

The judge's bailiff poked his head out of Castor's chambers. "Five minutes," he said when he caught my eye. I nodded to him.

Eric leaned in and put a quick peck on my cheek, then headed off for the elevators. I took a breath for courage, then summoned Tori and Juliet back into the courtroom with me.

Chapter 37

CHARLOTTE STAHL FACED THE JURY. Three times she walked back to her table, paused, then made her way back to the lectern, shaking her head. Finally, she folded her hands and began.

"Members of the jury," she said. "You've been patient. Diligent in your note taking. Attentive. I've been watching you. I know you've seen what I've seen and heard. What we have here is perhaps the most clear-cut case of murder I may ever prosecute.

"The defense is going to try to get you to believe that you didn't just see and hear what you thought you did. Ms. Leary is going to spin wild tales about ... you know ... I'm not even sure. But it'll be either that the victim in this case meant to take his own life or that he tried to pin the blame on his wife or some ridiculous combination of both.

"So I won't take up much of your time today. You've seen and heard enough. You know the truth. You know what's real. I know you're probably anxious to get back there and deliberate. So let me clear the way for you to do that as quickly as I can.

"You've been charged with determining the facts in this case. You've been charged with deciding whether Juliet Clay planned and murdered her husband. You have all the facts you need to come to a verdict of guilty. I've shown them to you. And for reasons I, as a prosecutor, cannot fathom, Cass Leary has shown you even more."

I followed my own advice to Juliet. I kept my face free from any reaction. I folded my arms in front of me and waited.

"Fact," Charlotte said. "Nathan Clay died of acute thallium poisoning. You heard Amelia Trainor's testimony. There was no equivocation or doubt. Whatever underlying medical conditions he might have had, Nate Clay's lungs shut down due to the neurological effects of thallium poisoning.

"Fact. Thallium was found both in the cupboard near the protein powder Juliet prepared for him and in the blender bottle by his bed. Fact. Nathan Clay drank from that blender bottle. His DNA and fingerprints were all over it. So were Juliet's.

"Fact. Juliet taped herself giving her husband those shakes. She made no secret of it. Ms. Leary will probably point that out as proof of her innocence. Why would a guilty woman be so bold? Why wouldn't she try to hide it? Well, I'll tell you. Because she tried to hide her guilt in plain sight. So she could try to fool you with that very defense.

"Fact. Juliet Clay had a history of violent outbursts against Nathan. The police were called on numerous occasions due to safety concerns. Her neighbors overheard her threatening to kill Nathan Clay more than once.

"Fact. Juliet Clay did her research. Her phone and computer had search histories going back weeks. She looked up different poisons. She settled on thallium. She read articles about other murders where thallium was used. Then, she set about trying to find some.

"Here's the part where my mind got blown. I'll admit it. The defendant's own lawyer provided you with the answer as to how that thallium got in Juliet Clay's hands. Beatrice Morelli gave it to Nathan because he told her he had a mouse problem. Juliet saw it. She researched it. She fed it to her husband. All this business about trouble Nathan had with his law partner is smoke and mirrors. An attempt to get you to focus on the irrelevant."

I jotted down a few notes. The jury was watching me, not Juliet.

"Finally, the defense made a big deal out of parading poor Bryson Ballard back on the witness stand. It was theatrics. Nothing more. It doesn't matter if Nathan Clay told him what to say. It matters that he knew he was dying. Of that, there can be no doubt. It matters that he wanted Bryson to know his mother had something to do with it. The rest is all noise.

"I don't know what the defense is going to stand up here and tell you. I really don't. That Nathan Clay took the poison on his own? Really? Think about that. Think about what Dr. Trainor told you the effects of thallium poisoning are. It shuts down your organs. Your lungs. You lose your hair. It might feel like your stomach is turning inside out. It is a horrible, slow, painful death. It is not reasonable to believe that Nathan Clay would have done such a thing. It is far more reasonable to find that he was poisoned without his knowledge. By a woman who wanted him gone.

"I thank you for your time. For your careful consideration of the facts. I know that you'll render the only reasonable verdict. The only possible verdict under the circumstances. And you'll find the defendant, Juliet Clay, guilty of first-degree murder. Thank you."

Still shaking her head, Charlotte walked back to her table, opened her blazer, and sat back down.

"Ms. Leary?" Castor said. "Are you prepared to deliver your closing at this time?"

I rose. "I am, Your Honor." Slowly, I walked up to the lectern.

"It's a good story," I said. "Perfect, almost. You want to hate Juliet Clay. She's pretty. Toned. Skinny. She's that tightly wound, needy mom who's desperate to be liked at the PTA meeting, the booster club, as your neighbor. She seems to fall for every get-rich-quick scheme there is. Leggings. Bakeware. Skincare. Diet shakes. I mean, it's endless. How can she be so gullible, right? Doesn't she know the neighbors all talk about her? They roll their eyes behind her back. You heard them. They told you.

"Nathan was better off before he married Juliet. They told you that too. His law partner also told you that. A gold digger. A trophy wife. You name it, Juliet fits the profile. She should get what she has coming to her, shouldn't she? I mean, she puts herself out there. On social media. She knows what she's doing. The more obnoxious she is, the more followers she gains. I mean, does she even know what they think? Is she in on the joke?"

Juliet blinked rapidly, trying to keep her tears away. My words hurt her. Good. It's what the jury needed to see.

"Only none of that means she's guilty of murder. The prosecution has a high burden. As well they should. The punishment for premeditated murder in this state is life in prison without the possibility of parole. But to get there, the state must prove beyond a reasonable doubt that Juliet planned the killing of her husband."

I walked to the end of the jury box. Half of them stared at me, the other half stared at Juliet.

"Juliet Clay is an easy target," I said. "For all the reasons I just laid out, you might want her to be guilty. She's asking for it. Who in their right mind would actually record themselves giving someone poison and then document their slow, painful demise? You watched Nathan Clay wither away right in front of you. Day after day. Week after week. And she posted it on social media. She went viral. Juliet Clay finally got all the attention she ever wanted.

"But here's the thing. You know she wanted it. You can feel her desperation to be liked in every video. It's compelling to watch. You can't miss it. Neither did Nathan Clay. He knew exactly how to feed his wife's ego to bring about her downfall.

"Yes. I'm telling you what happened. Juliet Clay is no murderer. Because there was no murder at all. There was a crime though. Only the guilty party is dead.

"It's horrible. Incredible. Shocking to believe. But Nathan Clay knew exactly what he was doing. For months, he refused to let Juliet Clay record him for her social media channels. Until the day he realized he could use it to destroy her.

"Theirs was a volatile marriage. We know this. He told Juliet he was fine with her extracurricular dalliances. But he wasn't. Of course he wasn't. And then, the unthinkable happened to him. He got a death sentence. He knew what it meant. He'd watched his own grandfather die of the same type of cancer. He knew the treatments proposed would only prolong his agony and he'd die anyway.

"He. Would. Die. Anyway."

I let my words hang for a moment.

"Members of the jury," I said. "Nathan Clay made a decision. He would take Juliet Clay down with him. He researched the poison on Juliet's laptop. A laptop he purchased for her. He knew the police would search it after he was gone. He found his opportunity when Juliet pressured him to be her guinea pig with the diet shakes. It was perfect. Use her own ego and need for attention against her. Let the whole internet watch as he drank the poison that she handed to him.

"Is it gruesome? Yes. Shocking? Of course. But Nathan Clay was dying anyway. The ravaging of his digestive system was happening anyway. When you know that, the horror of ingesting poison to hasten it isn't so shocking at all.

"Nathan Clay got a death sentence on March 10th. He knew he was already dying. He saw the opportunity to go out on his terms in Bea Morelli's barn. He swore his doctor to secrecy so Juliet wouldn't know about his cancer. Only his doctors knew and they were ethically bound to keep quiet. He'd already seen the thallium in Bea's barn. He saw Dr. Broyles one last time, then made arrangements to go out there and get his poison. He made sure the whole internet saw him guzzling down the shakes that Juliet made.

"Think about that. He got the poison from Bea Morelli's barn. He brought it home. He put it in the shakes and left it in the cupboard where he knew it would be found. But what if it wasn't? What if Juliet had found the powder and moved it or threw it away? Nathan Clay was a lawyer. A litigator. He knew the burden of proof you would have to weigh.

"He coached his stepson to say the right things. I know I'm dying. That's the threshold requirement for what we call a dying declaration in the rules of evidence. It's a very specific hearsay exception. He started researching it in April. After his diagnosis. After he got his poison. He said those exact words and made sure Bryson repeated them. He told him, time and again, make sure you tell them I said I knew I was dying.

"Think about it. What other possible explanation could there be? If Nathan knew he was dying and he truly suspected Juliet was behind it, why wouldn't he have called the police? Why wouldn't he have called an ambulance? He didn't because he wanted to die. He had researched thallium poisoning on Juliet's very own laptop. He knew there was an antidote, just like Dr. Trainor told you. If he called the police, he would have been taken to the hospital and treated with Prussian blue. His plan wouldn't work. And he wanted to die. He wanted the evidence he left to be found. And he wanted his stepson to provide the last connection so Juliet would be arrested and tried for his so-called murder. Then he could keep her from inheriting a dime of his estate or benefiting from his life insurance. He was a lawyer. He knew it was the ultimate way to screw her. Get her locked up. Penniless. Hated.

"I put to you, it wasn't a murder at all. It was a suicide. A twisted, elaborate suicide. If Nathan Clay were alive, he could be convicted of obstruction of justice, filing a false police report. Perjury, you name it. But he got what he wanted in the end. He got to die on his own terms and stick it to his wife in the process. It's the perfect death for him. And the perfect crime. Only Juliet Clay is innocent of all of it. There is reasonable doubt. A wealth of it. But there is something else. Something we don't often get in murder cases, even with a full confession. What you have, ladies and gentlemen, is an explanation. It's horrible and sad and tragic. But there was no murder at all. I trust you'll do the right thing and find Juliet Clay not guilty. Thank you."

I tapped my knuckles on the wooden ledge of the jury box and walked back to Juliet's side.

Chapter 38

"Don't move!" I shouted. "It's no good, Miranda. I hear you creeping around back there. You'll never make a clean getaway."

The floorboards at the back of the office creaked, further transmitting Miranda Sulier's location.

I heard her mumble an obscenity I didn't often hear her use. She said it even louder when the back kitchen door opened and Eric came in through the other side.

"You gonna cuff me?" Miranda said.

"Don't be so dramatic," Eric said.

"Don't think I haven't thought about it!" I called back. Miranda walked back into the main lobby with her hands on her head for effect. Eric came in behind her, rolling his eyes.

"Where is she?" I asked.

"Where is who?" Miranda asked.

"I'm not in the mood for games," I said. "She called you. You're in on it. Where's Jeanie?"

I could see Miranda's wheels turning. She brought her hands down and crossed them in front of her. Belligerent. Defiant. And guilty as sin.

"I'm not her keeper," Miranda said. "Jeanie's a grown woman. Plus, I couldn't have stopped her anyway."

"Did you try?" I asked. I heaved my messenger bag onto the receptionist's desk. We didn't actually have one of those. A grievance Miranda filed regularly. At the same time, she rejected every viable candidate I sent to her.

Miranda's face fell. "Yes. Cass, I swear. I tried."

I turned my back on her and went into Jeanie's empty office.

"You can't!" Miranda said. The woman was cat quick when she wanted to be. She darted around me and barred the door, holding her arms out wall to wall.

"Miranda," I said. "Don't think I won't pick you up and throw you. Jeanie's in over her head on this one. Bryson Ballard is still lying."

"And he's not under arrest either. Is he?" She looked at Eric. Eric spread his hands out.

"Not my circus," he said. "You'd have to ask the Woodbridge County Sheriff's Office."

"And they don't do anything you don't hear about," she protested.

"Or you," I reminded her. "Miranda, nobody's in trouble. Yet."

"You think that boy killed his father?" she asked.

I looked back at Eric. "No. I think his father killed himself. And I think he tried to frame Juliet for it and Bryson helped him. That's what I argued to the jury today."

"It's over? They're deliberating?"

"Yes," I said. "And Jeanie has made Bryson Ballard disappear."

The front door opened. My heart lifted, hoping it was Jeanie. Instead, Tori walked in. "She's not at her house," she said. "The neighbor said she hasn't seen Jeanie's car since early yesterday. No one's there. I looked."

"You broke into her house?" Eric asked. "You know what? I don't want to know."

"You're on leave, Detective," I said.

"She gave me a key," Tori said. "She has me feed her fish when she goes out of town. I didn't break into anything. Bryson's things aren't there anymore."

"Cass," Miranda said. "You don't think that kid would do anything to hurt Jeanie, do you? Eric?"

"No," he answered for both of us. "I don't think that's what's going on. I think the kid is running scared because he lied to the cops and he lied to the prosecutor and he initially lied on the stand. He's got some things to answer for, no matter how this verdict shakes out. But I don't think he's a danger to Jeanie. She's enough of a danger to herself."

"She's trying to help," Miranda said. "If she's on that boy's side, she thinks he's worth saving."

"I think you better tell us what you know," I said.

Miranda's eyes darted from me to Eric to Tori. She knew she was cornered. Her shoulders sank in defeat. She turned and opened the door to Jeanie's office. We all filed in behind her.

"You won't find anything in here," she said. "Jeanie knew you might come snooping. She took all the files she had on Bryson with her."

"She told you her plans?" I asked.

"Not exactly," Miranda said. "She told me she was going to be gone for a little while and that you'd be pretty pissed at her about it. And she asked me to give you this."

Miranda walked over to the desk and picked up a white envelope with my name on it. I took it from her and sank into one of Jeanie's leather chairs.

I opened the envelope. Jeanie always wrote with felt-tipped pens. In her looping scrawl, she wrote simply, "Trust me. Do your job and I'll do mine. Also, leave Miranda alone, you bully. J."

Shaking my head, I handed the note to Eric. He covered his laughter with a cough then handed the note back to me.

"I want to talk to that kid," Eric said.

"Isn't it too late for all that?" Tori asked. "I mean, the jury has the case. They're either going to believe us or they won't. Right? If the sheriff's office wanted to reopen the investigation, they would have by now. They're doubling down on Juliet as the murderer. What difference does it make what Bryson did or didn't do now?"

"You could appeal," Miranda said.

"Let's not go there yet," I said.

"He got to testify," Eric said. "Twice. There's no new evidence. No reversible error there."

"Do you really think Nathan Clay did all this to himself?" Miranda asked. "I mean, it's not like he just drank the poison and fell asleep and died. This took weeks. So every single day he had to make a decision to go through with this."

"Yes," I said. "It's what I think. I'm just not sure the jury bought it. I honestly have no idea what they're going to do."

"How's Juliet?" Miranda asked.

"Horrified. Terrified. She's worried more about Bryson than anything else. And she's furious with me for having a go at him on the witness stand."

"Well," Miranda said. "That sure doesn't sound like the actions of a guilty person. I'll be honest. I've never liked that woman."

"No one does," Tori agreed.

"But she's acting like a Mama Bear now," Miranda said. "You watch. If somebody tries to go after that boy of hers, I bet she confesses anyway."

"Come on," Eric said. "There's nothing to do here. Cass, let me take you home. Get a good night's sleep."

"You don't think they'll come back yet today?" Tori asked. It was after seven. The jury went into deliberations at two.

Miranda's phone rang in the outer hall. We all looked at each other.

"Check your cell," Eric said. I'd forgotten I'd turned the thing to silent when we were in the courthouse. I had three unanswered texts. It was ringing now.

"Court clerk," I said. Miranda had already scooted out of the office, headed for her ringing office landline.

"What's happening, Nancy?" I answered.

"Hi, Cass," Nancy Olson said. "The jury came back. They asked to meet with Judge Castor."

My heart tripped.

"They're hung," Nancy said.

"They're hung!" Miranda yelled from the outer office, reporting what her phone call was about as well.

"What now?" Tori asked.

"He's asked them to go back at it tomorrow morning," Nancy said. "But it doesn't look good. I just wanted you to know."

I clicked off the call and sank further into the chair. Praying it would swallow me whole.

Chapter 39

THE LAKE HOUSE became jury vigil central that night and into the next morning. I had a call with Juliet. She took the news as hard as I feared.

"They think I did it," she said. "They didn't believe what you told them."

"Half of them didn't," I said. "But they'll go back. It's not terrible news. It means we convinced some of them. It's better for us than it is for the prosecution. Just hang in there. I know it's hard."

She didn't ask about Bryson. I had nothing yet to tell her. I kept calling and texting Jeanie. Her voice mailbox was full.

Eric spent the night in the guest room. Tori camped out on the daybed in my home office. In about an hour, Matty, Joe, and Vangie were headed this way. Vangie volunteered to make us all dinner, if we got that far.

Tori sat out on the porch. We were in the middle of a typically weird Michigan November weather pattern. It was seventy-two degrees out there. Tonight, they were calling for frost. I walked out to join her.

"I wanted to tell you," I said. "No matter how this jury rules, you're ready."

"What do you mean?"

"I mean, after this, I think you should try a case or two on your own. You've worked your ass off."

Her beaming smile warmed my heart. Jeanie called Tori one of the strays we liked to take in. She'd come to us with no family. No real support system at all. Now, she was my family.

"That means a lot to me," she said. She pulled the ends of her sweater closer around her. That cold front was already starting to come in.

"Cass," she said. "Before Matty and the others get here, there's something I want to tell you."

"How's that going?" I asked. It was the first time I had. "Matty and you?"

Tori took a breath and blurted her next words out. "He's moving in."

It took a second for her meaning to sink in. "Wait, what?"

"Matty's moving in with me," she said.

"Oh dear."

"Look, I know this is weird for you. Matty's terrified to tell you."

"Matty's never been scared of me," I said. "But he should be."

"You're wrong," she said. "You're so wrong. Cass, he worships you. I often think your good opinion of him is the only one that really matters. He's so worried about disappointing you. He knows how often he has."

"Tori," I said. I couldn't help it. Anger flared within me. I loved them both. But I'd be damned if I was going to get lectured about my little brother. "I don't need you to tell me about Matty."

"Yes, you do," she said.

"Are you chastising me?" I asked. This was coming out all wrong. Tori was the last person I wanted to be at odds with.

"No," she said. "I'm sorry. No. Matty didn't want me to say anything to you about this. He's been working up the courage to tell you himself. He's afraid you'll disapprove. But Cass, he needs to know that doesn't matter. We love each other."

I let a hard breath out of my nose. "Really?"

"Yes."

"Tori, I love Matty. I'd kill and die for him. He knows that. But are you sure you know what you're getting into?"

"Yes," she said with such force, it seemed like she'd been holding that answer in for weeks. I realized she likely had.

"Yes," she said again, softer. "I really love him. We've kept all of this away from you and I don't think we should anymore. We're okay. Matty's okay."

"He might not be," I said. "Tori, you have to know that. My brother's ..."

"Not perfect," she said. "I know about his addiction. I know he has his demons. I'm not so naïve to think he couldn't relapse today, tomorrow. Someday he probably will. But I'm willing to take that road with him."

He's going to hurt you. I wanted to say it. As Tori stared at me, I knew I didn't have to. She understood my mind.

"It's worth it to me to take that risk," she said. "When you love someone, you can't just sit around and wait for the perfect time or for when life isn't complicated. If you do that, you'll always be alone."

I opened my mouth to say something, then clamped it shut. Eric's laughter reached me. He was coming down the driveway. My niece Jessa trailed behind him. He had Marbury in his arms. Jessa had Madison on her leash. Marby's paws were covered in mud.

"Come on, squirt," he said to Jessa. "You grab a towel and get ready to catch him. Marby hates getting wet."

Jessa ran ahead. Madison barked and yipped, racing to keep pace.

Matty's truck pulled into the driveway behind them. I turned to Tori but she was already on her feet, running and waving at Matty, her cheeks flushed. She couldn't wait to see him.

Matty came out of the truck and held his arms out to catch Tori. He kissed her. She went on her tiptoes and whispered something in his ear. Telling him she'd already spilled the beans to me. With his arm around Tori's small waist, my brother caught my eye.

"You okay?" My brother Joe's voice pulled me out of myself.

"Yeah," I said. "Just ... edgy."

"Sure," he said. "Come on inside. You worry too much, sis. They're going to be all right."

"You knew?" I said, looking back at Matty and Tori. They were kissing still. They looked happy. They weren't willing to wait for my approval or for things to not be complicated. I looked back at Eric as he dumped Marby into the small plastic pool I kept just for doggie baths.

I wanted things to be simple. Eric laughed. Jessa sprayed him with water. Marby slipped out of his grasp and ran across the yard.

Chapter 40

At ten o'clock the next morning, Jeanie finally answered my call.

"Forget it," she said, instead of hello. "Bryson stays where he is. It's not like I'm harboring a fugitive."

Tori came out of her office. I wasn't sure what tipped her off, but she stood in the doorway and I waved her in. I would have put Jeanie on speaker, but she'd know.

"Jeanie, where are you?"

"Taking a vacation," she said. "I haven't had one in years unless you count the time off I took getting chemo at Maple Valley four years ago."

"Nobody's coming after Bryson," I said. "At least, not as far as I know. They should have. Don't try telling me you don't know that."

"He's a kid!" she shouted. I pulled the phone away from my ear. "And he was under my protection and counsel. You knew that."

Screw it. I put her on speakerphone.

"Jeanie," I said. "I need to know the truth. Did Bryson help kill Nate Clay?"

She was breathing hard in the pause at the other end of the phone. "No."

"But he knew what Nate was planning all along, didn't he?"

"No!" she said. "He's a dumb, scared kid who got caught in the middle of two crappy parents. Juliet might not be a murderer, but she's still one of the bad guys in this, Cass."

"Bryson knew Nate was planning to frame Juliet. How much did he know?"

"No," Jeanie said. "No way. Whatever Bryson knew or didn't know, he's done talking to anyone without an immunity deal."

"Jeanie, I have a jury in the middle of deliberations. If Bryson has more information that could exonerate her, he has to come forward. Now. Before she's convicted."

"You don't know she'll be convicted. You've raised reasonable doubt. This will be over soon and everyone can just go on their merry way."

I rubbed my temples. This wasn't like Jeanie. Sure, she got personally invested in the lives of the kids she represented. My own family had benefited from that in immeasurable ways. But she'd never tried to cover up criminal behavior.

"Where is he, Jeanie?" I said.

She paused so long before answering. For a moment I thought she'd hung up or walked away from her phone.

"I don't know," she said. "That's the God's honest truth. I don't know. You think I'm hiding him. I'm not. I've been out looking for him. I'm afraid of what he might do."

"Is he suicidal?" Tori said, coming further into the room.

"I don't know," Jeanie answered. "He's a wreck. I told you. He is the victim of two really crappy parents. He feels guilty about Nate's death. I meant what I said. I don't believe he was some kind of co-conspirator. He was just a kid being forced to make grown-up decisions when he wasn't equipped to do it. He got in over his head. Nate Clay was everything to him. He was his way out of a really bad situation with Juliet and he was afraid his mom was about to wreck their lives again. Now he's scared to death he's going to go to jail too."

"But he knows his mother is innocent," I said. "He knows Nate's the one who spiked his own drinks."

No answer. Either she didn't know or she still refused to tell me.

"Jeanie," I said. "What if they convict Juliet? She's facing life in prison."

"Nate Clay did this, not Bryson," Jeanie said. "Come on. Has Sofia Blackfoot offered to reopen the investigation? Has Rafe Johnson?"

"They don't have all the facts," I said. "I did my best to present that to the jury, but some of them didn't buy it. I know that much. I know at least one member of that jury believes Juliet is guilty beyond a reasonable doubt. Right now, they're in there deciding what's going to happen with the rest of her life."

I heard footsteps downstairs. Heavy ones. My landline blinked as Miranda tried to call me on the intercom. Tori put up her index finger, gesturing that she'd handle whatever it was.

"Jeanie," I said. "You know what you have to do. And you know I've done what I've had to do."

Silence on the other end. I hated that she was angry with me. I hated that we were on opposite sides of this particular fence.

"I did exactly what you taught me," I said.

"Don't remind me," she said, but I detected a trace of humor in her voice.

The voices were getting louder downstairs. I looked out the door. Eric came up, followed by Tori, both of their expressions grim.

"Jeanie," I said. "I'm going to need to let you go."

"No, don't!" Eric said. "Jeanie, it's Eric. You should hear this too."

"What's going on?" I said.

"They found Bryson Ballard," he said. "He wrapped a car around a telephone pole on Lakeside Road."

I heard Jeanie gasp.

"Is he dead?" I asked.

"No," Eric said, loud and clear so Jeanie could hear too. "He's banged up pretty bad.

Jeanie, it was your car he was driving. I suppose you knew that."

I knew better. Jeanie never let anyone drive her car. Lord, he'd stolen it or at least taken it without her permission. She hadn't reported it.

"He's at Windham Hospital," Eric said. "Broken leg and some cracked ribs. But the cops on scene think he might have done it on purpose."

"I'm on my way," Jeanie said.

"If you tell me where you are, I'll send a crew to pick you up. On account of the fact you don't have a car, Jeanie," Eric said, meeting my gaze.

"Fine," Jeanie said. "I'm at the Harmon Arms. I'll be in the lobby waiting."

"I'll pick you up," I said.

"Cass," Tori said. Miranda was coming up behind her. "You can't. They need us in court. The jury has reached a verdict in Juliet's case."

Chapter 41

"Do we tell her?" Tori asked. She stood beside me at the defense table just before they brought Juliet in.

"Jeanie's going to be with him," I said. "He's given her his medical power of attorney since he won his emancipation. They won't talk to Juliet anyway. Let's just get through the next twenty minutes. Then we'll let her know."

If she made it that long. One of the deputies, Carleen Warner, came up to me. "She threw up in the hallway," Carleen said. "C.O. said they're going to put her on suicide watch if this goes against her. I wasn't sure she was even going to make it this far."

"Do you have it under control?" I asked.

"We've got her upright," Carleen said. I liked her. Carleen was six months from retirement and acting like it. She no longer cared who she ticked off. "She doesn't smell great, but I helped her clean up."

"Thanks," I said.

"Question is, can *you* handle it?"

Rafe and Charlotte came in. They were deep in conversation and didn't look my way. Behind them, Detective Blackfoot came. Stone-faced, she took a seat at the back of the courtroom.

The double doors opened. Juliet came in. Well, not so much came in, but was carried in. Two male deputies had a hold of her under each arm. She shuffled her feet. Her face had no color and her eyes were bloodshot. They got her to me. In the span of a day, I swear she'd lost another ten pounds.

"Juliet?" I said. I stopped myself from asking her if she'd be okay. She wouldn't. Not until those twelve jurors had their say. "All rise!"

Castor's bailiff called us to order. Juliet stood beside me, gripping the table for support. I shot a look at Carleen. She stood right behind us, ready to catch Juliet if she went down again.

"Cass," Juliet whispered. "I'm going to be sick."

"No, you're not," I said through gritted teeth. "Stay on your feet, no matter what happens next."

"Members of the jury," Castor said. "I understand you've reached your verdict?"

"We have, Your Honor," Juror number eight said. He was a younger guy, maybe thirty. He worked on an Alaskan oil rig for six months out of the year. It surprised me a bit they picked him as jury foreman. There was a retired schoolteacher in the back, Juror number two. She had an authoritarian air about her and was the oldest member in the box.

The clerk took the verdict from Juror number eight and walked it over to Judge Castor. He read it and handed it back to the clerk.

"I can't," Juliet gasped. "I can't breathe."

I took her hand. Tori took the other.

"In the matter of the People of the State of Michigan versus Juliet Ballard Clay, on the charge of first-degree murder pursuant to MCL 750.316, being murder perpetrated by means of poison, lying in wait, or any other willful, deliberate or premeditated killing, we the jury find the defendant ..."

"I can't!" Juliet shouted. "I can't. I can't."

Judge Castor banged his gavel. "Ms. Leary, please control your client."

"Hang on," I said to Juliet. My ears were ringing. She was hyperventilating.

Castor nodded to his clerk.

"We the jury find the defendant, not guilty."

I gripped Juliet's arm, willing her to stay on her feet.

"In the matter of the People of the State of Michigan versus Juliet Ballard Clay on the lesser included charge of second-degree murder pursuant to MCL 750.317 being murder by any other means not described in the previous statute, we the jury find the defendant, not guilty."

"Oh God," Juliet said. She slipped out of my grip, doubled over, and threw up on my shoes.

Chapter 42

"Will he see me?"

I stood outside Bryson Ballard's hospital room. Jeanie was there. Eric stood beside me. It would take another couple of hours before Juliet was processed out of the county jail. Tori was waiting with her and breaking the news about Bryson's accident.

"He's not very talkative," the nurse said. "He's extremely lucky to be alive."

"You sure he sees it that way?" Eric asked. Two state troopers were down the hall, finishing up with a witness. A Good Samaritan motorist had seen Bryson hit the tree and called 911.

"I'll be back," Eric said. He headed for the troopers.

"You can go in," the nurse said. "If he throws you out, that's on him."

"I appreciate it. Thanks."

Bryson looked awful. The left side of his face was already starting to swell. He'd broken his nose on the steering wheel. The fracture to his leg was less serious than we first feared. A clean break to the fibula. The doctor didn't even think he'd need a cast. Just a boot for six weeks.

"Hey, there," I said. Jeanie held a straw to Bryson's parched lips. He took a tentative sip but grimaced from the movement, clutching his side.

"Those are probably going to hurt the worst," I said. "Not much they can do for broken ribs."

"Is it true?" he asked. "About my mom?"

"The jury acquitted her a couple of hours ago," I answered. "She's anxious to see you."

Bryson's eyes went glassy. He turned his head and stared out the window.

"Do you want to see her?" Jeanie asked.

"I didn't try to kill myself," Bryson said. "I just looked away from the road for a second. I was stupid, not suicidal. Make sure they know that."

Jeanie looked unconvinced. "You'll talk to a psychologist," she said. "After that ..."

"After that, I can leave," Bryson said, his voice taking on a hard edge. I'd never heard him speak that way to Jeanie before. I also never thought he'd steal her car.

"The police are going to want to talk to you about a few things," I said. "You can have a lawyer with you."

"Can it be you?" he asked.

I shared a look with Jeanie. "I don't know. That's not a good idea."

"Bryson," Jeanie said. "You need to tell the truth about what happened with your stepdad."

"Don't call him that," he said. "He was my dad. I'll never have another one. She made sure of that. They should have locked her away."

"That isn't what you wanted," I said. "You came to me. You begged me to help her. Then you withheld information that could have accomplished just that. Did he put you up to it? Your dad? Was that the deal? He knew he was dying and he left you a road map for how to get her out of your life after he was gone?"

Silence.

"If you're my lawyer," he said. "Then you can't tell the cops anything I say, isn't that right?"

"I'm not your lawyer," I said. "But Jeanie is."

"You don't know what she's like," he said. "She's charming when she wants to be. But it doesn't last. Do you know how many things I got uninvited from because my mom rubbed people the wrong way? How many girlfriends of mine she ran off?"

"But she didn't murder Nathan," I said. "And you knew that, didn't you? You knew Nathan was poisoning himself. He told you. He told you he was dying. And he coached you on what to say to me and the police."

"Yes," he said. "I tried to talk him out of it. I promise. I tried to talk him out of it. He wouldn't listen."

"He told you he was dying of cancer?" Jeanie asked.

"Yeah," Bryson said. "He said he was dying anyway. He said he knew how to take care of me. I didn't lie. I told the truth on the stand the second time. I wish I hadn't. I wish I could have done what he asked. That's what he wanted. He made me promise. He promised *me* he'd make sure I was taken care of and that his way would keep her away from me and out of my life forever. I didn't know what to believe. I swear to God he never told me he was taking poison. He just told me there were some things I'd have to say if I had to go to court. He said this was how he could help me make sure I'd never have to see her again."

"You've already done that," Jeanie said. "Bryson, legally, you're your own man. That hasn't changed. You can see her, not see her, it's up to you."

He blinked. "She won't let that happen. She'll hound me. She'll try to grind me into a nub just like she did my real dad and Nathan. She ... she gets my head all turned around. She makes me feel sorry for her. Makes me think it's my job to take care of her. That's why I asked for your help. I felt guilty. It's been that way since I was really little. How messed up is that? I'm supposed to be the kid."

"You have the trust your father set up for you," Jeanie said. "It's intact."

"But she'll get the rest now," he said. "Isn't that how it works? Because she didn't murder him, the court will give her the rest of Nathan's money that he left her. Less what she owes you. Congratulations. She'll get to pay her bill to you with my dad's money, won't she?"

"You can leave," Jeanie said. "I'm not going to press charges on the car. You had permission to drive it."

"Jeanie," I started. She gave me a pointed stare.

"I gave him permission to drive it," she said, firmer. "That's the end of it. You can come back home with me, Bryson. I'll help you figure out your next move."

"I want a restraining order against her," he said. "That's my next move. I want a court to tell her she'll be arrested if she comes near me."

"She hasn't threatened you," Jeanie said.

"She's taken everything I love away from me," he said. "And I'm not staying in Delphi. You said I've got the money. You said I've got the right to decide for myself."

"Where will you go?" I asked.

"Anywhere. California, maybe. I have a cousin there. My real dad's sister's kid. We've messaged a few times. She's cool. She could help me find a job. Or maybe I'll finish high school there or get a GED. Join the army. Anything to get away from Delphi and Juliet Clay. I can do that. Right?"

"You can," Jeanie said. "I just don't know if it's a good idea."

"And you can't tell me what to do either."

With that, he rolled on his side and stared out the window again. He shut down from both of us. Jeanie tried to prod him, but got no answer. A moment later, the nurse walked back in to check his vitals.

"Come on," I said to Jeanie. "It's time to go."

I could still see Eric talking to the state troopers down the hall. We made our way to a small family waiting room, Jeanie and me. When we got there, she sank into a worn orange chair and started to cry.

"Hey," I said, sitting next to her. "You've done everything you can for that kid. You know that, right?"

"I know. It's just so damn tragic. And unnecessary. Nate Clay. Juliet. All of it."

"As troubled as Juliet is," I said. "Nathan was worse. He's the villain here, Jeanie."

"He manipulated that kid," she said. "And now he's hung him out to dry. I got a call from Johnson's office right after the verdict was read. They're trying to save face. They might bring Bryson up on obstruction charges. Thanks to me, if they do, he'll be tried as an adult. No question."

"Hopefully, it won't come to that," I said.

Eric walked up. "How's the kid?"

"Banged up," I said. "Scared. But he says he didn't intentionally hit that tree."

"Yeah," Eric said. "That's what the state boys are saying, too. Distracted driving. He's going to get cited. It's just a lucky thing he didn't hurt anyone else or himself too badly. Jeanie, they're asking about the car though."

"I let him borrow it," she snapped. "If they're ready to take my statement, I'm ready to give it."

"But ..." Eric stepped back just before getting plowed over by Jeanie. She charged after the troopers before they got on the elevator.

"Never mind my question about how Jeanie's doing," he said. "She's too close to this one, Cass."

"I know," I said. "And I don't believe for a minute she really gave him the keys."

"Well, she'll convince those two anyway," he said. "He'll probably be able to plead down the reckless driving charge without too much trouble. Pay a fine. Get his insurance premium jacked up. But other than that ..."

"Other than that, he's facing obstruction and filing false report charges."

"You think he's earned that?" Eric asked.

I didn't get the chance to answer. The elevator doors opened and Juliet Clay came running out. Her eyes wild as they connected with mine, she came shrieking down the hallway.

"My baby! Where is he? Bryson?"

The nurse came out of Bryson's room. She held her hands up. Two security guards appeared, likely drawn by the commotion.

"Are you Mrs. Ballard?" the nurse asked.

"I'm Mrs. Clay," she said. "Though I'll be changing that soon enough. I don't want anything to do with Nathan Clay other than I'll take his damn money."

"Mrs. Clay," the nurse said. "My patient doesn't want you in the room. If you can't calm down, I'm going to have to ask you to leave."

"Leave? He's my son. Cass, you have to do something. They can't keep me from seeing my son."

"They can, I'm afraid. Juliet, why don't you let me take you home? You have to be exhausted. Starving. Get some sleep. Take a hot bath. Just clear your head and give Bryson a chance to clear his. He's okay. Some minor broken bones, but nothing a few weeks won't heal."

"What's he telling you?" she said. "What's that little monster telling all of you people?"

Her face changed. Gone was her charming smile. "What are you telling them?!" Juliet yelled toward Bryson's closed door. "You think your father was on your side? You think Nate loved you? He used you, you little idiot. He used you to get back at me."

"Juliet!" I said. I grabbed her by the shoulders. "You need to calm down. Let Eric and I take you home."

"He was going to let me rot in jail. They planned it together. Now everyone knows it but they're still going to blame me for everything. Nate got exactly what he wanted. They'll all still think I did this. Or they'll think I'm so awful my husband would rather drink poison than be with me. He's ruined me. Have you seen what they're saying online? You have to help me get my social media channels back up. I have to talk to my followers directly."

"Let's go," Eric said. He put a hand on Juliet's back and led her back toward the elevators. She came, but not without ranting the whole way down.

This was the Juliet the neighbors saw. The one Ted Gorney thought had ruined Nathan Clay's life.

Maybe she had.

Maybe I was wrong about all of it. Juliet was innocent of murder. But maybe they were all villains after all. Nathan. Juliet. And even Bryson. As we finally got Juliet into Eric's car, I hoped the last bit wasn't true. I hoped there was still a chance for Bryson to escape all of this and break the cycle. Though I knew, the odds were stacked heavily against it.

Chapter 43

THREE DAYS LATER, I stood on the dock as the mid-afternoon sun tanned my face when it had no right to. We were a week from Thanksgiving. The boats were already shrink-wrapped and in the barn. But it was sixty-eight degrees and I'd let most of the summer go by immersed in Juliet's case.

The dogs slept on the porch. Marbury lay on his back, his legs splayed out. Weird dog. Madison whined in her sleep, chasing after some squirrel she never could catch.

It was quiet. Peaceful. The sun reflected off the water, glimmering like rolling waves of diamonds.

Leaves crunched as tires rolled over them in the driveway behind me. Eric parked his black truck in front of the garage and headed down to the dock to join me.

He took long, sure strides. He wore a pair of weathered jeans and a faded blue tee shirt. He'd come here to work. Later, my brothers were planning to pull the dock. It was so nice today; I meant to call them off. What's one more weekend?

There was something about Eric's expression that made me pause. Not grim, but serious. The dogs were finally alerted to his presence and scrambled down the porch steps heading him off before he could reach me.

I came up, bypassing the melee. Whatever he came to tell me, I figured it would pair well with a glass of wine. I poured two glasses and joined him as he came in with the dogs.

"Well?" I said, sipping mine.

"It took some doing," he said. "But Johnson's office isn't going to bring charges against Bryson Ballard. He's already on a plane for California."

My stomach dropped. I didn't know if I felt relief or something else.

"I suppose that's best," I said. "At least it'll give Jeanie some peace of mind. She's torturing herself over that kid. And Juliet Clay's up over a million followers on TikTok as of yesterday."

"Yeah," he said. He took the wine I offered, but hadn't yet drunk any.

"Well," I said, raising my glass to his. "We never did celebrate the verdict."

He gave me a half-smile and clinked glasses with me. "It feels like a weird thing to celebrate. I don't know; that one was just ..."

"Icky," I said. "I can't shake it either. It all just seems so sad. Those people wrecked each other, even if it wasn't murder."

Eric put his glass down. "Yeah." It was as if a storm brewed behind his eyes.

"What is it?" I asked.

"I don't know. It's like you said. They all wrecked each other. And for what? Nate Clay would have died anyway. Juliet would have just kept on being ... Juliet. And Bryson?"

"Is maybe already too far gone," I said.

Eric stared out at the water. It rolled today. Those shimmering waves nearly blinded me.

"Cass," he said. "I'm sorry."

He sat on the couch. I sank down next to him, but kept my distance a bit.

"What for?"

"For everything. For leaving. For putting you through all of that with Wendy."

"You did what you had to do," I said.

"We wrecked each other too," he said. "Wendy and me."

"No, you didn't. One of these days you're going to truly have to forgive yourself for not being perfect."

He didn't answer. He just kept staring out at the water.

"You know," I said. "I've been thinking. A lot, actually. I meant what I said. We made a pretty good team on the Clay case. I don't know if I could have solved that without you."

"It was ... fun," he said. "I didn't think it would be. Hell, half the guys in the department aren't even talking to me right now. They think I've crossed over to the dark side helping you out."

"Have you? Or would you?"

"What do you mean?"

"I mean, you never gave me an answer."

"Your job offer?" he asked.

"Yeah," I said.

He put his wine glass down. Rising to his feet, he put his hands in his pockets and walked over to the double doors leading to the porch.

"I talked to the chief today," he said. "He offered me a job too."

"Big day for you, then," I said. I got up and stood beside him. Lines of worry creased his face. Eric seemed to carry the weight of the world on his shoulders so often. So much of it had been about Wendy. But it had also been about his job as a homicide detective.

"You're going back," I said, trying to keep the disappointment out of my tone.

"They've held it for me," he said. "I can pick right up where I left off. If I want it."

He turned to me. Since he'd come back to Delphi, we'd been with each other. But we hadn't been together. He held a question in his eyes. Could he pick back up where he left off with me?

"I don't have a right to ask," he said. "I know that. I've put you through hell. What you did for me. With Wendy's trial. I never properly thanked you."

"Yes, you did. And I didn't do it for your gratitude, Eric."

"You were one of the few people who believed in me. I mean, really believed. Not just because you wanted justice or because …"

"I've missed you," I said. And I did.

"I know. And I also know you've had a lot of questions. I've owed you answers. We haven't had a real conversation about any of it. We just used Juliet's case as an excuse to avoid it. That's my fault too. I owe you more. I should have …"

"Eric?" I said. It came over me. Rising from the deepest need. A push and pull that finally broke, leaving me breathless, weightless, untethered until I reached for the one thing, the only thing that would center me to the earth.

I rose up on the balls of my feet, laced my fingers around the back of Eric's neck, and pulled him to me.

One breath. His. Mine. Inhale. Exhale.

His hands came around my waist. He smelled clean, strong, with a hint of the woods lingering in his hair.

He'd kissed me before. But this was something else. A question. An answer. A promise.

I drank him in.

His strong arms encircled my waist, lifting me up. His chest pressed against mine and I could feel his thundering heartbeat. He was just as scared as I was.

If the first kiss was a promise, the second was a demand. Eric's lips trailed down the column of my throat. His breath caressed the tiny hairs along my neck, sending a shiver of pleasure all the way down to my toes.

"Cass," he whispered and I'd never loved the sound of my own name on someone else's lips so much before.

"Yes," I answered back. Yes and yes again.

I don't remember how we made it up the stairs. I think we floated. As we did, my eye caught the crumpled paper from that fortune cookie I opened weeks ago. I'd taped it to the fridge.

The things you fear will lead to new opportunities.

I lifted the hem of his shirt, pulling it over his head. Eric's face swam over mine, his eyes hooded. Over his shoulder, waves of diamonds rolled to the shore.

ERIC SLEPT shirtless on his stomach with his arms splayed out on either side of him. I ran a gentle hand through his thick, dark hair, leaned over, and kissed the nape of his neck. His stomach growled so loud Madison woke up. She'd been sleeping in a ball on the floor near the doorway.

I kissed Eric again, then grabbed my phone. It was almost nine in the morning. We'd slept in.

Eric rolled to his side. When he opened his eyes, he had a brief moment of confusion as he forgot where he was. Then, when he saw me, his face lit up in a guilty smile that thrilled me to my core.

"What time is it?" he asked, his voice a ragged whisper.

"Late," I said.

He stretched. "Come here," he said, pulling me back onto the bed toward him.

"Oh no," I said. "I need a shower. And coffee. Lots and lots of coffee."

Eric laughed. "I'll take care of the coffee."

"I knew there was a reason I liked you," I said.

"Just the one?" Eric asked, raising a sinful brow. I felt my cheeks redden.

I found my robe and headed for the bathroom as Eric went downstairs to the kitchen. He was humming as I heard him pour water for the coffee.

Happy. We'd both slept like the dead and I couldn't remember the last time that had happened.

I pulled on a sweatshirt and a pair of boxer shorts and padded downstairs. Eric pulled a carton of eggs out of the fridge and had set himself to the task of scrambling them. The smell of sizzling bacon warmed my soul as much as the coffee.

"You never definitively answered me about the job offer I made you," I said. "Think about it. It could be good for you. Maybe it's time you put away your badge." I grabbed a piece of bacon and went to him. Eric was singularly focused on the eggs. Or avoiding my question. I wasn't sure which.

"Eric?" I asked. He smiled, but didn't look up from the frying pan.

Just then, I heard a car pull up the driveway.

"Oh crap," I said. "That'll be Matty and Joe. They're gonna want to get started on the dock."

Panic flared through me. Eric was wearing nothing more than his own boxers and a smile. There was no way my brothers wouldn't put two and two together. Eric caught my eye and I knew he had the same concern. Neither of us were ready for the inquisition yet.

"I'll handle it," I said. I grabbed another piece of bacon. Eric playfully swatted me with the spatula.

I went to the front door. Marbury and Madison were yapping at my heels, sounding ready to murder. Odd. They knew the sound of both my brothers' trucks.

I swung the door open. There, staring down at me with intense blue eyes and a deeply dimpled smile that used to turn my knees to water, was Killian Thorne.

He looked me up and down, making note of the boxers and my disheveled hair.

"Good morning, a rúnsearc," he said. "I've got a bit of a favor to ask of you. And I'm afraid I can't take no for an answer."

He stepped inside, kissed me on the cheek, and set his suitcase down at my feet.

Cass's mob lawyer past will come back to threaten everything she's built in Cold Evidence, the next page-turning book in the Cass Leary Legal Thriller Series. You won't want to miss it! https://www.robinjamesbooks.com/book/cold-evidence/

Newsletter Sign Up

Sign up to get notified about Robin James's latest book releases, discounts, and author news. You'll also get *Crown of Thorne* an exclusive FREE bonus prologue to the Cass Leary Legal Thriller Series just for joining. Find out what really made Cass leave Killian Thorne and Chicago behind.

Click to Sign Up

http://www.robinjamesbooks.com/newsletter/

About the Author

Robin James is an attorney and former law professor. She's worked on a wide range of civil, criminal and family law cases in her twenty-five year legal career. She also spent over a decade as supervising attorney for a Michigan legal clinic assisting thousands of people who could not otherwise afford access to justice.

Robin now lives on a lake in southern Michigan with her husband, two children, and one lazy dog. Her favorite, pure Michigan writing spot is stretched out on the back of a pontoon watching the faster boats go by.

Sign up for Robin James's Legal Thriller Newsletter to get all the latest updates on her new releases and get a free bonus scene from Burden of Truth featuring Cass Leary's last day in Chicago. http://www.robinjamesbooks.com/newsletter/

Also By Robin James

Cass Leary Legal Thriller Series

Burden of Truth

Silent Witness

Devil's Bargain

Stolen Justice

Blood Evidence

Imminent Harm

First Degree

Mercy Kill

Guilty Acts

Cold Evidence

With more to come…

Mara Brent Legal Thriller Series

Time of Justice

Price of Justice

Hand of Justice

Mark of Justice

Path of Justice

With more to come…